The Golden Plan

PSYCHIC SOLUTIONS, MYSTERY #2

PATRICIA RICE

Author's Note

My original Magical Malcolm series was built on the premise of an 18th-century realm where my Druidic-descended Malcolms had no rationale for their inexplicable gifts. The rest of society called them witches, while my scientific Ives did their best to figure them out.

In this series, I welcome you to my 21st-century universe of colorful, eccentric characters who march to different drummers and who will never fit into any niche you may wish to cram them into. They're not detectives or policemen. Following procedures might cause their heads to explode, except for legal, military-minded Jax—who does his level best to make them conform, except when he doesn't. But they always get the job done, even if they're dragged screaming out of their comfortable small town into the big, sometimes dangerous, world the rest of us live in.

I hope you'll join us for the journey!

PS: For those of you who think Conan Oswin in the first chapter sounds familiar, take a look at TROUBLE WITH AIR AND MAGIC (https://patriciarice.com/books/trouble-with-air-and-magic/), book two of my California Malcolms series, my first attempt at bringing my Malcolm/Ives characters into the 21st century!

One

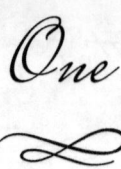

"JACK RABBIT. I COULD CALL MYSELF JACK RABBIT. SINCE I DON'T HAVE A NAME, would you mind if I stole yours? Name-stealing seems a common practice out here." Sitting in the California desert twilight, Damon Ives Jackson—or maybe it was just Damon Ives or No Nameatall—poked campfire embers while keeping an eye on the rabbit frozen in the shadows of a Joshua tree.

If he was the son of an identity-stealing killer, he needed to know that before he could proceed. For all he knew, he owed some poor family everything he ever earned.

Learning that his parents were frauds was a pervasive black cloud he couldn't blow off. He'd spent his career fighting fraud—irony at its worst.

The rabbit, of course, did not reply. Three days alone in the desert—maybe he was starting to hallucinate. Or having a psychic vision. Jax—the name he'd been called all his life—was almost envious of the women he'd met back east who thoroughly believed in their paranormal abilities. He could use a magical gift or two to solve his dilemma.

He'd best not think about the miniature whirlwind with orange curls he'd left behind. Evie would have something succinct to say about his current state, if she didn't murder him first.

The rumble of a vehicle hitting the ruts of the old dirt road intruded on his misery.

Jax accepted the incongruity of an approaching vehicle in the middle of nowhere. Someone had to be paying the taxes on acres of dirt. Maybe they'd shoot him for trespassing.

A Jeep parked next to Jax's old Subaru. He'd sold his classic XKE and his condo when he'd left Georgia. The Subaru had served him well as transportation and housing on his quest to find the answer to a decades-old mystery in California. He hated to return defeated, but he had few options left.

The man climbing out of the Jeep was tall and rangy and a total stranger.

"Lost, are you?" Jax asked before the intruder could speak.

"Thought you might be. You drove all the way from Georgia to commune with the Joshua trees?"

His license plate, of course. Just because Evie had taught him there might be magic in the world didn't mean most things didn't have a practical basis.

"You a ranger? I didn't think I was harming anything." Jax didn't get up or even bother looking at the unwanted visitor.

"Conan Oswin, not a ranger, possibly a distant cousin, though. Mind if I have a seat?" He folded up on the ground with the confidence of someone who didn't anticipate refusal and produced two beers from a backpack.

Cousin, huh. He'd been roaming this part of California for six weeks and had yet to find more than pieces of paper indicating the existence of the man who might or might not have been his father. He'd left a pretty wide search trail, so even this remark didn't surprise him. Jax popped the top of the beer can without a word. He'd learned interrogation at the hands of masters.

"Military, like my brother Magnus," Conan guessed. "Irritating as all hell when he gets silent like that."

Exactly. Jax took a sip of the cold beer and waited.

His companion stretched long legs encased in worn hiking boots toward the fire. "My sis-in-law leaves sticky trails all over the internet. Genealogy is Nadine's specialty. She has access to databases most people don't know exist."

Genealogy databases—DNA. Jax had submitted his over a month ago in hopes of learning who his real father was. He hadn't had any response yet. "I'm guessing Ancestry.com didn't send you out here to tell me I'm 88% Anglo-European."

"Actually, you're in the range of 20% Native American. As soon as the match to my family showed up, Nadine went on red alert. She's a trifle OC." The stranger looked like a laidback surfer. He didn't move a muscle that wasn't necessary and swept his overlong blond hair out of his face with a toss.

"Your family?" Maybe he really was hallucinating. Who in hell haunted DNA laboratories? Crazy people and cops.

He'd already seen the percentage. Native American explained his blade of a nose and easily tanned skin. But then, he'd always assumed he'd inherited those from his mother, who never claimed to be a Georgia belle.

Conan Oswin continued. "There are genetic markers distinctive to the Ives family, and we've both got them."

Jax ignored the twitch of confusion at being identified as an Ives. He wanted to be the Jackson he'd thought he was. This stretch of the Mojave had once been the ranch and mine of one Aaron *Ives,* a man he'd never heard of until a few weeks ago. The Franklin Jackson Jax had called dad, who had died in Georgia almost twenty years ago, had the fingerprints of Aaron Ives. *Why?*

Jax took another swig of the man's beer. Did he dare hope that this Conan Oswin person knew about the mysterious Aaron Ives?

"Don't know where you picked up the Jackson bit," Oswin continued. "But you sure got saddled with one of the Ives' crappy first names. We're Magnus, Conan, and Dylan. Try one of those on for size."

Damon Ives maybe-Jackson flung a pebble at the campfire. "Sounds like my theoretical dad must have known yours. I can't even call myself Jax anymore."

"Call yourself Alien Number One. Your name only matters to you. Choose one." The intruder didn't show the least curiosity in Jax's story—*because he already knew it?*

That thought caused more than a twitch. "You're an Oswin, not an Ives," Jax pointed out, irrelevantly. There were far more important questions to ask, but the name problem pressed on him.

"Big brother's name is Dylan *Ives* Oswin for a reason, just as you got stuck with the Damon *Ives* Jackson moniker." Conan took another swig of beer. "We're twigs off the old family tree."

"How did you find me in the middle of the desert?" Irritated that he was even having this conversation, Jax threw another pebble at the fire.

"Once Nadine reported we had a strange family member roaming around, I tracked you. We keep an eye on the Mojave. Heavy-duty illegal marijuana growers out here. They get mixed up with some bad mad scientist stuff, so we got curious."

"Can't say I've met any drug dealers or mad scientists yet." Jax watched him warily. "Even a satellite can't track me when my phone is off. For all intents and purposes, I should be invisible."

Conan snorted. "You're more visible here than in the city. Let's say Magnus and I are in the information business. You want to explain why you're here and want to be invisible? It's possible we can help."

Jax sipped his coffee. "You don't even know who I am."

"Georgia license plate, driver's license. . . Not a stretch. You want to know what's in your credit report?" Conan crushed his beer can.

Definitely the kind of thing Jax's hacker team would have done—and they were trained military intelligence.

"You're tracking a name that might not even belong to me," Jax retorted. "My birth certificate says Damon Ives Jackson, parents Franklin and Hannah Jackson. They died in a car crash nearly twenty years ago. I have just learned that Franklin's fingerprints belong to Aaron Ives, owner of this patch of dirt."

"Pretty danged clever for a lawyer to track property that might belong to him." Conan spoke with sarcasm. "Proves you might be entertaining."

Jax scowled. Talking to a human instead of a jackrabbit had its moments. He continued with the revelation that had sent him careening off track. "The Franklin Jackson I called father was actually Aaron Ives' *attorney*." It hadn't taken spy equipment to search databases, but connections had helped. "According to his death certificate, Aaron Ives died in a mining accident in that mound right over there that I'm not even going to call a mountain."

Conan eyed the rough hillside. "Lots of abandoned mines out here. Digging them up is seldom profitable. That means no body, right? When did he die?"

No body, of course. That would explain heaps and bunches. "Aaron Ives died months before *Franklin Jackson* arrived in Savannah, Georgia and took a job at Stockton and Stockton, LLC." Stephen Stockton being the man Jax had called his adoptive father since his birth parents had died. "Franklin was married when he arrived, and I was born a year later."

"Huh. Maybe he named you after his recently deceased client." Conan scuffed his boot in the dust, thinking.

"The client whose *fingerprints* his matched? What are the chances a military security clearance would have the wrong fingerprints?" Jax had verified the father he thought had died in a car accident had the same fingerprints as the man who had purportedly died in that mine. One man couldn't die twice.

Which meant his father might have murdered his attorney or vice versa.

"Slim to none," Conan agreed. "Send us what you've found. Magnus has government clearances even the president doesn't have. You're wondering who's buried in that mountain, aren't you?"

"I'm wondering *why* he's buried in that mountain. The land is so worthless that no one has claimed it. I'm still digging around in thirty-year-old records, trying to figure out who these men are. They died before DNA was an identifier, so even if I get some hits in a DNA database, they're likely to be distant relations like you." And his digging had apparently triggered Conan's sister-in-law. Interesting. So maybe he did have family out here. Spying did seem to be a genetic flaw.

"We need objects that once belonged to both men, see if we can pull DNA off them. You got anything of your father's?"

"Old legal files he worked on, maybe. Not much there. My father's executor sold off everything and set up a trust with the proceeds. I have a few old books and photograph albums dating back to my infancy but not before. And from what little I'm able to find, we'd have to dig up the mountain for the DNA of whoever, if anyone, is in the mine. Both men lacked immediate family. I've been traipsing all over this property, looking for anything resembling a house."

Conan typed notes into his phone. "I'll have Nadine poke around. Her family has abilities beyond the normal. Don't know if they'll be useful in this case, but digging through internet files is what Nadine does best."

Jax had people back home who could do that. He missed his team. He even missed Evie and Loretta and their craziness. None of them needed him. He'd arranged it that way. But after weeks of not finding out what he needed to know, he was wondering if he'd made a mistake by leaving. He didn't see how he could have done it any differently though. He couldn't live a lie.

But since meeting Evangeline Malcolm Carstairs, he'd stumbled into a world he didn't recognize. The man he owed for giving him and his sister a home, providing them with educations, and Jax with a job, a man he trusted and respected—had turned out to be a criminal fraud.

Flaky con artists running a psychic shop had turned out to be more honest than his respectable adoptive father and his wealthy business clients. And now Jax was sitting in the desert with a man who practically professed to being a spy and quite possibly related to him in ways he might never know. And this intelligent, knowledgeable spy was married to flakes just like Evie and her family, except they weren't flakes? They were geeks like his team?

The roar of a powerful engine cut the early evening silence.

His days of meditating with nature were over.

Two

Jax rubbed his nose. "Another of your spy family?"

"Probably not. Maybe the sheriff wants to see who's haunting the county's hills." Conan looked unconcerned.

Jax knew better. While waiting for the inevitable to arrive, he pretended the vehicle heading this way would pass on by into the empty desert. "What does one mine out here? I didn't think gold was accessible without heavy machinery."

"Anything from sand to quartz with a side order of chromium, I suppose. They used to use quartz to make silicon, which is why we have silicon valley, I guess, but it's made artificially these days."

The engine roared closer. A dust cloud formed against the pale blue evening sky.

He'd have to research mines and minerals. Jax sipped his beer while he watched an enormous Hummer spin to a stop next to his Subaru and Conan's Jeep. "Conspicuous consumption, much?"

"The question is, how did they find us? It's not exactly a beaten track." Conan watched with equal interest as the Hummer's doors heaved open. "Nadine has no reason to send anyone our way, that I know of. And even my Hollywood-excessive brother got rid of his gas-sucker since he got religion. Or a wife, same thing."

"Jax!" a child's voice squealed in delight as the Hummer's doors opened.

Shit. Loretta! He'd expected his team, not his ten-year-old ward. Jax stood to meet the onslaught.

The kid flew at him, braid flying, glasses bouncing. He wasn't much on hugging, but he opened his arms to the orphan he was supposed to be looking after. She flew into him, hugging his waist as if he'd been missing a thousand years. With exasperation, he watched over her head.

Sure enough, orange curls and a psychedelic T-shirt popped out of the passenger side. He didn't even bother noting which of his oddball fellows accompanied her. Jax focused on Evie's expression. She looked like she might murder him. Fair enough. He could handle that.

"Hey, pipsqueak. Are you here because you need my permission to buy a circus? Or has Evie been mean to you?" He hugged the kid and hefted her into his arms as shield against the approaching storm.

Loretta smacked his shoulder. "You vanished! Ariel was frantic!"

"How could you tell? Did she text in all caps?" Jax knew his neurodivergent sister well. Ariel was probably just as angry with him as Evie. Women simply didn't understand that a man had only his name and reputation to show who he was.

Jax glared at Roark, who ambled up behind Evie. The six-foot Cajun had grown out his hair lately. Muscled like a body builder, covered in tattoos and a roving assortment of metal, he'd once been part of Jax's military intelligence crew. He was studying the landscape while pretending he wasn't taking in everything about the stranger unfolding from the campfire.

"Conan, this is my ward, Loretta Post, her guardian, Evangeline Carstairs, and a man I thought was a friend, Roark LeBlanc. Conan Ives Oswin, folks. I am not dead or vanished and while I appreciate your concern, you can all go back to your regularly scheduled lives." He should feel glad that they were worried enough to come looking for him. But he knew them too well. They'd spent a good chunk of Loretta's money because they were curious.

"Hey, Conan." Evie nodded at the tall stranger, but she was doing her weird third-eye thing where she turned blank and insensible. "Funky aura, you got there," she declared, coming out of her spell and swinging to admire the buttes and desert. "Man, this place has stories to tell."

Ignoring Jax, she walked off.

Jax couldn't help it. Every time Evie dislocated everyone's expectations, he wanted to roll on the ground and roar with laughter. Jaws dropped all around, and she didn't even notice.

Damn, he'd missed her.

"She's really, really mad at you," Loretta whispered, then wiggled to get down. "But not silver dagger mad."

Good to know. The last time Loretta had reported that Evie's *bubble* was a sword, Evie had taken on the men who had killed Loretta's parents and almost got them all shot.

"Roark?" Conan asked. "How did a Cajun get called by a Scots name?"

The metal head shrugged. "Ma reads romance."

Conan nodded as if this made sense. "Looks like you have more than enough company." He pulled a business card out of his wallet and handed it over. "I'll look into those things we talked about. Keep in touch."

Jax wasn't carrying business cards and didn't think Conan needed one if he could find him in a freaking desert without having been introduced in the first place. He tucked the card away and returned to glaring at Roark as Conan strode back to his Jeep.

"Da women thought you were dead, man." Roark shrugged. "Ah couldn't let Evie and da *chevrette* come alone."

That was a crock, but he wouldn't call his Cajun friend on it. The dialect was a cover for a brilliant mind that had aced MIT with honors—although how he'd talked to his Boston professors was a mystery. "How the hell did you find me? And if you say *satellite*, you're fired."

Roark grinned and watched Loretta run after Evie, who was apparently speaking to thin air. "If you were keepin' up, *couillon*, you'd know we got our own business now. You can hire us, but you ain't, so you can't fire us."

"So you're being paid to locate me?"

"Huh, hadn't thought 'bout dat. Think your sister has money?"

"Given her math abilities, I suspect Ariel could own the world if she applied her mind to it. Knowing whether she does or not is another matter entirely." Jax couldn't tear his gaze from Evie. She was a flame against the growing darkness.

Roark poured coffee into a cup, sniffed, and dumped it into the dirt. "I got better in da Hummer. You want to rein 'em in and send them home or should I fix a pot?"

"Fix a big pot. Reining in might require a herd of cowboys." Fascinated despite himself, Jax abandoned the fire to follow Evie, who appeared to be conversing with a Joshua tree while sitting in the desert sand, legs crossed, and palms up.

"I think she's talking to an Indian," Loretta whispered as he reached her. "She asked if he wanted to join the sky father. Look, she's glowing!"

"That's just the sun setting." But the light around Evie was a little more intense than elsewhere. Jax decided the hills simply shed weird shadows.

A minute later, the sun must have shifted. She quit glowing, turned to look for Loretta, and spotted Jax. Without a word, she stood and punched him in the gut.

Exercising off his fury and frustration had him in better shape than he'd been in since the service. It probably hurt her small fist more than it did him.

"I'll tell Ariel you're dead and that we put a stone on your grave, shall I? Then you don't have to worry about anyone else anymore." She stalked off toward the Hummer.

EVIE NURSED HER BRUISED KNUCKLES. THE MAN WAS MADE OF STONE, LIKE THE Hulk. Her first impression of the arrogant lawyer had been the right one. Head of stone as well.

She must have drained herself pretty badly with that ancient ghost. She was so tired that even Jax looked good standing there with his dark hair all tousled —he had hair! Who knew? She'd only seen him in a military buzz cut. That skimpy mesh thing he had on revealed far more than his uptight lawyer clothes ever had. She was so furious with him that she wanted to claw out his eyes, but she'd have to do it while drooling. Why couldn't men who looked like that ever have brains?

He had brains. With a sigh, she waited beside the Hummer for Roark to unlock it. Jax had lawyer brains, not people brains. Poor Loretta was clinging to the ornery cuss as if he were her real father. The tadpole *deserved* a real father. And Ariel needed a brother who would be there if she needed him. And the man sat out here, sulking in the desert.

Evie was dying to hear why he was in the desert, surrounded by ghosts. The air shimmered like water mirages, encircling her with auras. She couldn't fix them all. Most of them probably didn't want to be fixed.

The men were making coffee, ignoring her. She kicked up dust and considered walking back the way they'd come, but it was almost night, and for all she knew, there were wolves out there. Weren't the animal rights people trying to bring back wolves?

She'd never been farther than Myrtle Beach. She hadn't realized one place could have so much dust and no one but ghosts anywhere in sight. Wasn't California supposed to be crowded? Well, it was June, in the desert, probably not the right time for visiting. For someone from South Carolina, the lack of humidity was refreshing.

She climbed up on the hood of the Hummer, lay back against the windshield, and studied the stars popping out. She had to admit, if one wanted to sulk, this was the place to do it. She closed her eyes and let star energy fill her.

"Evie, Jax wants to know how we found him," Roark called, disturbing a lizard climbing up to join her.

"Try explaining, see if he believes you." She was tired of people not respecting her talent. Roark was clearly insane to listen to her. Well, given his tats and metal, Roark was clearly insane, period. One would have to be to put up with a contrary bastard like Jax all these years. It was very peculiar knowing two such different men were best buddies.

"Ariel lost contact with your phone back at that gas station down the road three days ago," Roark was saying, in clear American English for a change. He probably wanted to sound convincing. "So we just started there. Guy said you asked about the Ives mine and told us how to find it."

Evie grinned. Roark obfuscated the truth so well, he should be the lawyer.

"The *ghost* told us how to get here," Loretta corrected. "The gas station guy had the IQ of a rock, but the ghost heard our question. When Evie asked if he wanted to go to the light, the ghost told her the Ives mine was in Glass Mountain. So we asked the sheriff how to find Glass Mountain."

"It's a small world after all," Roark added dryly. "And the sheriff didn't even throw me in the clink for looking dangerous."

"Intimidating," Evie called. "My cousin said you were *intimidating*. Everyone knows you're a creampuff and not dangerous."

Jax spurted coffee out his nose.

With a sigh, Evie slid off the car. "Open the door so I can get my tea. I'm not drinking your rotgut."

"We're not making tea. You're going back to your hotel," Jax ordered. "It's cold out here at night and the Subaru only holds one sleeping bag."

She could argue with that, but she wouldn't. She wasn't sleeping with the bastard. "We don't have a hotel. We got off the plane, rented the Hummer, and came straight here. These two idiots were worried about you, and I was worried about Ariel. We hoped—" She was angry but she politely amended that cruel lie. "We *thought* we'd find your carcass being picked bare by vultures."

She was pretty certain that biting his cheek meant Jax was laughing at her. She wished she hadn't given her water gun to Ariel to drive off marauding pests. Sometimes one had to take drastic measures to keep all that male testosterone in check.

"You promised me Harry Potter World! Can we go tomorrow?" Loretta asked.

Harry Potter World made more sense than stomping through a desert after a meathead who didn't have the grace to die. Of course, Jax vanishing in the desert was the reason they'd promised Loretta this trip. He'd scared the tarnation out of all of them. They'd have to find cellphone reception before she could text his poor sister.

Evie didn't wish to admit—even to herself—how relieved she was that Jax was alive and just exhibiting his usual jackass nature. She didn't want to raise Loretta alone. The improbable situation that had left this special Indigo child in her incompetent hands was Jax's duty. "Harry Potter is why we're here. It's your summer vacation."

Jax lifted his coffee mug in salute. "Have fun. Travel safely."

"Jax, my man, you're as dumb as a kumquat," Roark said in disgust. "I brought these women across the whole cotton-pickin' country to help you, and you want to send them to Harry Potter World? Did you eat your brains?"

Oh, swell, that did it. She was supposed to *help* a man whose bones ought to be shredded by vultures by now? She came out here to reassure Ariel, not help Jax, who didn't have the brains of a kumquat, granted. Since Roark hadn't unlocked the car doors, she marched down the road. There had been some shacks a few miles back. She'd hiked farther.

"Evie!"

Footsteps pounded up behind her. Jax was a jogger. Her short legs couldn't possibly stay ahead of his long, muscled ones, so she didn't even try. Her mother made a big deal out of tarot and crystal ball predictions, but people were so damned predictable. . .

Jax grabbed her waist and dragged her up against him. *That*, she hadn't predicted. Goddesses above, but the man was solid steel and smelled of masculine sweat, musk, and dust. No showers in the desert, she guessed. She almost swooned, although admittedly, that was more lust than his stench. She grabbed his thick shoulders to balance herself and regretted it instantly.

"Evie, this is my problem. I don't want to drag you into it." Now that he had stopped her, he slowly released her.

Perversely, she wrapped her arms around his neck and stayed right where she was. Maybe this was how one got through kumquat lawyer heads. "I thought we were *friends*." She dragged that straight out of her gut, so it came out an almost guttural growl.

He wrapped his arms around her, hard, and rested his head against hers. "How can I have friends if I come from a long line of murderers or spies or who knows what?"

"Damn, you do have kumquats for brains. And a walnut for a heart, just like Loretta said. Your friends *know* you. You're a literal-minded, ruthless control freak, and yeah, you've probably killed in war zones, but your walnut heart has potential, and there isn't anyone more honest." She grabbed a fistful of his short hair and yanked his head upright. "Why, by all the heavens, do you think we're out here?"

"To bury my vulture-pecked, control-freak bones?" he asked with a hint of humor.

"Yeah, that." She dropped her arms and pushed away. "Why Glass Mountain?"

Just like that, he surrendered. "Because that's where Aaron Ives is said to be buried. This was his land. And if fingerprints are to be believed, he also died that night with my mother and is the man who might be my real father."

"So there's a good chance that if anyone is buried in that mountain, it's Franklin Jackson, the man you *thought* was your father?" Evie knew she was quick at deductions. That's why she'd started her Psychic Solutions Agency, even with the addition of Jax's team, she now had to call it Sensible Solutions, which was probably a lie because there was nothing sensible about what she did.

"Damn, you're good." Jax took a deep breath, ran a hand through his tousled hair, and nodded. "Do you think you might find his ghost?"

Evie grinned so wide she thought her cheeks might break. Damon Ives Jackson was admitting that she might talk to ghosts?

"Only if I can get back in time to file for election as Afterthought's mayor." Establishing her priorities, she headed back for the campfire. "I'm not giving the mayor's cronies another chance to steal the town."

Three

"WE CAN'T GO GHOST HUNTING TONIGHT. THERE'S AN AIRBNB DOWN THE ROAD, and what passes for a diner, if you haven't eaten." Deeply unsettled, Jax returned to officer mode and directed his troops. He kicked out the fire and gathered his supplies to fling into the Subaru.

Holding Evie that close—had felt way too necessary. He needed distance to continue his mission.

As soon as he unlocked the car doors, Evie inserted herself into his passenger seat. One thing he could say about the capricious genie—she wasn't shy or lacking in confidence. Or maybe she just didn't give a damn.

Nah, Evie gave everything to others. That was probably what was making him nervous. He didn't want to be one of her projects. *Mayor?* She seriously wanted to be mayor?

He'd just asked her to look for a ghost. That was equally as improbable, bordering on insane. He'd baked his head in the desert long enough. "You don't mean to leave Loretta with a loose screw like Roark? He's likely to take the Hummer off-road to see how fast he can go."

Evie raised a pointed eyebrow and nodded at the Hummer. Loretta was bouncing up and down and excitedly buckling herself into the front passenger seat. "You want to tell her she can't sit there? I've read his aura, remember? Roark is a total gentleman, if you give him a chance. He's the favorite uncle she doesn't have."

14

Loretta had just tragically lost both parents—twice. The kid hadn't believed them dead until they'd found the bodies nearly a year after they'd disappeared. Now she was having to adjust to an entirely new life with a distant arm of her father's family, weird strangers she hadn't even known existed. Evie had to keep reminding Jax of that fact because he was a poor excuse for a human being.

He was a damned lawyer, not a child psychologist.

Sighing, he strapped himself into the driver's seat and drove away from what might have been his home had his father lived. Or not.

"The chance of finding any ghost is small." Evie spoke as teacher to student, maintaining that comfortable distance he needed. She was probably reading his *aura*. "Millions of people die a year. Most move on to the next plane. Those remaining don't necessarily make their presence known. Or can't."

"You're already making excuses for failing," he countered. "And I have other sources. I just thought as long as you were here. . ."

"You'd what? Pacify me? Lovely." She crossed her arms and glared at the dusty ruts in his headlights.

"Look, dammit, Evie, I'm not a believer, okay? I wasn't raised to give a crap about souls rising to heaven or any of that religious crap. Dead people are worm fodder. Whoever those people were who claimed to be my parents and died that night in their car, they've been cremated, ashes to ashes. I have no means of proving their genetic connection to me, no more than I can prove anything about a body buried in a mountain. I'm clutching desperately at straws, hoping to put together a straw horse, at least. You're one straw among many."

"And a straw horse is all you'll have when you're done. There are real living people who need you more." She turned and glared at him. "But because you are quite probably genetically connected to a man who was apparently about to turn his own partner in as a criminal fraud, I'm going to make a wild guess that the man in the mountain did not die by accident. And that there's more to this story."

"Yeah, I think so too." Jax sighed in relief that they were back on solid ground. Evie had a flaky mind that took paths his more straightforward one couldn't. "I've been digging through records. Aaron Ives and Franklin Jackson were partners in the Glass Mountain mining operation. They both graduated high school here and went to Stanford together. Aaron was both engineer and lawyer and ran his father's mining company. Franklin inherited his father's practice. Apparently both their fathers died decades ago, and I've not been able to trace any other family."

"Except Mr. Oswin."

"Conan found me, or his sister-in-law did. I sent my DNA in, hoping to find relatives. If she's using that sample and my local inquiries, she's working with a private database and a spy network larger than Roark's."

Evie hummed in appreciation but didn't comment. Jax understood. He could see where an obsessive-compulsive like Oswin's sister-in-law might be handy to know. But Evie was ADHD. Dog-walking with a side of shop clerk, while running for mayor and helping his team start a detective—*solutions* —agency was simply one minor example of her eccentricity.

Roark and his military partner Reuben had dishonorable discharges preventing them from obtaining the licenses real detectives needed, no matter what they called themselves.

And Jax was pretty sure mayors and detectives were a conflict of interest, without throwing in the psychic bit.

He continued. "I don't have DNA samples from either Ives or Franklin to prove any genetic connection. I have birth, marriage, and death certificates with the name Franklin Jackson on them because he was presumed to be my father. Obtaining legal certificates on Aaron Ives is taking more time since I don't even know his birth date or if he was ever married. There is only his obituary in the local newspaper." Jax steered the car off the road into a dirt yard in front of a tin shack.

Evie stared out the windshield. "This the diner?"

"This is Marge's house. The diner is over there." He gestured at a ramshackle cabin across the road made of leftover plywood and aluminum siding haphazardly tacked together. "Marge has a. . . heck if I know what she calls it. A teepee? She rents to idiots who think it would be cool to spend the weekend in a desert and gaze at stars."

Had Evie been any of the ambitious women Jax had dated back in Savannah, she would have shoved him out the door, taken over the car, and driven straight back to LA and swimming pools. Instead, she pondered the shacks without blinking—which meant she'd gone into one of her trances again.

When she returned to the moment, she nodded and climbed out without argument. Loretta was already out and examining the bottle tree in the yard.

Jax had stayed with Marge his first night here. The facilities weren't as bad as they appeared from the outside. Marge didn't like just anyone stopping by.

Evie produced a cellphone. "You were *three miles* from a signal. You deliberately camped out there with no signal." She tapped into the phone.

It was weird watching Evie with a phone. When he first met her, she'd said she didn't want one, that it distracted her from her observations. But once one had a kid—they became essential. Nice that she was willing to adapt for Loretta, but Evie wielding technology. . . was almost scary.

Jax figured she was notifying Ariel that he was alive, and she hadn't killed him yet. Or they were plotting to box him up and ship him home.

With grizzled hair stuffed under a purple ball cap with a golden eagle on the front, Marge plodded down the concrete block stairs. "Lawyer man, you're back, with friends." She eyed his group with curiosity.

"They tracked me down. Are you booked tonight? Evie and Loretta aren't accustomed to camping rough." Jax and Roark had spent over a year in Afghanistan, not all of it at headquarters.

"Sure thing. You boys heading back out or want to park your vehicles here?" She waddled down the rock-lined path to her fenced-in backyard.

"Roark?" Jax turned to the inked Cajun who'd provided the military with protection and intelligence before Roark had been booted for insubordination. Jax knew better than to order his friend to do anything unless he was being paid.

Roark shrugged. "*Ça va.* Got a spare blanket? Desert gets cold."

"I got quilts," Marge called back. "You're welcome to use them."

"*Merci beaucoup,*" Roark called after her. In a whisper, he added to Jax, "You paid her well, didn't you?"

It was Jax's turn to shrug. "It's a wooden wigwam in the middle of nowhere with a hot tub and good wine, neither of which Evie or Loretta will appreciate. Want to have them sleep in the cars?"

He was trying hard not to wish he could share that tub and wine with Evie.

"Want me to take the kid back to LA and Harry Potter World?" Roark asked cynically, reading his mind.

"Yeah, I do, and you deserve that fate for encouraging them. But it won't happen, so let's get quilts for you. I have a sleeping bag." Knocked out of the rut he'd been digging, Jax trudged after the women, wondering how he'd got into this ludicrous situation.

Leaning against the cabin, waiting for the quilts while Roark explored their surroundings, Jax decided asking Evie to hunt for ghosts had been his mistake. The perceptive genie squirmed into any opening offered. He didn't need more baggage. That's why he'd sold his house and his Jag and headed west.

Before he could ponder the error of his ways, Evie emerged with an armful of covers. "Loretta and I are heading over to the diner. You need that tub." She shoved the quilts at him just as the kid emerged, jabbering about wigwams and Marge's distorted bubble.

"Marge is old enough to be your grandmother. She has a muddy aura and ulterior motives for living on the edge of nowhere. She's not poor. Watch your back." As if she hadn't blown a hole in his peace, Evie took Loretta's hand, and the two of them wandered off.

THE NEXT MORNING, ROARK AND LORETTA TOOK THE HUMMER BACK TO LA, leaving Evie and Jax to climb Glass Mountain in search of Jax's ghosts. Beating the ground with a stick to chase off snakes, Evie had second thoughts about her choice.

"Did Marge's aura tell you she's not poor?" Jax demanded, in lieu of polite conversation.

"Her aura is a muddy gray in her root chakra, and she's seriously cautious, possibly to the point of paranoia. She probably went through everything in our cars during the night."

"That doesn't tell me she's rich." Jax took the hill at an unreasonable rate, not sounding concerned about having his car searched.

Evie followed Jax more slowly, swinging her stick. "Come on, Jackson, use your eyes. She was wearing a Rolex, and she had a hot tub in the *desert*. Her shack was air-conditioned, with no visible sign of electrical wiring. I'm guessing she has a private solar panel set-up out of sight. The electric company doesn't bury wires in a place like this."

"I read documents, not people." Sounding irked, Jax handed her a water bottle. "You should have gone to LA and had a little fun."

"My head is scary enough without having imaginary creatures from a theme park in it."

Roark and Loretta had bonded over computer games. Evie had a feeling that despite his brilliant mind and educated background, the Cajun hadn't had much of a childhood, and his inner child needed nourishment. Loretta would have more fun at the theme park with him, while Evie did what she knew best —hunt ghosts.

"Do you even know where the mine is?" She slugged the water and shouted at Jax's back. The man had to be half goat.

Trudging up the hill, she wondered if she could Google hotels with spas in LA. And if relaxing in hot water might focus her spinning thoughts. And if snakes preferred dawn to emerge. Plus, some of the spirits out here were really disgusting. She ignored the one in rags miming being hanged, complete with gaping tongue and bulging eyes. Sociopath probably deserved to die.

"There's a mine." Jax reached back to grab her hand and haul her over boulders from an old mudslide covering the road. "There are a few timbers at the site, what appears to be a collapsed depression, and we're walking the remains of an old road. But this place is littered with old mines. I may need to hire someone who understands mining maps to find the right one."

"Have you looked up whoever took over Franklin Jackson's law office? If Franklin and Ives were partners, the office might have their personal files." Liking Jax's rough hand around hers too much, Evie yanked away and stopped to admire the scenery.

Unfortunately, chaparral looked the same everywhere she turned.

"I left them for last. I'm disinclined to appear like a desperate heir hoping to score a windfall, and I don't have any other good excuse." Not even breathing hard, Jax continued upward, giving her a nice view of his tight butt in jeans.

She could think of two things at once. Better go with the obvious. "Money is generally the root of all evil. Let's hope you're *not* an heir."

"Cliché. Money can provide food and shelter. But if there's evil to be had, money can be one factor. I wouldn't rule out lust, envy, revenge, and all that, though. You need to be open-minded."

Evie snorted. "About evil? Listen to the bigot who believes all psychics are frauds. But I'll agree it's probably safer to avoid anyone who might be connected to Ives and Jackson until Loretta and I can take a look at them."

Jax hooted. "Right, that's exactly what I mean to do, fling two females into a potential snake pit first. If you come out alive, maybe I'll go in."

Evie picked up a pebble and flung it at his back. "I'd be far more useful reading auras of people who may have known your father than climbing a hill to nowhere."

Jax turned and waited for her to catch up. "You keep demanding respect, but you need to respect what *I* do. It's not all about you, okay? Roark is better at ferreting out info on the internet than I am. Let him do his job. Once we have a defined path to follow, we'll know if your talents can advance our cause. Admit that knowing more about people helps you read them."

Evie pondered that as she studied the collapsed hole in the ground he'd brought her to. "Different observances," she concluded. "When I first met you, your aura said you were a ruthless killer. But *observation* allowed me to understand you were ex-military, so your killing days might be behind you. I didn't act on first impressions but waited to see how you would behave."

"And now?" He poked around a pile of scorched lumber, scattering the snakes and scorpions into the brush before heaving the boards aside.

"I see you growing beyond your anger, so I know the anger isn't all you are. First impressions simply show me how to approach someone. Knowing who someone is allows me to see potential."

He kicked aside what might once have been tar paper. "Well, it's hard to know someone if all you have is a genealogy chart and a packet of papers. And it's hard for me to understand what you can determine that might help." He studied what appeared to be a large stone cairn buried beneath the rotted boards and tar paper he'd just kicked off.

"A memorial." Evie studied the stones, but she didn't see any aura that might indicate an ectoplasmic presence. Finding the ghost of Jax's long-dead father—or partner—would be too much to hope for.

"All it tells us is that someone may have died here. If there was ever a shelter or storage or any indication that people mined this area, it's vanished without a trace." Jax kicked a loose stone.

"Not quite without a trace. You have those old timbers to start with." Evie crouched down and pried some of the smaller rocks loose. The cairn was hip high and constructed with boulders large enough to discourage disturbing the pile. "And there are ashes mixed with the dust indicating the rest of the timbers may have burned. See, the silica in the dust sparkles. But this gray stuff. . ."

"Could simply mean a hunter had a campfire." Jax crouched beside her.

"The timber was up here for a reason. You've found a mine, although it might not be the one you want. The stones, however, suggest a deliberate memorial. Someone wanted what happened here to be remembered. People often put mementos under them." She pried more of the smaller stones loose.

"We shouldn't disturb a gravesite," he protested.

"If you don't believe in spirits, why do you care? And it's a memorial, not a grave. We can rebuild it when we're done."

"You're entirely too familiar with the dead." Abandoning his unthinking hypocrisy, Jax removed the rocks in an orderly fashion, lining them up by size.

"Duh. I may have a passing acquaintance." Evie messed up his arrangement by haphazardly dropping the stones she removed behind her. "Why would anyone go to the trouble of stacking all these rocks, then hide them under timbers?"

"Private memorial, maybe. If I didn't want curiosity seekers poking around, I'd make certain it was covered in spiders and snakes. And if the timbers are the remains of a mine that collapsed, it would also be part of the memorial. Hold up a sec." Straining muscled shoulders under a thin T-shirt, Jax carefully dislodged one of the boulders on the edge.

At sight of the piece of plastic beneath, Evie offered a little prayer to any spirit watching over them. She didn't sense any ghosts, saw no auras, but unlike Jax, she respected those who had gone ahead. She helped him remove the stones in the area he'd chosen.

"A circuit board?" Jax wiggled the plastic out.

"Would it contain data?" Evie studied the plastic bag and its contents in disappointment.

"Unlikely. Heat and dust destroy electronics. I can have Reuben take a look but don't expect much. If this memorial is related to my father, he left California before I was born. The board is likely to be older than I am. Finding a machine to even *read* it might be problematic." Jax set the small board aside and dug around in the dirt the plastic had covered.

As part of Jax's team of renegade hackers, Dr. Reuben Thompson was a computer engineer, among other things. Reuben had known exactly how to return her great aunt's ancient Apple computer to operation, not that it was of much use. But if anyone could examine a thirty-year-old circuit board, Reuben could.

"There's writing on the back of this." She showed him what looked like Sharpie markings with a number and initials.

"We'd need a code breaker." He returned to digging. "There's metal under here."

Excited, Evie stood and hunted around for something that would make a better digger than her fingers. A rusty iron spike stuck out from the discarded timber. Checking for creepies, she pulled it out. It might hold up.

Jax had his army knife out, digging into the dirt they'd exposed. She scraped with her spike.

"Looks like an old iron pipe." Jax sat back in disappointment.

"And some old fencing?" Seeing the corroded chain link, Evie began pulling aside more rocks. "Aunt Felicia has a metal detector. She says people who really want to hide gold in the ground have to hide it under iron pipes and chain-link fences and stuff that will confuse the radar."

"Huh. Looks like old junk someone buried to me." Jax heaved rocks, then dug some more.

If it was just old junk, she'd raised his expectations for nothing. He'd send her home and sulk out here for the rest of his life.

And she damned well needed Jax to come home and help with Loretta. He'd saddled her with the kid—well, Loretta had found her first. Evie might be Loretta's cousin, but she knew she wasn't in the least bit maternal. She'd sent Loretta with *Roark*, the crazy Cajun, for heaven's sake! Because she'd wanted Jax's respect. Damn, she needed to straighten out her priorities one of these days.

Jax yanked out a rusty old pipe and flung it aside. "There's another baggie. Plastic really doesn't ever rot, does it?"

"That's the argument anyway." Evie scraped at the dirt around the second sealed plastic bag until Jax could tug it free. "Not gold."

"But a treasure trove to me." Jax carefully opened the seal and produced a disintegrating photograph from a newspaper. "I haven't had time to search ancient newspaper microfiche."

Beneath the crumbling paper was what appeared to be a big brass key similar to the one Evie had been given when she'd set up Loretta's bank deposit box. But it was the photograph that held their attention. The caption read, "*Aaron Ives (right) and Franklin Jackson receiving an award for their achievement in bringing jobs to San Bernardino County. The Ives Silica Mine will provide components for the new electronic voting machines manufactured by Sovereign Machinery.*"

Jax pointed at the taller, broader of the two men. "That's my dad."

The man labeled *Aaron Ives.*

Four

Despite his birth certificate, he wasn't Damon Ives *Jackson* but Damon *Ives*.

Aaron Ives had not died in a mining accident. He'd stolen his partner's identity. Jax and Ariel might actually have family they knew nothing about.

The orange-haired genie was tenaciously refusing to leave him alone after that earth-shattering revelation.

She sat now, cross-legged on the bed in Marge's B&B, revealing tanned legs beneath tiny shorts. "Did you set alarms on the car so Marge can't snoop?"

Jax rubbed his two-day-old scruff and tried not to look at temptation. "What would she find? I keep my ID with me. And the baggies from the mine are in here. You can sleep on them. I've checked for bugs—technical and entomological. The place is clean."

"Your call." She shrugged and tapped into her phone. "Huh, did you know it takes five-hundred years for one of those plastic baggies to decompose? That's even better than a safe deposit box."

Evie had sent Loretta and Roark home without her. And right now, with his head swirling in fifteen different directions, Jax was almost grateful she'd stayed. He'd be even more grateful if she showed any sign of interest in going to bed with him.

Instead, she and Loretta were entertaining themselves by exchanging text messages while the kid and Roark waited at the LA airport for their flight after their visit to Harry Potter. Roark needed to get back to work, and the desert wasn't any place for a kid—unless they wanted to buy tents and dune buggies.

Jax had promised to drive his Subaru back across country as soon as he was done. He'd made an appointment for tomorrow to interview the attorney who had taken over Franklin Jackson's practice. And after that, he had to attempt to find the box to match the brass key.

Evie, being Evie, had perceptively refused to leave him to deal with his discoveries alone. Jax didn't know how he felt about that. He'd been looking after himself and his sister since he was twelve.

"Safe deposit boxes are lousy places to keep anything," Jax muttered, while he used his laptop to dig through online files with the abysmally slow internet. "No one has safe deposit boxes anymore."

But this was very definitely the key to one. And someone had buried it where even a gold prospector wouldn't find it.

"Loretta says they're boarding shortly. Want to text her before she goes? Now that your phone is working again," she added dryly.

Right. The kid was being extraordinarily well-behaved and not protesting being sent home while her guardians remained behind. She was probably planning on burning down his office—except he didn't have one anymore. Jax pulled out his phone and typed MAKE ROARK BEHAVE.

HE BOUGHT ME A WAND XOXO

Jax thought those last letters were hugs and kisses, and they warmed his icy heart. He didn't deserve them, but he sent her hearts and flowers in return. Loretta had been a neglected genius all her life and didn't expect much from adults. He feared Evie's off-the-wall family wasn't much of an improvement, but they were at least family of sorts. He wasn't.

"Will your sister mind looking after the kid for a few days?" Jax glared at Roark's text, which included a middle finger. Did emojis even have middle finger salutes? He'd have to look someday. He returned to his laptop.

"Gracie's a teacher and has time on her hands in summer. She has a kid to keep Loretta company. I promised Gracie a proper salary for being chief cook and bottle washer. They'll be good. My main concern is Reuben and Roark alone in my basement. I hope I have a house to go back to." Evie bounced off the bed and rummaged in her duffle. "If you're spending the night on your computer, I'm getting in that tub."

Working through his files, Jax tried to imagine what she'd wear in the spa. His eyeballs crossed. Evie had curves even a Renaissance artist couldn't do justice to. She was simply too vibrant to be caught in oil. He thought his head might catch on fire.

He'd been celibate too damned long.

Telling himself she hadn't offered an invitation, he continued digging into anything he could find on Aaron Ives, Franklin Jackson, the Ives Silica Mine, and Sovereign Machinery, the latter simply because he didn't know where else to go with this.

He had a storyline worked out to give Jackson's former law firm since, after all, he had a birth certificate showing that Jackson was his father—even if that photo proved he wasn't. Probate had been filed twenty years ago, so he should be able to use his letters from the court to open the deposit box—provided it was in Franklin's name and provided they'd guessed right about the enigmatic notations on the back of the circuit board.

All he found on Aaron Ives was that he'd grown up here, went to Stanford, and instead of getting rich in San Francisco, he'd returned to his family's land, where his father had apparently ranched and prospected. Jax had already looked up the worthless property. Ives Silica Mining had disappeared with the mine collapse. He had a reported date of death from the obituary listing the victim's only next of kin as deceased. Poor sot.

Except it must have been *Franklin Jackson* who had died in that mine since Aaron Ives was very definitely the father Jax remembered.

And then, recalling Evie's warning about Marge, he realized this was an unprotected internet connection and shut down. He really was losing his edge. As he knew from painful experience, it was much too easy to allow emotions to overrule the brain. Confirming that his father wasn't who he said he was had shaken him.

He'd been twelve when his parents died in the car wreck. He had photos from that time period. And Jax knew he pretty much looked like the damned mysterious Ives and not Jackson, who'd been lean and small, with lighter-colored hair in the photo. Conan Oswin's purported DNA connection to the Ives family added one more nail to the case he was building. Jax knew his square-boned face and size resembled Conan more than it did the pretty-boy lawyer in the photo.

Too exhausted to think, Jax stood and stretched. Evie hadn't returned. He studied the California King bed Marge had provided. He could sleep in the Subaru as he'd been doing. But he'd like to share that tub. . .

Wine would be good about now, but he didn't expect Evie to be drinking it.

She didn't even drink coffee. She was an ethereal being from another dimension, certainly not from the world he grew up in. He stepped out on the deck to where the blue lights under the water lit the yard. Evie was no more than a shadow against the night.

Knowing he was out of his mind to do so, Jax pried off his shoes and yanked off his sweat-dried shirt.

He stood over the tub as he unbuckled his belt. Evie opened one sleepy eye and murmured, "Finally."

With that acceptance, he dropped his khakis and slid into the water with her.

She hadn't opened the wine, of course. He left it unopened. Closing his eyes on temptation, he allowed the heat to soak into his sore muscles.

"Lust is a good color for you." She nudged his toes.

Dutifully keeping his eyes closed, Jax let her steer his mind to the inane. Maybe meditation would calm his roiled thoughts. "What color is that?"

"Orange, mostly, although you're hiding it under the water. Orange under blue lights. . . interesting." She rubbed her big toe up the sole of his foot.

"So I look like a red and orange rainbow in a blue sea?" He could almost handle the inanity while his mind melted. He had no business becoming involved with Evie Malcolm Carstairs. She was bad news from every logical angle. And with no job, he had nothing to offer.

"Rainbows are faint. Your energies are powerful. I have a bad habit of being attracted to men with powerful energies. Want me to get out so you can soak alone?" Her voice was quietly seductive.

Or that's where his head was anyway. "This is probably a bad idea," he thought he agreed.

"Oh definitely. You *abandoned* us. I'll never forgive you for that."

Which nicely reminded him that he still didn't know if his father had killed his partner, dumped him down a mine, and stolen his identity for reasons unknown. And that he hadn't checked the tub area for listening devices.

Either understanding that he wanted distance or bouncing on to some new thought, Evie shoved out of the water and reached for a towel.

He caught a good eyeful of lush, naked curves. Evie was shaped like a miniature Marilyn Monroe. He'd never been into the curvy type before, nor petite, but damn. . .

She padded away, leaving him to curse his need to be honest and straightforward and a real stupid brick.

Evie studied the small adobe building Jax parked next to, the one with a sign stating Pendleton Law Offices as if the building had a lot of offices, and they were all staffed by Pendletons. Pretentious. "You're not lying," she insisted, carrying on the argument that had started when they set out this morning. "You really are inquiring about Aaron Ives for a client. You just happen to be the client."

"But you pretending to be the client is a lie." He shut off the engine and climbed out.

She shot out of her seat before Jax came around to help her out, which he did, occasionally, when they weren't fighting. Although it was pretty hard for them to share the close proximity of a car without fighting. They had issues, lots of them. Driving across country ought to be entertaining.

Seeing Jax naked except for his knit boxers had not helped the tension. Definitely superhero six-pack and that ripple of dark hair between his pecs had revved her engines more. She had to put her blinders on and focus. . . Yeah, like that had ever happened in her whole entire life.

"I'll pay you a dollar to hire me. I want to know about Aaron Ives. You can't just ignore what you want because you don't have any evidence." She marched up the stone sidewalk to the door.

"You'll promise not to talk about auras and spirits or anything to distract from the hard cold facts I want to lay down?" He caught the door handle before she could open it. He wasn't a large man, but he was still twice her size. Still, it was the steel gray of his eyes that demanded respect.

Evie sighed. She understood his need to be in charge. "Fine. I'll be a mute idiot. But if you don't mention Ives—"

"I know, I know, the result will be on my head." He opened the door for her and led her into a small, carpeted lobby with touches of Southwestern décor.

Wearing a gold pin of an eagle with a fish in its claws, a stout receptionist with short, iron-gray hair greeted them expectantly. Her aura held the darker hues of red—grounded, survivalist colors. Hints of muddy green and blue warned she had a few issues with self-esteem, but without knowing the woman, Evie couldn't judge her.

When Jax introduced himself as Damon Jackson, the receptionist looked disappointed and maybe a little confused. "From something Mr. Pendleton said, I thought you were Franklin Jackson's son. I imagine there are a lot of Jacksons in Georgia, so that was foolish of me. He'll be right with you."

Evie nudged Jax. The damned dense man didn't know opportunity when it grabbed him by the throat. Well, mostly, he didn't know how to lie without planning ahead.

Jax glared but rather than let Evie speak, he did. "Franklin Jackson *is* my father. Did you know him?"

The receptionist still looked confused, but she smiled at a memory. "He gave me my first job in this office. I never thought Franklin would marry. Goes to show how wrong we can be. You must look like your mother."

Ding, another piece of the puzzle nailed. Jax did *not* look like Franklin, verified by someone who'd known him well.

"So I've been told," Jax said genially.

Evie wondered if that was truth or lie. He was good when it mattered.

"How is your father doing? I wish he'd stayed in touch. We missed him around here."

"We lost him in a car crash when I was just a kid. It's nice to hear good things about him though, so thank you." Jax's southern hospitality didn't come naturally, but it did rear its head upon occasion.

"Oh, I'm so sorry! No wonder he never brought you back to visit his old stomping grounds."

"So you were here when he sold the office?"

The woman's smile dimmed. Evie checked the desk but there was no name plate.

"He closed the office after his partner died in that dreadful mine collapse. The next thing I knew, he'd sold the place, lock, stock, and barrel and took off for some job back east. But he gave his staff recommendations, so we were all hired back. It was a long time ago, I suppose. Forgive an old woman's reminiscences." A buzzer rang and she gestured toward a door. "Mr. Pendleton can see you now."

Evie had the distinct feeling that the secretaries behind the glass window to the right were listening to every word. She wanted to linger, but Jax grabbed her elbow and steered her in, intent on his own defined goal and not her— admittedly—blurry one. As they left, the receptionist was already reaching for her phone—to tell her friends about Franklin's son? And how much he *didn't* look like his father. Or how much he looked like his father's partner? *That* could make for some good gossip.

The man behind the desk was old enough to be Jax's father. Balding, with gray hair, wire-rimmed spectacles, and trim enough to show that he exercised regularly, he stood and offered his hand. "Damon Jackson? This is amazing. I haven't heard from Franklin in decades."

Evie tuned out while Jax went into his spiel about his parents dying, yadda yadda. It gave her an opportunity to examine Pendleton's aura. He appeared to be a nice, if not very exciting, man. She gauged from his lack of interest that he hadn't known Franklin Jackson as well as his receptionist, but she saw curiosity, presumably at Jax's presence.

She tuned back in when Jax laid the key on the desk.

"In going through my father's effects in search of something else recently, I came across this, along with this cryptic code." He added a note of the letters he'd copied from the circuit board.

Not a flat-out lie. He was a lawyer, after all. But he still hadn't said the magic word. Now seemed an opportune time.

"And then I came along." Evie smiled at both men. "When I asked about Aaron Ives, it seemed an auspicious reason to visit our origins." She came from a family who knew how to obfuscate and embellish.

"Ives?" Pendleton's gray eyebrows rose.

Evie smiled like a half-baked simpleton with wind between her ears. "He was a partner of Jackson's, wasn't he? That's why I hunted down Jax. I'm trying to match DNA but not making a lot of progress."

Jax smoothly picked up her trail. "It seemed a long shot that you might have thirty-year-old files, but along with the bank box situation, we didn't see any harm in trying."

Evie figured he'd like to muffle her, but she wanted to move forward. If they couldn't explore California and hot tubs, she needed to go home, file for mayor, and get back to business.

"Hmm, I see. Well, genealogy is a fascination, and from all I know, Ives was an interesting fellow. I never really knew him, of course. He died shortly before I bought Franklin's practice. I think it might have been his death that caused Franklin to pack it in and move to the opposite coast. They'd been boyhood friends, if I remember correctly. So you might be on the right track. It's just too old to follow."

"You knew my father?" Jax asked.

Pendleton shrugged. "Not really. I bought this law practice through a company that sets up these exchanges. We met when we signed the papers, that's about it. His clients were all highly respectable and his files were in excellent condition. As an attorney yourself, you can understand the importance. Since Ives had already perished at that point, I had no reason to open his files, if there are any. All that material was scanned and digitalized decades ago."

Bingo. Pendleton was far more technologically advanced than the law firm where Jax had been working, where half their files were still paper and stored in boxes.

"But y'all can access the Ives' file? And maybe Franklin Jackson's, since they were friends?" Evie asked eagerly, leaning forward and laying on the Southern accent. She wasn't in the habit of flashing cleavage, but last night had awakened dormant hormones. Pendleton was distracted enough to remove his glasses to clean them.

"Yes, yes, I imagine I can. Both files? Hmmm, there would be a fee, of course."

"Thank you, sir. Of course, we'll reimburse you for any time you spend on us." Jax jumped in, forcing Evie to sit back. He tapped on the key and the code. "My research indicates there was a Bank of Mojave thirty years ago, which would correspond with the BoM on here. We're hoping the number is the box number. I know California code is strict on descendants accessing safe deposit boxes, but I have all the paperwork from my father's death. Can you verify that the Monarch Bank currently occupying the same address would be the new name?"

"If you have the probate letters releasing Franklin Jackson's assets in your name, you should be fine. I can't verify that the safe-deposit boxes weren't emptied when the bank changed ownership or that the fees were paid on the box. That's a real longshot, son."

"I know, but it's intriguing, isn't it? Like finding a treasure map. One has to look. But discovering what we can of Aaron Ives for my client is the more pressing business. How long do you think it will take for your secretaries to track down the material?" Jax scooped up the key and dropped it in the pocket of his jacket. He wasn't wearing one of his suits, but the blazer looked sufficiently preppy for a lawyer on vacation.

"We're not busy this time of year. Give me your business card. I'll need to verify there is no other next of kin and that a DNA report is sufficient relationship to release the files. Then I'll have them transferred as soon as they're located." Pendleton stood. "It's been a pleasure doing business with you. It's good to know that Franklin's son turned out to be a gentleman. You favor your father strongly, if my memory recalls."

Whoops. Not what the receptionist had said.

Evie didn't even have to study Jax's aura to know it shot excited lights from his root chakra. The lawyer had just verified that the man from whom he'd bought the firm had *not* been Franklin Jackson, but a man who looked like *Jax* —who looked like the Aaron Ives in the photo. How had Ives pulled off such a fraud?

When they left, the gray-haired receptionist was talking earnestly with a large older woman tottering on spiked heels. Dressed in a designer suit and dripping diamonds, the older woman appeared to be an important client. There would be no way of questioning the receptionist again. Dang. And the secretaries in the other office were on the phone and the computer—already responding to Pendleton's request?

Incongruously, Diamond Lady sported a purple ball cap with an eagle pin similar to Marge's. She stared after them as they approached the door. Evie felt an itch between her shoulder blades as they let themselves out. Should she have investigated a *client's* aura? That didn't seem practical.

They were both silent once they were in the car. Jax started the engine and drove down the street to the bank they'd looked up last night. It wasn't a large town. Evie enjoyed the Spanish-style architecture and the weird trees and flowers, but small-town people were predictable. She had this notion that eyes followed them everywhere.

Were there people here who remembered Aaron Ives well enough for Jax's resemblance to stir old memories? Ives must have assumed the identity of his friend and partner, pulled up roots, and transplanted himself clear across the country for a very good reason.

"Judging by the marriage certificate, my father married just before he moved to Georgia." As if following her train of thought, Jax parked in the bank lot and stared out the windshield. "His mine had collapsed, possibly with his best friend and partner inside. So Aaron Ives abandoned his land, sold Franklin's law office, married his girlfriend under a false name—and ran for his life?"

"If he was anything like you, he was running *toward* something. I can't picture you or him as men who would turn tail, even if they're protecting loved ones. Although, I suppose your mother could have been persuasive." Evie offered Jax a compelling smile, traced a finger down his square jaw, and purred seductively. "Your father may have been running from a killer, who could still be on the loose. Want to go home and keep me safe?"

Jax's snort was almost a chuckle. "You win. Goals come first, running, later. Let's see how many noses we need to twist to find out about an ancient deposit box."

While Nose #1, the first bank clerk, called for her supervisor, Evie unfocused and amused herself by letting her third eye explore the small lobby. Most of the tellers had normal, dull auras—about as expected. A broad-shouldered hulk in loose work shirt, jeans, and boots entered—wearing a purple ball cap. Must be a local sports team. His aura was muddy and angry, but that went for a lot of people these days. He frowned at the deposit slip desk as if not knowing what to do. He confirmed that impression by pulling out a phone to call someone.

Nose #2 arrived, brimming with curiosity but unwilling to open the deposit box. Evie began to feel as if they were a circus on parade. This nose led them back to an office, at least.

Nose #3 was a manager who finally accepted the documentation Jax presented, then called Pendleton just to be certain it was legal. As if the security box were his own, the slick-looking young man in a fancy suit grudgingly pulled up files on his computer.

"We still have an account in the name of Franklin Jackson, with that birth date and social security number. The only transactions are withdrawals for safe deposit box fees. Originally, there was no charge for the fees. They would have sent out notices when that policy changed. Apparently the address we had was no longer forwarding. We've gone to paperless statements since then. Let's see if the box is still there." He led them back to a secure area where they signed books, and he picked up a second set of keys.

Amazed that their request had worked, Evie bit her lip and kept silent for a change. She'd read up on deposit boxes after Jax's earlier remarks. He was blessed that the bank hadn't sold the building and thrown all the box contents into storage. Valuables had a habit of disappearing in storage.

The bank manager tested Jax's key. It worked. He removed the box to a private viewing room and left them with it.

"I think I'm shaking," Evie whispered.

"Take pictures for Ariel," he whispered back, opening the lid.

A most excellent idea. It kept her from slipping into la-la land. This new phone had its uses, she decided. She videoed everything he removed from the box—mostly papers. No treasure maps or gold. But to Jax, those papers might be worth more than gold.

"Aaron Ives's birth certificate. Deeds to his land and mining company. His graduation certificates and law license. This box did *not* belong to Franklin Jackson. It's proof that Aaron Ives existed." Jax was still whispering as if they were in a library.

"So why did he steal his partner's identity?" She had no phone reception in here, but she set up a text message to go as soon as they walked out. Jax's sister had known they were coming here today. She had to be fretting.

Jax opened a brown, expanding document case. "We can't read through all this now. Let's pick up something to eat, find a pretty view for lunch, take a look, then head home."

For some reason, that sounded ominous. Evie helped him place the fragile certificates into the folding file. "Wouldn't digital records have been better?"

"These certificates date from *before* 1990. The world wide web was barely a gleam in one guy's eye at that point. Scanners ate RAM and only businesses had them. I have no idea what shape Franklin's digital files will be in when and if we receive them." He tucked the folder under his arm as casually as if he carried newspapers and led the way out.

She let him get away with mansplaining because it was interesting. Thirty years ago was probably from before Jax had been born and well before she came into existence. She might have grown up poor, but she'd always known an internet.

It took forever to close out the box and transfer the remaining bank account to Jax. The box fees had eaten into the balance. Once upon a time, Jax's father had probably replenished the funds—until he died. The current balance would have run out in a few years. They'd majorly lucked out.

Evie was starving by the time they walked away. She waited until they pulled through a fast-food drive-in and were on the way down the road before she asked, "Can I start reading now? Or do you want to wait and look first?"

"Right now, I'm so rattled, I want your Cousin Orbis to see them."

That was pretty rattled. He'd never met her psychometrist cousin and didn't believe in psychometry. "That might be a smart thing to do, but I don't think we can wait three days before reading through this."

"I know. This looks like a good place where we can read them in private." Jax looked grim as he steered the car into what appeared to be a casino parking lot.

Evie had noticed a dirty pickup truck with a crumpled fender following them from the bank and the fast-food joint, but it was basically a one-road town, so she tried not to worry too much. It drove on past on the desert two-lane.

Her sense of paranoia didn't entirely diminish—probably because intelligent, educated men didn't vanish or commit fraud for innocent reasons—but the truck faded from her worries.

The parking lot overlooked a lake. A lake among cactus and tumbleweed boggled her mind and distracted her easily distractible thoughts. Jax parked in between two RVs, so they were practically invisible.

"You don't think we're being followed, do you?" She could tell from his aura that he was as uneasy as she was. Maybe he'd noticed the truck too.

"No, but I take precautions if we're talking about murder." He dug into his hamburger box. "What would make a man pretend to be dead?"

"If we're talking murder, two things." Evie greedily sipped her drink, then opened up her salad. "His partner getting killed, in a place where *he* was supposed to be? I mean, lawyers don't generally go down in mines, do they? If Aaron Ives suspected the collapse wasn't an accident, he wanted to keep himself and his new wife from being murdered too." She paused for effect, then added, "Or he could have killed his partner and run off with his money."

"Since my father never struck me as a killer, and we certainly weren't wealthy, let's set aside the latter possibility for now. Aaron Ives married my mother in Vegas under the name of Franklin Jackson. Surely my mother knew him as Ives?"

"Did her family know him as Jackson or Ives? Who witnessed their wedding—oh, right, Vegas. It could have been Elvis." Evie poked a tomato and tried to imagine a terrified couple fleeing across the country because a friend had been murdered. "So, if someone died in that mine, it was most likely Franklin, since he was never seen again. And Aaron presumably thought it wasn't an accident. Why?"

"That's what I'm hoping is in those papers." Jax nodded to the back seat, where he'd stashed them. "I want them all copied and in the cloud before we go much farther."

"Are we good to go then, if Pendleton can email you what he has? I need to get back and file the election paperwork before the deadline." Evie hoped he would say they were leaving immediately. Even geriatric killers from thirty years ago made her nervous.

He scowled. "Can't Afterthought find anyone else to take the mayor's job? Just because we uncovered his fraud doesn't mean you're obligated to take his place. Let's face it, even your mother is a better candidate than you."

She stole one of his fries and flung it at him. "Someone with ethics needs to clean house. If I don't do it, then we'll be stuck with Paul Clancy, a stooge from the town council who'll do the mayor's bidding, even from jail."

"Fine. It's your time you're wasting. I can probably do most of my interviews by phone, now that we have these documents and Pendleton is sending us what he has. I don't like hanging around anymore than you do." He opened his phone and began searching. "We're near I-40. If we're ready to head home, I'd rather find a place down the road to scan and mail this stuff. I'm not showing anything resembling a FedEx office ahead though."

Evie was playing with her map app much more slowly. "Wow, this really is desert. Look, there's Needles! Isn't that where Snoopy's brother lives?"

Jax shot her an incredulous look. "Right. Think he has a scanner?"

"Probably. But Yucca might be closer. There are two places there. Are you sure we shouldn't read some of the papers first?" Evie finished off her salad and rewarded herself with a big chocolate chip cookie.

"You read while I drive." He finished off his burger, wiped his hands, and reached behind the seat for the folder.

Evie handed him half her cookie. "Sweeten up, tiger. I've never seen the West before. Drive slowly and let me enjoy it between pages."

The look Jax gave her was smoldering and nearly melted her spine. Three days in the car with all those hormones. . .

With a sigh, probably of frustration, Evie pulled out the first of the yellowing documents. "Herewith and henceforth. . ." She stopped reading. "Really? You really want me to read a contract?"

Jax halted the car before it left the parking lot. "Do you drive?"

Evie widened her eyes and shoved the papers into the folder. "I have a license, honest. I just don't have a car. Can I put it in power drive?"

To give him credit, he didn't roll his eyes. "You drive, I'll read. Then you can enjoy the scenery."

She really could kiss him. She refrained. They played musical seats, and Evie happily pulled out of the lot, following the GPS lady robot's directions and heading northeast. "I was made to drive. I have eyes in the back of my head."

Jax removed the papers from the file and read silently, for which she was grateful.

A few minutes later, he whistled sharply. It wasn't a good whistle.

"What?" she demanded. She couldn't look at him. It had been a while since she'd been behind the wheel.

"Stockton and Stockton were the attorneys for Sovereign Machinery."

S&S was the firm Jax had worked for, until Stephen Stockton turned out to be running a form of fraudulent Ponzi scheme involving stealing from client escrow accounts.

S&S was where Aaron Ives/Franklin Jackson had accepted a position after moving east. He'd been investigating Stockton's fraud when he died in a car crash.

Well, crap-a-doodle.

Five

WHILE EVIE DROVE, JAX TOOK PHOTOS OF THE MORE IMPORTANT DOCUMENTS AND shot them to Reuben, Roark, and Ariel. One was the partnership agreement between Franklin and Jackson leaving the mine and the law firm to each other. He whistled and sent that off.

This material was too important to be left unsecured. He was debating how much needed scanning when he noticed the car slowing down. Evie had been driving well over the speed limit with the rest of the traffic. He glanced up to see if there were cops along the roadside.

She pulled in between two lumbering semis.

"Tired? Want me to drive?" he asked.

"I'm not pulling off the road in the middle of nowhere. Keep an eye out for a battered silver F100 with a taped front fender." She tapped her fingers impatiently on the steering wheel as they practically crawled down the road.

Jax pulled up his map app and began checking off-ramps. "We're almost in Yucca. I doubt it's big enough to lose anyone. Why would anyone follow us?"

"No idea. I saw the truck when we pulled out of the bank and the drive-through but figured one-road-town, you see the same vehicles everywhere." She checked highway signs and her rearview mirror. "I thought we'd lost him at the casino."

Jax realized she hadn't been lying when she said she had eyes in the back of her head. Evie's ADHD had benefits. Once focused, she managed to look everywhere at once and process what she saw in instants. He would never have noticed the cars around them. "When did you spot him again?"

"They must have been waiting for us to leave the casino. They've been about three cars back ever since. I tried speeding up, but they've stayed right there for miles now. Or I'm being paranoid and playing games. Six of one, half a dozen of the other."

"Ramp ahead in two miles. We can pull off, cross the bridge, head the other way, see if they do the same."

"Two miles, cool, got it. I've always wanted to play cops and robbers." She pulled from between the semis, hit the gas, passed the line of trucks, and almost missed the ramp on the far side, correcting to hit the pavement, and speeding up to the narrow two-lane.

"Damn, you drive just like you grew up in California."

"My mother taught me defensive driving. You really don't want to know." She pumped the gas pedal over the bridge.

Jax watched the highway below. "They're stuck with the semis. You have two minutes on them."

"Flat land sucks." She took the ramp back to the interstate going west.

Jax couldn't argue with that. He watched but the pick-up didn't follow. "They missed the turn or we're cracking up. They have another opportunity to turn around in a few miles, and then it's just desert. Watch for a gas station. This car gets good mileage but their tank is bigger."

"So is their engine. But it will give us a chance to see if they turn around."

The desert didn't harbor much in the way of gas stations. They were practically back in the town where they'd started before they found one. Jax filled the tank while Evie hunted for directions to a UPS or similar store. He kept an eye on trucks passing on the interstate, but the angle wasn't good. The Subaru was pretty well hidden behind a building, so maybe they'd lost them. Or Evie had been imagining things.

"Let me drive again. You find the copy store and keep an eye out." Jax knew he was capable of vehicular homicide if threatened. Evie wouldn't be. The whole scenario had his nerves hopping. "I think I've sent photos of the most vital information. I still want to scan and mail the whole package so R&R can be working on it."

"You don't think someone has been waiting around for thirty years to see what's in that box, do you? That's kind of crazy." She slid into the passenger seat. "Mr. Pendleton and the bank manager seemed to be perfectly harmless. I can't imagine they set thieves on us over a bunch of old papers."

"We don't know we were being followed, but if we were—the receptionist recognized my name. Mr. Pendleton had his secretaries looking for my father's old files. We talked to four people at the bank who know what we were after. For all that matters, Marge lives just on the boundary of my father's old ranch and might have gossiped about how much I looked like him. It's a small town. Gossip spreads. The question would be *why*." Jax followed the phone's directions to a small mail service office Evie had located.

"Did that old contract contain anything interesting besides the law firm connection?" Evie peered around as he parked. "No silver F100, but people could be watching for this car. Give me the keys. While you're scanning, I'll divert them."

"You're having a little too much fun with this." Jax tucked the document file under his blazer and studied her. Short, with huge crystal-blue eyes, tousled orange curls, and wearing a bright red T-shirt that said *I should come with a warning label,* Evie needed a warning label, for certain. Bad guys wouldn't even look twice, and she'd have them wrapped in knots before they knew it. Or he was insane. Probably the latter. But she was right. Diversion couldn't hurt.

"More than one contract, mostly for what appears to be motherboards. I'm no engineer, but apparently my father was. It appears he was doing more than mining silicon. I can only assume the contracts are evidence of some sort, or he was as paranoid as we are. Take your pick."

"Then the circuit board we found might be evidence too. Use mail and not UPS. You can send the box to the post office in Afterthought and not use my address." She popped out of her seat, took his keys, and slid beneath the wheel after he exited. "If you're not here when I get back, I expect you to be in fast-food city across the street. I'll hit the horn, hard, so you know I'm there."

"You watch too many TV shows." Except she didn't own a TV. Jax slammed the door and watched Evie peel out of the parking lot. He checked to be certain no one followed her. She immediately turned down the side street and into a trailer park. Huh.

It took half-past forever to scan all the material and upload to his cloud account. Then he had the clerk package up the original documents and send them express to himself via Evie's post office. No point involving any other names, in case the clerks talked too. He could hope Afterthought's post office was as safe as a bank until R&R could pick them up.

While he texted his team the info, he watched out the window for battered silver trucks. A filthy white Subaru bearing a magnetic placard advertising a construction company pulled into the parking lot instead. A 4x4 stuck out the rear seat window, with a red flag tied to it. It took half a minute before he recognized his own car.

Going outside, he glared at the imp leaping from the front seat, dangling his keys. "It's a damned good thing that isn't my Jag." He snatched the keys away.

"I think we need to head for LA. It's easier to get lost there. And then you need to sell this baby so we can take a plane home. I'm nervous about leaving Loretta and my family alone." She fled to the passenger side and climbed in without further explanation.

That sounded unpromising. "I have a trunk full of gear," he protested, backing out of the lot. "Last-minute plane fare is expensive." And his savings were dwindling rapidly.

"My ticket is paid. Checking your bags is less expensive than buying gas across the country. Plane ticket might be a little more than hotels and food, but we need to go home. I hope you're not seriously attached to this car." She crossed her arms and glared out the windshield, occasionally checking the side door mirror.

She'd already programmed her phone for directions. Jax followed the instructions back to the highway debating how attached one could become to a used Subaru.

"What happened?" Lacking her ability to look every which way at once, he scowled and relied on her instincts while he navigated traffic and the route.

"There are cop cars at Pendleton's office. And a battered F100 on a side street, where a driver could watch. I took a photo of his license plate."

THE INSTANT SHE MENTIONED COPS, JACKASS TRIED TO TURN AROUND AND GO BACK to the law office. Evie grabbed the steering wheel. "Maybe Pendleton found something in those files implicating your father in murder. He might have called the cops on us. Keep going."

Muttering obscenities, he obeyed. "Text R&R. See what they can find out."

As long as he kept driving toward LA, Evie texted his hacker team. She didn't know how to find police or sheriff reports on a phone. She just had this really bad feeling. . .

Maybe the bad feeling was from *not* going back to the office to see what was going on. She didn't like running away any more than Jax did. But not being followed seemed more pertinent to their well-being. She kept checking over her shoulder to be certain they hadn't been picked up again.

Surprisingly, Jax didn't argue too hard about flying home. There may have been something in those papers he wasn't telling her about. That would be just like him.

They ran the car through a car wash in LA, threw away the sign and 4x4, and sold it for more than enough to cover airfare on the economy airline she'd taken. Apparently, the demand for 4-wheel drive in LA was higher than back home.

By dinner time, Evie was sinking into the hard airport seat with relief. "Teach me to drink wine. I want to be blotto for the next hours." She had time to fret over nice Mr. Pendleton now, but she was helpless to do anything. Blotto would prevent jumping out of her skin.

"We have no good reason beyond paranoia to believe we're being followed or that Pendleton called the cops on us." Jax was already sporting a sexy unshaven appearance that would look even better if he'd been wearing one of his tight T-shirts instead of the stupid blazer. "Let's have a nice dinner and relax, then you can sleep all the way home."

Evie was trying to focus on the here and now and not the emotion roiling beneath the surface. Jax's normally narrow red aura had awakened with a vengeance. The killer streak was still there, not completely hiding the lust. But the muddy gray of guardedness and a strong protective streak had sprung up. Straightforward, honest Jax was never muddy. This trip was messing with his head.

"Unless you have access to an executive lounge, I'm gonna guess *nice dinner* is a euphemism for not fast-food. If they have chocolate, I'm on. Can I charge it to Loretta as part of my travel expense?" Evie dragged herself up, hauling her duffle. She traveled light. It didn't take much room for T-shirts and shorts, which were about all she owned.

"Asian or Irish?" he asked, checking the terminal map. "Chocolate probably requires Irish."

"Beer. I can do beer. Or Irish coffee with whipped cream and chocolate! Lead on and give me the hard stuff."

Having checked all his gear at the desk, Jax took her duffle and swung it over his back. "It's midnight back East. Think anyone has read those documents yet?"

"They'd text you if they found anything, but yeah, I'm gonna bet your buds are dissecting every paragraph. Unless we have clients who want more than raccoons chased from their attic, which probably ain't happening." Evie took the booth the waitress led them to and decided the seat was far more comfortable than the one at the gate.

At least, this way they wouldn't be spending days together in that little car. And nights sharing a motel room. She seriously needed to move past this attraction to a control freak who saw nothing but his immediate goal—which wasn't her. She'd learned from family experience that men just didn't hang around weird women very long, and she wasn't the type for part-time flings.

Jax was way too attractive for a part-time fling. He was heartbreak territory. With Loretta in the mix—she needed to keep her distance.

"Your Sensible Solutions agency needs better social media presence. Reuben and Roark are the opposite of social. And you don't want Loretta involved in that internet swamp. So it has to be you. Are you posting about this trip?" He ordered two beers and perused the menu.

"What, exactly, should I post? I met a Navajo ghost and sent him on? We uncovered a key at an abandoned mine following nothing that I had anything to do with? I never learned to sell myself. I've always accepted that I can do things others can't and thought people would respect that." Tired and disgruntled, she studied the menu.

"What you do is subtle, so yeah, you'll be lousy at running for mayor. I need a job. Pity I don't live there or I'd run." He slumped against the vinyl seat and sipped his beer. "Wonder if Ariel will let me move in since I'm paying the rent."

"Face it, your sister is a hermit. I have a huge house. R&R are in the cellar. Loretta wants to claim the attic. You can have the first floor, and I'll take the second. Find an office by the courthouse and hang out a shingle or set one up in the empty carriage house until I can afford a car. You might only get drunks looking for bail as clients, but it's a job that doesn't require much thinking. I assume your father's case will take most of your time, unless your adoptive father hires you to defend his crimes." Evie thought she might need a good head shrink for offering her home, but Jax was Loretta's guardian just as she was. He ought to shoulder some responsibility.

She carefully didn't mention that.

"I'm not a defense lawyer, and after paying back his victims, Stephen has less money than I do, so it's just me and you. Huh, we both need media gurus. Or I could paint park benches with my photo and a logo, *Call Jax for the max bail*. Needs work." He looked as tired as she felt.

"*Jax for the Max*. Except you're not really Jax, are you? *Ives for Your Hives* doesn't ring any bells." Evie fought the urge to slide in next to him and give him a hug. He'd lost his identity, his job, given up his house and car. . . A hug was hardly enough.

"*Ives for your Lives*, except that double pronunciation reeks. Have to do TV ads so people could hear it. And why in hell are we talking advertising?" He pulled out his phone.

"Because something bad may have happened in the office of a nice, helpful man we just talked to. We may have lost our opportunity to see your father's files. We may or may not have been tailed by unknown suspects, and we're clueless." Morosely, Evie dug into the shepherd's pie she'd ordered. After only eating a salad at lunch, she was starving, but the day's tension had churned her stomach into a gnawing monster. She hoped potatoes were soporific.

Jax held up his phone screen.

It was only a small note on a local newspaper website about the passing of Caleb Pendleton in his law office. Only survivor was a daughter in Oregon.

"Damn. Well, they didn't say suspected murder. At least we know they're not after us." Evie poked at her pie. "Only a daughter. Kinda sad if all you have at the end of the day is a bed to sleep in and a job to go to." She might be closer than most to the spirit world, but that didn't mean she took death lightly. Still, her paranoia returned realizing they might have been the last clients Pendleton saw.

"Better than a tent on the street. For all we know, he belonged to all the charitable organizations in town and had an active social life. We should send flowers." Setting aside his phone, Jax dug into the steak he'd ordered.

Because she knew his sister stayed awake most of the night, Evie snapped a photo of Jax looking tired and delicious and chugging beer and sent it to Ariel.

Ariel responded with a photo from what appeared to be a high school yearbook. It looked exactly like Jax if he'd been fifteen years younger—except judging from the clothing and the name beneath, it wasn't Jax. Evie showed it to him. "Your sister has been busy."

"Aaron Ives," he read. "*Damn.* Buzz cut, like mine, except I wore mine long in high school."

Evie took the phone back and studied the screen. "Same jaw line. Same gray eyes, nice tan. Ives must have dominant genes. I can't see any evidence of your mother."

"The tan doesn't wear off," he said dryly, chugging his beer. "Mom had dark hair too. Tall, for a woman, if I'm remembering clearly. I was just twelve when they died, so my perspective may be off."

Another image appeared on the screen. This one showed a serious youth with a narrow, pale face, glasses, and a hank of brownish hair falling into green eyes. She showed it to Jax. "Franklin Jackson, same year."

Jax looked resigned. "I should probably text the Oswins with the information so they can add me to their genealogy charts. Maybe they can find out more. Or I can wait for the DNA report."

His phone pinged. They both looked at it.

"We could pretend we're on the airplane," Evie suggested.

"It might be Ariel with more pictures." Jax looked rightfully doubtful, since his sister had been messaging Evie.

"Not unless you texted her first, which you never do. Maybe it's the Oswin person you met. He's at least in this time zone. It's nearly ten. We need to be paying the bill and heading for the gate." Unlike her mother and Great-Aunt Val, Evie didn't possess an ounce of precognition, but she still sensed an ominous message behind that ping.

She'd had a bad feeling about cops at Pendleton's office, and he was dead. She should pay heed to her instincts—except, in Jax's universe, not checking a text message wasn't happening.

Finishing his beer and gesturing for the waitress, Jax swept the phone off the table and punched the buttons. "Police report. Reuben's been hacking."

"Surely the cops have better security here than in a small town like. . ." That was a stupid thought. A desert small town wasn't any different than her hometown just because it was in California.

Grimly, he turned the phone toward her. He had the screen widened to make it easier to read.

Gunshot to the temple, suicide.

"Nope." Evie pushed away her plate. "Nope. No way. That man had no reason to kill himself. He was murdered."

She got up and left for the ladies' room.

She'd wanted to be a detective. She hadn't wanted to cause murders in the process. Now what the dickens did they do?

Six

"THERE IS NOTHING YOU COULD HAVE DONE," JAX INSISTED TIREDLY THE NEXT morning as they climbed out of the van in Evie's driveway. Their flight had been uneventful, but without business class seating, he felt like tuna squashed in a can. He'd have to get used to poverty.

Reuben had met them at the airport in the team's stripped-down utility van for the long haul back to Afterthought, which hadn't been much more comfortable.

"You said yourself that ghosts seldom manifest immediately after a violent death," he continued their exhausted argument.

"I could be wrong. It's not as if I'm that experienced." Evie heaved her duffel over her shoulder. "Or there might have been other spirits who saw something. I should have gone back instead of running home. Poor Mr. Pendleton deserves better than to be dismissed as a suicide! No wonder I'm only a dog walker. I'm useless."

Jax agreed with the sentiment about Pendleton, but sending Evie back there was *not* the solution. Her safety was more important than a stranger's ghost, but he was argued out—a sad state for a lawyer.

"Ain't useless," Reuben called from the back of the van, where he was unloading Jax's gear. His tribal scars emphasizing his angular jaw, his top knot still adorned by a bone, Reuben matched Roark in scariness, but he was more of a nerd than his partner. "Bubble witch needs you. Your mama needs you. And you gonna be one funky mayor."

On top of being unable to solve the mysteries they'd left behind, it was damned dispiriting hauling his few possessions to the servants' quarters of Evie's—*her aunt's*—home. He'd hit some lows before, but this was a new bottom. Afghanistan had probably been more devastating, but at least he'd had a home and job to go to afterward.

Jax loaded up with his gear and luggage, thinking he'd have to sleep on them. They wouldn't fit under the narrow bed in the bedroom off the kitchen where he'd slept before he'd taken off to California.

"I have no media presence," Evie informed them, sounding as depressed as he felt. "I won't be mayor."

It was all his fault she wasn't her usual bouncy self. Jax added guilt to his list of miseries.

Loretta ran down the street, presumably from the tarot shop Evie's mother owned. "You're back, you're back! Can we have chocolate milkshakes to celebrate?"

The kid had more money than the entire town but could still get excited by ice cream. Jax thought there was a lesson in that, but he was too tired to learn it. Her excitement almost made him smile though. When had anyone ever greeted him with such cheerfulness? His elderly adoptive family hadn't exactly been the warm and welcoming sort.

Evie opened her arms to hug their ward—as he hadn't. "Tadpole! Where's your magic wand? I need you to turn me into a toad."

"Harry Potter doesn't turn people into toads," the kid said with scorn, leading the way into the house. "He fights evil. I need to conjure spells for the wand to work."

Jax wondered if fighting evil with a magic sword was as exhausting as doing it in courtrooms. Hauling his bags up the kitchen stairs, he addressed Reuben and Roark quietly while Evie and Loretta chattered and dug through the refrigerator. "Anywhere we can have a talk about those papers I sent?"

"Cellar. I can beat Reuben's score on Pac-Man while we talk. Not much to tell you, though." Roark stacked boxes inside the bedroom by the kitchen door.

"A crap player like you can't beat a firefly," Reuben retorted.

"Decent meal first," Evie shouted at them. "Brains don't work without being fed."

"Man, it's good having a cook again." Roark helped himself to the coffee machine Jax had bought for himself, back in the days of luxury.

Communal living should be entertaining. Maybe he could talk his hermit sister into letting him move in with her. Although he'd need a car again if he lived out in the woods.

"So, do I still call you Jax? Or you want to be Demon now?" Loretta asked, sliding into her place at the breakfast banquette. The kid seemed to know everything going on.

"Demon!" Evie called. "I like that."

"Better than Dam, I suppose." Jax took the bench across from her. "But I prefer Jax, if I get a choice. It's what my parents called me." To solidify their stolen identity? Or dare he hope they were honoring a lost friend?

"Did you have fun with Aster and Gracie?" Evie slid what looked like a pancake with chocolate chips in front of Loretta.

"They have a trampoline in the backyard! And Aster may be learning to talk to dogs." The kid slathered the pancake with peanut butter, then topped it with whipped cream.

Jax hoped Evie was fixing something more edible for the adults.

"Mavis said she's running for mayor," Reuben said out of the blue, taking the seat beside Loretta.

Jax winced and sighed as Evie slammed down her spatula, turned off the stove, and stripped off her apron.

"I assume you didn't really want breakfast?" he asked the idiot nerd across from him.

"Reuben doesn't have people smarts." Loretta contentedly dug into her pancake. "And Evie only has to cook for me."

Wordlessly, Evie walked out.

Roark reached over the table to swat his friend, then scooted out of the booth. "I can fry eggs."

"He burns them," Reuben muttered.

Nope, communal living was not going to work. Jax couldn't abandon Loretta to go after Evie. . . But R&R had been looking after the kid these past days. What in hell did he know? Except that he was hungry, and he didn't want to do a witch fight on an empty stomach.

Jax slid out of the booth to see if Evie had started buying bacon yet. The refrigerator had 2% milk and eggs but no bacon. He found ham slices, though, and amazingly, bagels. He dumped a bagel into the toaster, rescued an egg from the griddle, and fixed a breakfast sandwich for himself. The clowns could fix their own.

By the time he had his food ready, Loretta had polished off her dessert breakfast and was patiently waiting for Reuben to move his carcass so she could deposit the plate in the sink. Muttering, Reuben slid out to fix a bagel and steal a rubbery egg.

"Let's go find Evie," Jax suggested to the kid. Maybe Evie and her mother wouldn't fight in front of a kid. "She's tired."

"Her bubble isn't sparkly," Loretta said, as if agreeing. "Can I have a bite of your sandwich?"

"You didn't give me a bite of your pancake." Jax left his culinary-deficient friends to haggle over who washed the dishes and set out for Afterthought's Main Street.

Evie was a prickly explosive even when things were normal. Nothing was normal right now. Jax expected the roof to blow off Mavis's shop at any second.

"You knew I was filing for that job as soon as I got back!" Evie was shouting as they stopped in the doorway.

"The Universe has spoken. You would quit the moment something more interesting came along," Mavis countered with a vague wave of her hand.

Jax figured Mavis was right, but that wasn't the point. He directed Loretta down the street. "Why don't you run down and buy a box of donuts? That will cool them down."

"Their bubbles are big," Loretta answered enigmatically, holding out her hand for money.

The line between his ward's expenses and his own was being cut pretty fine. He handed her cash and she happily skipped off.

"You don't even have the business sense to sue the city when they steal your land! You'd be telling the council their futures instead of paying attention to what needs doing." Evie's argument needed more focus.

Jax stepped in between mother and daughter, thinking he really needed his head examined, but he apparently had nothing better to do than get his head shot off. *Magicked* off. "You're both right and you'd both make lousy mayors. You're people oriented, not business oriented. Admittedly, a female on the city council would be a nice change of pace, but half the town is Black. Wouldn't that be even better?"

Identical crystal blue eyes glared at him. Well, *glare* was probably too strong a word. Evie had slipped into one of her blank trances, and Mavis was crinkling her already wrinkled eyes. Jax thought maybe that was a psychic glare. While they were quiet, he continued, "The council is all white male. That has to end. I'm assuming they're all the mayor's cronies?"

"Next council election isn't for two years. Mayor's position is only open because Mayor Blockhead got himself arrested. Paul Clancy just filed papers. He's one of the council's own," Evie said in indignation. "I know everyone in town. And since I'm the reason the mayor had to resign, I have recognition now."

"It took a *team* of us to bring the mayor down. It will take a team to elect someone new. The council has a team, you don't." Jax suspected he was being selfish in wanting Evie focused on Loretta so he could go his own way. But he was also pretty certain he was right. The town knew Evie as a bubble-headed dog walker—which might be better than a self-serving fraud, admittedly.

"I have my family! I can round up a team. And before you say I can't focus on the details. . . I *know* that. So I'll use my salary to hire people who can." She said that triumphantly. "I just want to bring diversity and honesty to this town."

"And keep them off Witch Hill," Mavis muttered. "And get us the pharmacy they promised."

"Fine then, if you're agreed on your goals, work together to find a candidate who represents them. You have what, two weeks before the final filing date?" Jax sighed in relief as Loretta burst through the door carrying a box of donuts.

"We could send Loretta out as a scout to find the best bubble in town." Evie gloomily helped herself to an apple fritter. "I can scout for honest auras. But neither tells us if they're capable of doing the work."

"Which is why government always ends up in the hands of lawyers." Jax held up his glazed donut. "No, I'm not running. You don't need another white man."

"Reuben's Black and smart." Loretta studied the box carefully before choosing an éclair. "But his bubble is twisted."

"And he's not a resident yet and he's not a people person. We are." Mavis stoically took her seat behind the counter and ate a plain donut.

Jax needed to get back to his team and discuss what they'd found in his father's papers, but he felt oddly compelled to continue this senseless argument. "I'm from Savannah. I don't know anyone here except you and your family. I can't help. You need to start making lists of likely candidates—beside yourselves. Then go out and study them in whatever way works for you. A candidate needs to think beyond his own needs."

"I can help." Loretta cheerfully darted behind the counter, found pen and paper, then settled in the window seat. "I can start with my teachers."

Evie chewed on her donut and eyed them all with suspicion. "Fine. You do your thing. I'll do mine. I have dogs to walk and a business to run." Not looking at Jax, she walked out, again.

"You have a black cloud on your horizon," Mavis told him. "You need her. The town doesn't." She produced her tarot deck and lost interest in the discussion.

Swearing to find a job and get the hell out of Podunk as soon as he could, Jax stalked to the post office in hopes his express documents had arrived. Puzzles were a better use of his time than figuring out female emotions. He needed to know who he was before he could work out what direction to take next.

And maybe text Conan with his new information and ask about Pendleton. Maybe the old man committed suicide over something in the papers Jax had requested. Maybe he didn't. He simply disliked loose ends like potential killers roaming free.

EVIE HURRIED THROUGH HER DOG-WALKING DUTIES INSTEAD OF DRIFTING AS USUAL. The men were down in her basement, plotting without her. She needed to be there.

She was still mad at Jax and Mavis for stealing the idea of mayor. She was creative and hardworking and knew what the town needed. Why should some pettifog who couldn't see beyond dollar signs have the job?

But the whole time she walked the dog and worked off her anger, Mr. Pendleton lingered at the back of her mind. She *knew* he hadn't committed suicide, but how could she prove it from here? And why should she? The only reason she could conjure was that his killer might be after Jax and those papers.

Which not only meant that Jax and everyone around him might be in danger, but that someone rich and important had something to hide. Those were old papers involving old businesses and dead people. No one from back then should care about a defunct mine—*unless they'd killed the real Franklin Jackson.*

Even so, a common ordinary killer wouldn't be paying attention to a safety deposit box or Pendleton's law office. A hired criminal would have moved on —or already be in jail for something else. Pendleton's death should have nothing to do with Jax, except that it happened after their visit.

Desperation and the hope of riches had led the murderously inclined to kill Loretta's parents. Had Jax's father been caught up in something similar?

And frighteningly—at least one of those contracts in his father's files had been drawn up by Stockton and Stockton, the same law office that had helped former Mayor Block with his land fraud. So maybe S&S had a tradition of coloring outside the lines—probably a professional hazard for people in a position of power who knew too much. Lawyers knew how to cover their tracks.

It was extremely odd that Jax's biological father had crossed the country to work for a shady law firm. She didn't want his father to be one of the bad guys.

After delivering the last dog to its owner, Evie clambered down the cellar steps into the playground Reuben and Roark were currently calling home. At least they appeared to be working and not playing with her aunt's ancient Pac-Man machine.

The document file from the safe deposit box was on the pool table. She feared they'd opened Pandora's Box.

Jax had the papers lined up in stacks. Reuben the tech nerd was taking apart the circuit board they'd found at the mine site. And the Cajun former military intelligence officer sat in a space-age gaming chair with three computers, streaming information across screens while his fingers flew over the keyboards.

Not one of them was speaking—typical.

"I can't read auras on computer screens. I'll have to go back to California once you have a list of suspects." Throwing ammunition on the fire to get them talking, Evie helped herself to the first stack of papers in Jax's arrangement.

"No crime, no suspects," Jax muttered, not looking up.

"Suspects right here in River City," Reuben corrected. "Too many rich old men. We need a revolution."

"Uh-huh, so we can put rich young men in their place. Unless you want poor ones with guns. Revolutions always work so well." Evie sat cross-legged on a fat decorator pillow and tried to focus on the contract in her hands. As before, the names *Stockton* and *Ives* stood out, along with the Sovereign Machinery part. The rest made no sense.

"First rule of the revolution, no lawyers allowed," Reuben said absently as he tested whatever mechanical contraption he was messing with.

"Who writes the laws, then? The army?" Jax had out his electronic notebook, making notes.

This wasn't going anywhere.

"Will y'all stop it?" Evie shouted at them. "Tell me what you found."

They looked at her blankly. All right, they didn't know where to begin. She had to orchestrate. She pointed at Reuben. "What's with the circuit board?"

He brightened. "This PCB you found is for an early electronic voting machine. It's primitive but the basic components are the same as today's models. These are embedded systems, so all the info is on the board with the electronics to submit it. The microchips require silica, which presumably came from the Ives Mining Company."

"Along with the silica mine"—Jax pointed at one of his stacks—"my father had contracts to create the microchips. Sovereign bought his chips to install in the PCBs of their voting equipment."

PCBs? Circuit boards? But Evie deduced the gist of it. "This is all about thirty-year-old voting machines? That might have been exciting back then but is anyone using those machines now?"

"Hope not." Roark finally spoke up. "Some genius discovered da machines could be programmed to switch votes a quarter of the time. Dat's easy enough to make a difference in any race. Sovereign got sued and shut down."

"So this is all past and done?" Evie gestured at the projects they were working on. "We can close up and go back to raccoon hunting?" That had been the job her Sensible Solutions Agency had taken on before she left to track Jax.

"Opossum," Reuben corrected. "And baby possums. The lady wasn't happy but she paid us anyway. She really wanted ghosts."

Danged good thing she was good at processing different topics at high speed. "I trust we got paid?"

"*Mais oui.* Used it to replace da tires on our van." Roark returned to scanning screens.

"So why are we still working on voting machines?" She made a mental note to see what kind of machine Afterthought was using. Buying used machines would be just the kind of thing the council would do.

"Because Stockton and Stockton wrote these contracts, Franklin Jackson examined them, and Aaron Ives was supposed to fulfill them." Jax looked grim and tired. "As we now know, S&S is better known for making money than being cautious. And Aaron Ives *didn't* end up in the bottom of a mine but went to work for S&S, and Franklin vanished."

"So, we can deduce that either your father murdered his partner to make a killing in the microchip market, or he got furious about his friend's death and decided to pull a switcheroo to catch a murderer?" Evie wanted the *people* underpinnings of this case. "Gotta say, I'm not liking either alternative."

Jax scowled. "We can assume that using his partner's identity, my father accepted a job at the company hired to draw up the contracts, maybe a job Franklin had already been offered. We have no idea why. At the time he was hired, Sovereign had not been caught with fraudulent machines. That came much later, well after the mine closed and the microchip company shut down."

Jax's aura had returned to murderous. He was too honest to cover up criminal possibilities, even when it came to his newly discovered father. If they didn't solve this puzzle, he might strangle to death controlling all that boiling fury. Or explode. That would be messy and not good for Loretta.

"So, it looks as if your father, posing as Franklin Jackson, was rewarded for keeping his mouth shut about the mine collapse?" Evie watched, but Jax's aura only got tighter.

Relentlessly, she continued. "So, what happened a dozen years later, when he died? You thought he was investigating Stephen Stockton's Ponzi scheme and got himself killed. But your adoptive father claims he didn't even know he was being investigated, and that your father got fired because the firm uncovered his real identity."

Evie scrunched up her nose to puzzle that out. If Jackson and Ives were in California, and S&S was in Savannah, chances were the law firm had never actually met the pair. The switch was possible. Who had connected the California company with a Savannah law firm? She studied the documents again but they used corporate names that meant nothing to her.

Jax didn't look happy and didn't argue with her conclusion. Instead of dying in a car accident, his parents could have been *murdered*. For what? Or committed suicide? Prickles ran up and down her spine.

"Someone at Pendleton's firm is sending us all the old Franklin files Jax requested—including correspondence. With Pendleton dead, there's no one there to give that order." Roark nodded at the paper pouring from the printer. Apparently caught up in the mystery, he dropped his Cajun accent.

"No one to countermand it, either," Jax pointed out.

Roark ignored the correction. "I'm printing some of the more interesting stuff. Wonder how much a company gets paid to fix votes?"

Wow, she hadn't gone that far in her thinking. "Enough to kill for?" Evie grabbed the correspondence rolling off the printer. "Even to this day?"

"We don't know that. But if Pendleton died for these files, we're all in danger." Jax snatched half the sheets from Evie's hands.

"So is the person who sent them. Or we're all paranoid or bored." Evie scanned the letters looking for glaring guilt, but the devil was always in the details. She had to read each one, line by line. "These are all over thirty years old, on Ives Mining letterhead, signed by Aaron Ives. But Franklin was partner, wasn't he?"

"Possibly a silent role, since he had his own practice and presumably knew nothing about mining or microchips. Start-ups require cash and Franklin may have invested." Jax dropped the papers he'd read and reached for the ones Evie discarded.

"I'd like to get my hands on one of those voting machines," Reuben announced. "I can see how this baby functions, but I need a machine to follow the connections. A newer one would be good."

Roark printed out a short list. "Lookin' like Sovereign settled the voter fraud suit. A few minor players got slapped with fines. The major ones rolled the operations over into a new firm called DVM. This here's a list of stock-holders in the Southeast."

"Stockholders *here*, not California?" Evie grabbed the paper. "Oh, yeah, baby, even I recognize half these investors. Is it legal for politicians to own a company that makes voting machines?"

"What isn't legal is doctoring the machines, if that's what they're still up to." Jax looked at the list and whistled. "Most of these guys have been in office for years. Maybe we can hand this over to the FBI?"

"The feds opened their case against Sovereign twenty years ago—right about the time your parents got themselves killed." Roark went silent as he stared at a file he probably shouldn't have accessed. "We might oughta take a look at the case they compiled."

If it was an FBI file, she didn't want to know. Evie reached for the document folder they'd found at the bank. "Put the original material in here. I'm sending it to Cousin Orbis. I want to know what the man who put these in the safety deposit box and buried the key was *feeling* when he did it."

She knew the men were worried when they didn't argue.

Seven

THE NEXT MORNING, JAX CONTEMPLATED CHEWING NAILS AS HE WALKED UP AND down the streets around the county courthouse, trying to judge whether to sink his last dime into setting up an office here. He needed an income. His most lucrative choice would be a position with a corporate firm in a city. Only, he'd never wanted his cushy corporate job at S&S. He'd wanted a career in the diplomatic corps.

But Afghanistan had put an end to that. The military had made him paranoid. He'd only accepted his adoptive father's offer of a situation in S&S because his real dad had worked there. The distrust of authority he'd learned in the military had led him to wonder if his parents' death *hadn't* been accidental, so he'd been investigating—until Stephen Stockton had been arrested on the Ponzi scheme. With his suspicions that the firm wasn't what it should be confirmed, Jax had quit in disgust.

There might be more evidence to be found at S&S, but after Stephen's arrest in the land scheme along with Mayor Block, official fraud units combed through the office now. He was better off investigating from the outside.

He didn't believe his biological father had been killed because of Stephen Stockton's fraud. His adoptive father wasn't much of a killer. Hell, Jax didn't even know if his parents' accident hadn't been just that, an accident. It was too late to go back and investigate speed and tire tracks after twenty years. He'd read the report. It was worthless.

But voter fraud. . . there was a subject he could dig his teeth into. Except he couldn't make a living at it. Aaron Ives hadn't left any fortune, just acres of arid land.

Neurodiverse and unprepared to survive in the real world, his sister had been living with their adoptive father when all this came down. Stockton's house was up for sale now, removing Ariel's safe place. Jax had to support her as well as himself. They wouldn't starve immediately, but an income beyond his fees from Loretta's trust was required.

Finding a For Rent sign on a respectable brick building housing a CPA, another attorney, and a dentist, Jax called the number on the sign. He was unsurprised to be directed to the first-floor accounting office.

A lank-haired blond wearing a gray suit met him in the reception area. "Geoff Hayes, CPA, pleased to meet you. Damon Jackson, right? You're the guardian for the little rich girl?"

So much for keeping Loretta's identity secret. After the bodies of her parents had been dug up outside of town, everyone knew who she was. "Co-guardian," Jax acknowledged warily, shaking the accountant's hand. Maybe this was where he should start trying on a new name.

"Ha! Maybe we could work a deal. I've got a great office upstairs, over-looking the courthouse. You steer her tax work my way, and I can give you a discount, throw in the utilities." Geoff led the way up the stairs. "I'm talking to Paul Clancy about partnering with me as a financial advisor. He's an invest-ment broker and on the town council, good fellow to know."

So, this was where it started, the old *I'll scratch your back* routine, the good ol' boy network. Jax got a discount office, Loretta got overcharged for her taxes. Hire Clancy to handle her wealth, and he'd invest in the locals who paid him favors, regardless of what it did to Loretta's accounts. Little by little, the money got siphoned off, and very few would be the wiser.

"Her father already hired a tax guy and advisor in Savannah," Jax said, checking the cleanliness of the stairway. It seemed well kept. "We don't have a reason to change. He knows the accounts."

"Ah, well, can't blame a guy for trying. The office is prime property, should attract good clients. Heard you were from Georgia. Got a license for South Carolina already?"

"Yup, fresh out of law school I applied for multiple licenses. I wanted vari-ety." He'd not wanted to work for Stockton. But life happened.

A smaller office across the hall bore the plaque of a construction company. At least it wasn't the one that brought Mayor Block to his knees.

"You're planning on keeping the kiddo in school here?" Geoff unlocked the door.

"Yeah, Loretta likes it here, and this is where her family lives. I'm still debating whether I need to live here too. Just thought I'd take a look around, see what opportunities are offered." Jax stepped into an unfurnished reception area with new carpet, large windows, and newly varnished woodwork.

"Got the mayor's case coming up in the Grand Jury. That'll be a big one. I could hook you up with some of the attorneys handling the contracting companies. Bunch of subcontractors caught up in that who don't deserve the grief." Geoff led the way to an office off the reception area. "All new carpeting. Refurbished the restroom too."

"Did an attorney rent this before?" Jax looked out the undraped windows. The building was on the opposite end of town from Evie's house, but he could see the school from here.

"Yup. George Norton had it for decades. We almost couldn't remove the stench of ancient cigars. Place has been non-smoking for decades, but he still sneaked one occasionally. His family might sell you the practice for a good price. They don't live around here. They just want the old fella's cash."

"Now that's a deal I might be interested in. If I bring you my tax work and direct my clients to you, can we still talk about a discount?"

Geoff pounded him on the back. "I knew you were a straight-up fella. Let's go down, and I'll buzz George's family, see if we can come up with some numbers."

Taking on construction clients caught up in the land fraud could lead down interesting paths. If there was also a built-in clientele. . . Jax would be following in the footsteps of Franklin Jackson *and* Aaron Ives. Both were small-town lawyers. He just wouldn't have to deal in mines and microchips.

Maybe he could call his office *Jackson and Ives Attorneys*, honor the names of both men—and confuse the hell out of anyone who came looking for him. Jax almost smiled for the first time in weeks. Evie's wild fantasies were contagious. And the idea of killers coming after him raised his adrenaline so he felt more alive again.

Of course, after thirty years, any killers were probably geriatric.

Obtaining numbers on the office and the practice he might buy, Jax said he needed time to think them over. It had all come together a little too handily, which made him wonder how much Evie's meddling family had to do with it.

They'd certainly heaved out Mayor Block fast enough once he'd been caught red-handed. Jax was almost intrigued enough to stay in Afterthought just to figure out how Evie's family operated.

After a satisfying talk with George Norton's widow, Jax headed for Evie's to join R&R in the cellar. Before he could reach the back gate, he ran into Evie's striped-hair cousin Priscilla. Today, the stripes were maroon, and she wore drab brown that matched the mouse color of her hair. She stroked Evie's Siamese cat as she rocked in the porch swing. Of all the Malcolms he'd met, Pris was the spookiest.

"Ariel needs a cat," she told him, without inflection.

"My sister dislikes changes in her environment. She has more than enough to cope with living in a new place," he countered. And how in hell would Pris know what his sister wanted? It wasn't as if Ariel communicated in any normal manner.

"She's lonely. She needs a pet. A cat can take care of itself." Pris calmly stroked Evie's cat, not looking at him or using an argumentative voice, just stating facts, apparently as she saw them.

"Evie would not like giving up her cat." Jax had had stranger conversations. He wasn't certain when.

"Psycat understands people."

Psycat was the Siamese. "Ariel would be better off with the raven. It would stay outside." So, he was losing his marbles. Why not?

"La Chusa?" She finally expressed interest. "Iddy won't want to give her up."

Jax had been told that Evie's cousin Idonea trained animals to understand human speech. The veterinarian's spooky raven certainly appeared to. He wasn't accepting that the animals talked back, though. "Evie won't want to give up Psycat."

"Psy chooses who he stays with." She put the cat down. "I'll think about this."

She sauntered down the front walk without a farewell. The cat sat on the porch, eyeing him.

"Is Evie home?" he asked the animal, out of sheer frustration with the world.

The Siamese daintily took the stairs down to the driveway and led the way back to the cellar. Jax rolled his eyes and followed the creature. At the cellar entrance, he rang the makeshift bell his team had installed in their eccentric hideaway. One of the panels partially lifted with a spooky creak.

"Need better hydraulics," Reuben called from below. "You'll have to open it yourself."

The cat preceded him. Downstairs, Evie swept it up and said, "Feeding time. Psy has you trained already?"

Jax admired Evie's short-shorts, but he also appreciated the way she made living in a cellar feel normal. Her acceptance of the world as is eased his aggressive need to change and improve. Probably not a good symbiosis but one he needed right now. "I simply asked the cat where to find you. Your cousin Priscilla thinks Ariel needs a pet. I'm thinking she had Psycat in mind, so I may have prevented a catnapping."

"Yeah, Pris is like that. She rearranges things. But a pet isn't a bad idea, something to look out for besides herself, like a turtle. I'll ring up Iddy and ask." Evie headed for the stairs.

He was tempted to ask Evie about taking George Norton's practice, but he wanted to ponder it a while longer. "Warn Iddy that Pris might be after the raven next."

Evie's grin lit the dim cellar. "Oh, that is choice, thank you. Mavis called to say you should take the job. I hope you know what that means." She headed up the stairs, hopefully to prepare food for more than the cat.

Jax turned to find his friends watching him with interest. "What? You think I ought to buy a law firm because the local psychic says so?"

From their grins, Jax guessed his badly damaged friends thought just that. They'd finally found a home—where they weren't the only crazies.

WHILE EVIE PREPARED LUNCH BY FLINGING TOGETHER CANS OF BEANS AND tomatoes and whatever vegetable was still alive at the bottom of the refrigerator, Loretta read the lists of potential mayoral candidates her family had spent the morning gathering.

"Honest people, for the most part." Evie pondered the list as she chopped peppers. "Reading their auras doesn't tell me if they're capable of running for mayor or doing the job."

"Mrs. Thomas is Black and runs a school. She should be good." The principal had been first on Loretta's list.

"Mrs. Thomas is an educator and the teachers need her. We need someone who understands *business*. And are we doing the right thing by discriminating according to race? Or gender? Should we be looking at either of those, really?" Evie cut up a half-dead carrot and added it to the broth. She needed to go shopping.

Or hire the cook Loretta's allowance covered. Having spending money just confused her.

"Only look for people who know business?" Loretta pushed her glasses up her nose and studied the lists as if she were studying for college exams. "There's Mr. Williams who runs the hardware store."

"Hank? He's old and thinks Apple is a fruit. Besides, he's already on the council. Keep going."

By the time Jax wandered in, Loretta had multiple lists labeled Black, Female, Business, Combination, and they still hadn't decided. They even had cantankerous Gertie from the café in the line-up, although they hadn't decided whether she qualified as Black *or* Female. She definitely ran a business, though.

Jax examined the lists, but unfamiliar with most of the townspeople, he wasn't any help. "What we need to be doing is make lists of chores to be divided. This place is turning into a commune."

"Engineers take out the trash. Lawyers pay the bills." Evie dumped an open box of rice into her kettle. "Children make their beds and do their homework. Dog walkers walk dogs."

"You don't own a dog, and you're making lunch."

"I cook and talk to ghosts. We go where our talents are. Engineers can wash dishes and make their beds. Lawyers go to work so they can afford the bills. It's simple. Are you staying then?" Evie had been stewing ever since she'd heard about him talking to George Norton's family, and he hadn't thought to mention it to her.

"What do you know about George Norton and his clientele?"

A wave of relief swept over her. Finally, someone appreciated her talents. She almost kissed him. Being into self-preservation, she shot Jax a grin instead. "George was Mayor Block's lawyer and handled his real estate business as well. Don't pay them for that part of the practice if the mayor is going to jail." Trying not to do a happy dance, she got out the last of the ham and threw that in, too.

"Ah, now that's the most practical information I've received so far. I'm guessing the mayor has hired a criminal lawyer for his defense, but he'll need access to all those real estate contracts for Witch Hill. I'm now thinking I'll empty my savings to get my hands on that firm."

Evie couldn't help it. She turned from the stove and hugged her straight-laced lawyer tenant. "I'll loan you my bicycle so you can get to work faster."

"Your bicycle has no tires. I checked." Jax crushed her against him for half a moment, before setting her aside. He smelled deliciously of hot male with a hint of spice.

"That's the old bike. Loretta and I bought new ones, remember? Or you could buy one of Toby's old Harleys. The mayor is probably selling off every-thing he can get his hands on to pay for his defense, and his garage is full of his son's junk. I am a fountain of information. Ask, and ye shall receive." Evie returned to stirring her soup, gratified. She might not be the next mayor, but she could be the power behind the throne—as soon as she decided who would sit on it.

"Huh, a Harley might work. I should go visit Ariel and see if she needs a pet. You do know it's June and this house has no a/c and hot soup is the last thing we need?" He checked the fridge and removed the prepared tea.

"Soup is what you get when the fridge needs cleaning. Being warm on the inside should make your outside feel cooler."

"Yeah, right. Loretta's allowance should cover a cook." Jax added ice to a glass.

Evie had heard that before. She glanced around the straight-out-of-the-sixties kitchen and grinned. "Do cooks like avocado green?"

Jax sucked down the entire glass of tea before answering, probably to prevent rolling his eyes. "Not even harvest gold. Do you have any bread to go with that soup?"

"Rolls in the oven. Tell the guys I cook but do not serve. If they want to eat, they need to come get it. And wash up after, being engineers and all."

"You're nuts but a good nuts." Jax jogged out the kitchen door.

"He jumps from Harleys to pets to soup and cooks, and he thinks I'm nuts?" Evie ladled a mug of soup for Loretta and popped the rolls from the oven.

"You're contagious." Loretta sipped contentedly from her mug. "And a good cook. You should get my cook's allowance, but I should decide what to spend it on. If there's money for a cook, then there's enough to take me to Disney World."

Evie laughed. "You're a chip off the old block. Bet your dad was good at bargaining."

At least she had the kid's respect and a perceptive kid at that. She could live with that. Humming, Evie dished up her own lunch and sat at the counter. She supposed she ought to serve meals in the dining room but clearing the table of debris was too much trouble. And expecting the men to sit down to a formal table would be too much to ask.

The room filled with testosterone as three giant ex-Marines poured through the back door, obediently washing at the sink before filling soup mugs and grabbing rolls.

Jax's phone rang. Setting down his lunch, he answered it without looking. When his face froze, Evie checked his aura. The red killer flares were back, and his expression hardened into that square-jawed ruthlessness she'd first noticed about him.

"Right. Got it. Will do. Thanks for the warning." He shoved the phone in his pocket. Without a word of explanation, he snatched another roll and started for the door.

Evie grabbed an overripe peach from the fruit bowl and flung it at his broad back. When he didn't turn around, Reuben and Roark joined the game, using spoons and salt cellars and anything loose they could fling. Their aim was more deadly.

Jax halted with the back door half open and glared at them. "What?"

"Your aura is not subtle, meathead." Evie glared back. "You're feeling murderous. Who warned you about what?"

"Am I going to have to tell everyone about every call I receive if I stay here?" he demanded.

"Your bubble shrinks when you don't." Loretta nibbled at her roll and watched him with curiosity.

"I can live with that." He stormed out.

"No, he can't," Evie and Loretta said at the same time.

Without being told, Reuben and Roark shoved rolls in their mouths, picked up their mugs, and carried them after Jax.

Eight

"Oh, for punk's sake, she has you brainwashed already?" Jax asked in disgust as his friends appeared on the back porch, stuffing their faces, presumably to find out what was *shrinking his bubble*. Gah, he'd have to take on Norton's practice and move into his office just to have a life of his own.

"Food," Reuben muttered, finishing his mouthful of roll. "Games. Running water. All good. *Punk*?"

Jax assumed that meant they wanted to appease Evie to stay here. He got that. He didn't have to like it. He ignored the reference to his new vocabulary —because Evie was brainwashing him on that, and he was a damned hypocrite. But she was right, kids shouldn't be subjected to the language he'd used in the military.

"We got your back, *couillon*, so you might as well tell us." Roark glugged his soup as if he hadn't eaten in days.

This was what happened when he lived with others. Jax appreciated his sister's need to be a hermit. People interfered. He was used to doing things alone.

"Look, we need a dividing line here." He thought furiously, trying to find a way of separating his private life from his business one. Without a real business, that was laughable. "I'm supposed to pay you when you help me out. If I'm sinking my savings into buying a practice, I can't pay you. You need to be looking for real jobs."

"Got one." Reuben poked at his mug of soup with a spoon, inspecting it for inedibles. "Sensible Solutions. We have three more contracts lined up. Newspaper played up Evie's ghost-talking and us hunting down evidence, so now everyone thinks they got ghosts or cheating uncles. Word spreads. Evie's like this big happy balloon floating above the town advertising our services. You don't get what she does because it's outside the norm. You have to watch her in action."

Jax had watched Evie in action. She was a loose cannon with a lit fuse that sparkled like a kid's Fourth of July toy—until she exploded. "I don't think *you* get what Evie does. Did you know she's taken martial arts training? And she's damned good." If he hadn't had the same training—and if she wasn't half his size—she'd have maimed him for life when she'd thought he threatened Loretta a few months back.

"That bit of a thing?" Roark asked scornfully. "Might be good for keeping the kid in line."

"Fat lot you know," Jax said in scorn, thinking of how she'd cut in and out of speeding semis like a race car driver. Loose cannon knew no fear. Which scared the shit out of him.

There was a point to ponder when he woke up with nightmares of Evie exploding like an IED. Or vanishing from his life as his parents had done. He was a head case.

"Evie's not the point," Reuben argued. "You can't keep treating us as if you're still our commanding officer."

"You never followed orders when I *was* your officer," Jax reminded him.

"Well, yeah, because we got brains and know how to use them. Thing is, now we're all on the same page. We gotta have each other's backs." Reuben finished off his roll and looked as if he wanted to go back for more. "If that phone call was someone warning you off, then that affects all of us."

Jax clutched his mug in frustration. "If you have paying jobs, then you should be doing them instead of messing with my problem."

Roark snorted. "We threw out our hooks. We'll reel the customers in when ready. We don't make solvin' problems too easy or we don't get paid da big bucks. That's petty stuff. What you have is major. We want the juicy cases."

"You're not likely to get paid for uncovering thirty-year-old crimes!" Jax paced the dirt yard. Evie needed a gardener. And a landscaper. And now he was thinking like her and so out of focus, he didn't know what his problem was.

Reuben sighed, put down his mug, and cuffed Jax upside the head. "Been wantin' to do that for some time. It's not about *money*, dummy!"

Jax punched the top-knotted nerd's arm in retaliation, but Reuben's lanky frame held muscles, and he didn't flinch. At the same time, Jax understood what his friends were saying. The pair had been living in a utility van, doing his scut work since they'd been shafted out of the service. They'd never been interested in more than improving their equipment so they could do their jobs better.

"Twisted bubbles," he muttered, using Loretta's description of them.

"Yeah, we got dat." Roark took a seat on the sagging back step. "Twisted brains, too. You can thank the Man for that. But we know what's good for us and this gig is good for now. You wanna give it up, go ahead, move out, make your fortune, let dat walnut soul of yours stay shriveled. But you wanna do what's right, we here to help."

The Man being the military that had turned them into killers, then spit them out when they crashed and burned and weren't needed anymore. That had been a high price to pay for school loans, wanderlust, and a juvenile quest for justice and world peace.

"There isn't anything you can do in this case. That was Conan Oswin on the phone. Roark, you met him. He claims to be some distant relation of mine and hinted that he has some connections with the intelligence community."

"Yeah, I looked him up." Roark grinned, unrepentant. "He's got cred."

Jax figured he had. "He says the coroner called Pendleton's death murder. He was most likely unconscious from a blow to the back of his skull before someone held a gun to his temple and shot him. The sheriff is looking for me and Evie."

Both men whistled.

"Whatcha gonna do?" Reuben asked.

"Call the sheriff. I'd rather not drag Evie into this if it can be avoided. Now do you see why I didn't say anything?"

"He'll want to talk to Evie. You can't hide da facts. She needs to be right here when you call so she knows what you've said. She's right, you know. You're a jackass." Roark gathered up the mugs and stalked back inside.

"Jackrabbit," Jax muttered. "What kind of sound does a rabbit make?"

"Kissy noises." Reuben followed his friend back to the kitchen.

"So much for having my back, dolts," Jax shouted after them.

Damn, but they were right, in their own warped way. He was protecting

Evie. She wasn't Ariel. She was a grown woman who'd never needed his protection in the past. The world probably needed protection from her.

Psyching himself into believing all that shit, Jax called the number Conan had given him. He gave the person answering his name and number and looked up without surprise as Evie trotted down the steps with a fresh mug of soup in hand.

"Loretta and I have decided on the next mayor. I'm off to twist arms. Have a nice day." She handed him the mug and swung on her heel to march away.

Pedal to the metal, full speed ahead. "Evie!" Jax shouted after her. "Pendleton was murdered."

TIMES LIKE THIS, EVIE REALLY, REALLY HATED BEING RIGHT.

"Do you think he believed us?" she asked worriedly when they were off the phone with the sheriff's department.

Poor Mr. Pendleton. If he'd died because of her, she'd hate herself forever.

"Sheriff has no reason to, one way or the other. He knows we couldn't have killed him while we were in his office, because Pendleton was still alive when the bank manager called him. We were surrounded by witnesses. He's just gathering evidence. I'm sure he'd like to point a finger at us if he can. Calling someone local a killer can cost him an election." Jax paced the backyard.

Evie had sent Loretta off to help her cousin at the vet clinic so the kid didn't have to overhear this and worry. "How will we find out who did this, so the killer doesn't come after us too?"

She was grateful that Jax had been very careful to not give away their contact information other than his cell number and his former law firm's address. That still didn't mean she couldn't worry.

"*We* are not finding out anything! We have no way of knowing that Pendleton's death has anything to do with us. Let the sheriff do his job. Go find a mayor." Jax quit pacing and aimed for the carriage house.

"We were the last people Pendleton saw. He probably called up your father's files right after we left. We *might* be responsible!" Evie fretted and followed him down the drive. "I knew we should have gone back. I can't do anything from here. Let me send that photo I took of the F100 to your Conan friend. Can he do anything with it?"

68

"I'll give it to him to check out." He threw open the big barn doors. "But this case is not on your doorstep. You have no reason to be involved."

"No reason? A nice man may have died because of us! And there's a killer on the loose. And I *hate* being a suspect!"

Evie gasped when Jax grabbed her arms and lifted her from the ground. "You cannot personally solve all the world's problems. Lay off, Evie. Stick to one thing at a time. Find a mayor."

SuperMachoMan was back. She'd kicked his shins when he'd tried manhandling her before. But she knew Jax better now.

She grabbed his thick shoulders and kissed his nose to make his head spin. "Then you have to do the same. Forget your father's papers and go start your new law office."

She wriggled away before he could tighten his hold. The hormone thing was a real nuisance when she needed to keep her attention-deprived head. Living in the same house with so many people around them. . . Very bad setting for quickie sex. Which she didn't do, she reminded herself. She had a kid to think about now. And Jax made her so angry sometimes, she could just spit.

She had no intention of giving up on poor Mr. Pendleton, but he didn't have to know that.

Jax took an unsteady breath, then set his square jaw. "Fine. I'll make some calls, be certain Norton had a good practice. Who's your choice for mayor?"

"You won't know her. I'll let you know once she accepts. If she accepts. She's not exactly crazy, so that may be a large *if*."

"Got it. Mavis going with you?"

"She's already filed for herself, so no. I'll set fire to her filing papers if my candidate accepts."

Still miffed at her mother, Evie left Jax to his calls. She was a little anxious about making the contact with her potential candidate, but this was a task she'd set herself. She couldn't ask her family for help. Yet.

It was just a good thing she had a mission or she'd go crazy worrying about killers and how they might be connected to voting machines and mines and Jax's father. Grabbing her new bike, Evie pedaled to the outskirts of town, past the school, to the sprawling brick building housing Larraine Fashions.

Larraine Ward was an enigma. Evie was fairly certain Ward had been born a Larry, but her taste in ladies' fashion had garnered her awards and scholarships from design schools. She'd returned to Afterthought wearing women's clothes, and her success was such that she'd withered anyone daring to mock. Evie wasn't clear on why a well-known designer had returned to her small-town roots when she could have succeeded in fashion centers around the world, but Ward knew how to run a business—and that's what the town needed. Along with honesty.

Evie didn't know if Larraine would remember her, but the designer would have to live in a bubble not to know Evie's family. So she approached the impressive, modern lobby and model-thin receptionist with a confidence she probably had no right to feel.

"Hi. I'm Evangeline Malcolm Carstairs. I'd like to speak with Miss Ward about a matter of some importance to the town. Do I need to make an appointment?"

With colorfully decorated fingernails longer than Evie's nose, the receptionist punched a button on a phone line. Evie didn't bother studying the woman's presumably stylish clothes and chic hairstyle. At five-two, Evie could barely find clothes in her age group. She could never hope to achieve any degree of fashion and wasn't much interested in trying, so she didn't relate to anyone who did.

She studied the art on the walls instead. The canvases were mostly color and line and not recognizable objects, but against the brick walls, in the sun-drenched lobby, they were dramatic.

"Miss Ward will see you now. First door on the right." The receptionist pointed at a hallway.

Evie figured she was out of her mind to come here, but it beat worrying about stone-cold killers and why they'd murder a nice old lawyer. Her main concern should be how she might study the fashionista's aura without looking like a space cadet.

Loretta had already approved of Ward's bubble when the fashionista had done a presentation on careers at school. Evie was fairly certain what Loretta perceived as a bubble was a person's soul. If Ward had a good soul, anything else was just gravy.

The designer opened her office door before Evie could knock. "Come in, come in, tell me what I can do for my little hometown."

Aided by sky-high heels, Larraine Ward towered over Evie. Gorgeous brown skin highlighted in gold glitter announced her mixed heritage. With her black hair severely pulled back in a knot and flashing fake eyelashes long enough to cause breezes, Ward was dramatically gorgeous. Wearing what appeared to be a peach-colored 70's jumpsuit with flared legs and arms in a fabric that clung to her slender frame, she swung back to a desk almost as striking as she was. Made of what appeared to be onyx and mahogany, the desk stretched long enough for a pool table.

"Don't you even want me to introduce myself?" Evie asked, not hiding her amusement. "I could be a con artist." Which Jax had accused her family of being often enough.

Ward waved a heavily beringed hand. "Your mother found me a ride to Savannah for a competition, and your uncle gave me a place to stay while I was there. I remember the good folks. You were just a wee little thing and told me my aura looked like a rainbow. You were right on."

Evie relaxed and took the high-backed leather chair offered. "Then you don't mind if I look to see if your aura is still a rainbow?" She didn't wait for a response but opened her third eye and read the messy, dramatic hues of a creative soul, an older one tinged in gray.

Ward looked more amused than wary. "So, am I still rainbow-colored?"

"I don't think that part of you changes," Evie admitted. "You're a creative. Your energies are off the scale. You have as much potential for murder as doing good, but you're at peace with yourself. Loretta, my ward, met you and says you have a large soul. That doesn't mean you can't be as petty as the rest of us, just that you're less inclined to be so."

"Oh, you're good, maybe even better than your mother. She told me I had a good future if I accepted myself. It's amazing how much a few kind words can mean. She gave me courage. I needed that back when I was a poor, skinny teenager thinking I'd have to kill myself because I didn't fit in anywhere. I try to pass on that good deed any time I can. So, what do you need from me?"

Evie studied the expensive office and the sophisticated designer behind the desk and sighed. "Probably too much. I set my sights high, but I may have bitten off more than Afterthought deserves. We need a new mayor, someone who isn't one of Mayor Block's cronies, someone not involved in real estate but who wants to work for the benefit of *all* the people of this town, not just the rich ones."

Ward whistled, and Evie thought maybe—beneath the skillfully enhanced cosmetics—she caught a glimpse of the designer's inner unconfident teenager. She'd overstepped her boundaries this time.

"You do live in another dimension, don't you?" the fashionista said in a more thoughtful manner than the grandiose one she'd been using. "I like that, but reality shatters dreams."

Evie sighed. This was where she never got any respect. "I'm twenty-five-years old and have a higher than average IQ and more than the usual amount of understanding of how people work. Setting high goals is how the human race achieves great things, although I accept that success comes with failure."

"But we're talking Afterthought here, not Mars. You're asking a small, mostly unsophisticated and uneducated populace to accept what much more urban areas won't."

"Asking you to run for governor might be a different case, but I know Afterthought pretty well. Despite whatever you may have experienced growing up, you're respected now. Our schools are more diverse and creative than twenty years ago. Education makes for smarter voters. My main concern, now that I've seen this place, is that you won't have time for us."

Ward was no longer diva-smiling. "I can make time, if you convince me I won't be ruining a chance for someone more electable. I'm aware that the town council has put up their own candidate. Paul Clancy sells stock. His career depends on everyone knowing his name. Voters prefer people they know and don't like change. You must admit, I'd be an enormous, possibly divisive, change—like your mother, who is also running, am I correct?"

"See, and that's why we thought of you!" Evie sat forward, hoping she wasn't fooling herself because this was what she wanted. "Mavis is running only because no one else stepped up. We both know she's not up to the job, but she needs to respect whoever else runs. When we first started talking about ideal candidates, we started with the basics—a candidate ought to represent *all* the town, not just the white male business part. But then it got messy because if we picked a well-known Black businessman, we might be discriminating against a white female who knew business just as well."

Ward chuckled. "So you chose someone who has it all? That won't get me elected."

Evie sat back in satisfaction now that it seemed Ward might be interested. "No, what will get you elected is your business acumen, your generosity, your well-known name, and the support of a community that has known you since birth. Clancy is not a native."

Ward leaned back and clasped her slender, beringed fingers with their red-polished nails. "You phrased that very nicely. I'm not necessarily agreeing with your interpretation, but I thank you for your open-mindedness."

Evie waved her unpolished and ring-less hands. "This is not about playing nice. I'm no politician. To get where you are now, you had to be. To prove my point, let me be blunt and address the elephant in the room—sex. People in a rural town do not often meet flagrant. . . what's the current terminology here?"

"Transgender? Nonbinary?" Ward suggested, looking both interested and amused.

"Perfect, thank you. The fact that you're not hitting me over my ignorant head proves you're secure enough to handle the epithets the other side will fling. And the more mud they sling, the more the people who like you will cheer you on. And people *like* you." Evie stopped to take a breath. She hadn't known her head held all these words. But she couldn't stop now.

She dived back in. "You've brought real business to town. You employ hundreds of people who would be picking cotton otherwise. You offer your workers benefits that help their families. This is a small town. Half the voters will be related to your workers in one way or another. Get them to the polling booths, and you're a shoo-in."

Ward pointed a finger. "There's the catch. How do we drag people to the voting booth who have given up all hope of making a difference?"

Evie stood up. "That's where you come in. You need to make them believe in the impossible, give them hope, offer them an underdog to root for. There are only two weeks left to file. I've done all I can. My family will back you, but we're not politicians. It's your decision. All we can do is hope you make the right one."

Ward remained seated, eyes half-closed. "I'll think about it. If nothing else, you've made my day."

"I live to serve!" Evie let herself out, crossing her fingers and wishing she had a magic wand.

Larraine Ward could put Afterthought on the map. Evie didn't expect that to mean she got any more respect, but she'd settle for knowing that she'd made it happen.

Nine

THE NEXT MORNING, JAX HALTED HIS NEW, USED HARLEY ON THE LANE LEADING TO his sister's house to answer his phone. The whistled "Ya Got Trouble" refrain greeted him.

"Rube, if you're going musical gay, go to New York City where they at least have theaters. And update your repertoire while you're there." Jax shoved his sweaty hair off his brow and scanned the sparse piney woods concealing Ariel's cottage. He spotted one of her security cameras and waved.

"I grew up on the oldies. New ones don't have the same flair," Reuben complained. "Y'know how we said that old Sovereign Company your father worked with reinvented itself as DVM? I've been tracking those new DVM voting machines. Did you know we've got some right here in River City?"

Afterthought barely had a pond and no river, but Jax got the message. "No, I did not know that. You think the town council will let you in to tamper with them?"

"They have an election coming up. Shouldn't someone inspect them to be certain they are all functioning?"

"And you want to be that inspector?"

"Damn right. I want my hands on the new PCBs, see how they compare with this old one. Looks like the machines go through the county attorney. Got strings to pull?"

From that, Jax deduced Reuben was studying the county's contracts, he hoped, legally. "Who's the county attorney?"

"George Norton."

Jax pounded his helmet against his knee—as opposed to pounding his head against a tree. "Hell, no mayor and a dead county attorney. What are we getting into?"

"Opportunity, my man, opportunity. Find something legal-looking in Norton's files, put my name on it, and I'll take it from there."

"His personal practice shouldn't include the county's files," Jax warned. "And I haven't decided for certain I'm buying it."

"Buy it. You have a damned good thing going here—unless you really want the city life." Reuben punched off.

Growling irascibly, Jax returned his helmet to his head. He had liked his city life well enough—the fancy restaurants, first-run films, leggy ladies who didn't require rings. But he had *liked* his restored XKE and condo, too. He'd given them up without a second thought to pursue his family's secrets.

He wasn't much into metaphor and allegory, but he figured that said something about him. Or the difference between *like* and whatever. . . *passion*? He didn't do passion. He was an objective observer. City life and never knowing his neighbors had allowed that.

He had an uneasy notion that living with people like Evie and her family ripped objectivity to shreds. Is that what he wanted?

He kicked the Harley into action and rolled up to Ariel's cottage. She monitored the cameras and she'd know he was here. Back in Savannah, when she'd finally started leaving the house and taking taxis, he'd hoped his sister was becoming a little more stable.

Being thrown out of the only home she could remember had been a setback.

NEED A PET? he texted, knowing she wouldn't respond to anything indirect like *Hey, howdy*.

PET?

Any response at all indicated interest. He dug in his backpack and produced a young box turtle he'd found alongside the road. He held it up to the porch camera.

She sent him a smiley face. That was a good sign. Jax produced the fish pellets the guy at the hardware store had recommended, along with a handful of dandelions he'd yanked up. He spread the turtle buffet on the porch and set it down. The turtle poked its nose from its shell to inspect it. Jax knew Ariel was watching when she sent a hugging emoticon.

Now that he had her attention he texted: NEED ANYTHING?

She replied: CHECK EMAIL

He'd been avoiding it all day. Fighting a prison sentence, his adoptive father had been sending demands for affidavits and requests for Jax to be a character witness and so forth and so on.

Worse yet, after Jax had quit the law firm, Stockton and Stockton had descended into a shambles with two of their principals gone. The firm emanated a constant stream of questions he didn't feel inclined to answer.

Jax checked his VIP messages and found the one from Ariel.

It merely contained an attachment. He opened the file and squinted at the small newspaper headline: *Mine Collapse Kills One*. He wouldn't inquire as to how Ariel accessed microfiche.

Damn and double damn. The article didn't include much he hadn't already ascertained, except a paean to Aaron Ives, the young man who had owned it—and who hadn't actually died. Why had their father abandoned that damned land his family had owned? And who the hell was paying the taxes?

He sent Ariel a thank-you emoticon and shoved his phone into his pocket. He had to get back to his research. Somehow, he needed to juggle checking into George Norton's practice, voting machines, and a thirty-year-old murder that might be related to a current one.

That required Evie's leapfrogging mind—and apparently his non-communicative sister and a pair of hackers.

Buying a practice in Afterthought meant putting down roots, giving up childhood dreams of traveling the world in the diplomatic corp. He had more experience with the military and government now than he had in his idealistic youth. That dream was tarnished.

His thirst for justice might be better served on a smaller scale. His background wasn't such that he might aspire to positions of government authority, with the freedom and power such positions wielded. He might, however, hope someday to become a judge and wield justice. To achieve that, he couldn't traipse the world.

He'd got as far as he could finding clues about his dad's death working at Stockton. Time to make the next step—going off on his own.

Settling down in a tiny town of whackos—*Ariel likes it here.*

Loretta was here too. He had been appointed as her guardian. Someone sensible should look after her well-being. Evie hadn't bargained to take on a ten-year-old by herself. Even Loretta's distant relations on her mother's side had refused that responsibility.

Jax supposed, if he told her family about Loretta's money, they'd capitulate —but they'd informed him they were done raising kids and would put her in boarding school. Loretta had already got herself kicked out of one school and run away from the other. She was happy with Evie and public school.

And then there was the big juicy land fraud case he could elbow into if he stayed here. Yeah, maybe it was time to start adulting, and a small town was a good place to begin.

He aimed the Harley at the bank.

$\sim$

"SENSIBLE SOLUTIONS," EVIE ANSWERED THE RING FROM AN UNKNOWN CALLER. She figured getting the name out there was good advertising even if it wasn't a client—which it usually wasn't, since this was her mother's number in the phone book.

Standing in for Mavis at the shop, she completed a sale for a crystal while the person on the other end of the line hesitated.

"I'm looking for Evangeline Carstairs," the unfamiliar voice replied.

Hmmm, Evie didn't generally use her father's name. Where had she used it last? With Larraine Ward—*and in California*. She pulled together her scattered thoughts, waved off her customer, and focused. "Speaking."

"This is Officer Reilly from the San Bernardino County Sheriff's office. We need you to sign your sworn statement concerning the Pendleton case. What address shall we use? It will need to be notarized."

They'd only given the sheriff the address for Jax's old Savannah law office, avoiding any connection with their real location. Evie knew zilch about police work. She could just be overly suspicious. It happened. But she wasn't giving her address to this stranger.

"The law office of S&S is fine. My lawyer will have notaries. I hope you've caught the terrible person who killed a nice gentleman like Mr. Pendleton!" Her theatrics needed a little work.

"We called the law firm, and they didn't list you as a client—"

"For good reason. Just send it care of Mr. Jackson as we said. It will be fine." Evie tried to think of a *good reason* if anyone asked. She was a famous film star?

"It's unusual for witnesses—"

"We were strangers passing through, not witnesses." Evie cut off that line of thought. If this was someone fishing for info. . . A reporter? "I have to go. Good-day."

She punched off, wondering if she ought to be worried. How had they found the phone number? Another customer entered, and she forgot about it.

Loretta arrived after Mavis returned, and Evie set aside her dust cloth. "I was just about to hunt lunch, tadpole. Have you had any yet?"

"Iddy offered an eggplant salad, but I said I had to get home or you'd be lonely." Loretta skipped alongside Evie as they took the sidewalk route around the block to home.

"Lonely." Evie snorted, thinking of her house full of men. "You'll need to work on your story-telling. Tuna salad sound better?"

"Is it awful to eat fish?" Beneath her dark bangs and large-framed glasses, Loretta looked serious. "Iddy makes me feel bad about eating anything that walks the earth, but fish are in water."

"Plants are alive. Maybe most of them don't walk, but they're alive, and there is evidence they know when they're hurt. So is it better to yank the fruit off an eggplant or the leaf off a lettuce? I prefer the Native American way of thanking the earth for its bounty and returning the gift by making the world a better place."

"So maybe I can grow up to be an environmentalist and save the tuna from toxins and overfishing." Loretta skipped happily.

With her wealth, Loretta could do a lot more, but Evie preferred to keep money out of it. Loretta had the brains and the good vibes to do it on her own. "Listen to your teachers and learn, and you'll work it out one day."

"Oh, Iddy said Ariel emailed. She wants you to deliver turtle food and a turtle house, if you have time." Loretta ran up the stairs and into the house, presumably in search of tuna.

"Good thing I'm used to being errand boy," Evie muttered as she followed in her ward's footsteps. But she wasn't complaining. Jax's sister roused her insatiable curiosity.

Reuben and Roark were in the kitchen preparing a pitcher of iced tea. Evie gave them credit for at least attempting to look as if they were preparing their own lunch. "Security camera showed we were heading this way, right?"

Unabashed, they filled a glass for her. "We didn't think you'd like us rummaging in your fridge."

"Aunt Val's ex-husband liked parties. They knocked out a wall to add that fridge. It might be half a century old, but it holds enough for two armies. You can put your stuff in there. You do know how to grocery shop, right?" Evie sorted through cabinets and refrigerator for salad ingredients.

"For beer and chips." Roark helpfully opened the cans of tuna.

"The microwave in the van is small. We nuke frozen meals." Reuben studied the celery that Evie pushed at him.

"Loretta, toast some of that stale bread, will you?" Evie directed her troops at the point of a knife. "Fine, then I'll make meals. In return, you tell me what fun things you discovered today."

"If we don't tell you?" Roark asked, simply because that's how his mind worked.

"You can go back to your hole, and Loretta and I will take our salad over to Ariel." Evie had seen how Roark's aura spiked whenever Jax's sister was mentioned. She wasn't ashamed of using her secret knowledge.

"That's just plain mean. This isn't rocket science. We can figure it out." Reuben whacked at the celery.

"You should wash the celery and cut off the ends and the bad spots first." Evie waved her knife. "You want to go through the spice drawer and figure out which ones go with tuna?" She handed an onion to Roark. "Know how to peel and chop one of these?"

"Hey ya, I can do dat. Mama made hot sauce, y'know?" He settled on a counter stool and started peeling.

"Did you send off that package of Jax's documents? I don't know if Orbis Junior can learn anything from touching paper, but we should try."

"Fed Ex. You paying us back?" Reuben painstakingly scrubbed his celery and picked at bits that looked brown.

"The allowance I get from Loretta's trust will cover it. So, the old contracts from Jax's father—have you figured out their importance?" Evie broke eggs and started on her homemade mayonnaise.

"Nah, that's for Jax. What we've got is more fun." Reuben took his celery to a cutting board she shoved at him. "That old PCB you found was made by Sovereign Machinery. Shareholders included Ives and Jackson, plus the original Stockton from Jax's law firm. They hung with some mighty fine fellas."

"Hoo yah, baby." Roark cut professionally at his onion. "The big money for Sovereign came from back here, which is probably how Stockton got involved. Ever heard of the Swensons?"

"Swenson Fisheries?" Evie held up her can of tuna. "Used to can tuna. I think they made cat food and maybe canned soup and things? They were pretty big when I was a kid."

"*Ça c'est bon.* Dey had a big plant down in Luziana." Roark laid on the accent.

Evie had learned that Roark's parents were from Louisiana, but they'd split up when he was a kid. He'd spent a lot of time with different families and earned a scholarship to MIT. So the accent was his childhood speaking. How he came by a Scots name and survived Boston accents was a story for another time.

"Canning and fishing have been a dying industry for a long time." Reuben meticulously cut up the celery as he spoke. "The family started putting their fortune into up-and-coming industries, like electronics."

"So Swenson Canneries helped finance Sovereign Machinery?" Evie tried to speed up the storytelling.

"Right on, sister." Reuben handed over his precisely chopped celery. Evie handed him another stalk. He stoically took it to the sink. "Better yet, Gustav Swenson had a son who wanted into politics. And said son had a handful of California friends with deep pockets—"

"Not *Augustus* Swenson?" Evie asked in incredulity. "We are not talking the California senator? How did we get from east coast fisheries to California?"

"By way of Granny Marilyn Swenson, Gustav's wife. She's from a family of California real estate moguls. Did the Hollywood thang when she was young, met Gustav at some society benefit in the sixties, decided wealthy east coast influential family better than *nouveau riche* Hollywood, and they formed a power couple on both coasts."

Reuben's middle-class professional origins peeked out when he got wound up, Evie noticed. "That was w-a-a-ay back before my time. Is Gustav even alive now?"

"Nope. He was an old man when he married Marilyn, the Hollywood not-a-star. But she's still going strong. Between Gustav's tuna fish fortune and her family's real estate contacts, she had tons of connections to help her son get ahead in California."

"And they still own the fisheries *and* the voting machine company?" Evie raised her eyebrows. "So, Augustus, the senator, is what, pushing sixty these days? And thirty-some years ago, when Sovereign was forming, he was in his late twenties?"

Roark added the onions to the bowl with the tuna. "He was working with his mother's family in California real estate back then. With all that money and mama's contacts, he ran for some local office, and invested in the new machines that were supposed to handle the elections of the future."

"Except the machines cost too much." Reuben added his celery to the bowl.

"And nobody wanted to spend a lot of money on new-fangled machines, and voters hate change." Evie mixed in her mayonnaise and some pickles and stirred the bowl. "So they should have all lost their shirts."

"But they didn't. Sovereign's original owners may have been young up-and-comers, like Jax's dad and partner, but they all had powerful, wealthy families."

"*Except* for Ives and Jackson," Evie reminded them. "They appeared to be essentially orphaned."

"But Ives owned a valuable silica mine and Jackson owned a powerful law office in the district young Augustus was running for at the time. Jackson and Ives weren't small change. They had what it took to set up the mining business *and* the machinery business and the locals knew them. They were the front office. The VIPs just provided funds and stayed out of the picture." Reuben inspected Evie's bowl, nodded approval, and took his usual seat next to Loretta in the breakfast nook.

Evie's people radar spun with all this input. "So, Jax's father and partner were appointed to talk towns into buying their fancy new voting machines?"

"Yup. Cutting edge equipment. If they could have lowered the cost, they would have been on the brink of big time."

"Would they have known their microchip was going into a circuit board that didn't work right?" Evie had been fretting around that. Someone had left that crooked board under the memorial for a reason.

Rube thought about it. "In early days, probably not. It would have taken a lot of use before the error was noticeable."

"Where's the fun part?" Evie spread out the salad on the toast and pointed Roark at the tomatoes.

"Sovereign kept chugging, even after Ives and Jackson fell off the map. Front men weren't essential once the machines were introduced. Augustus won his local election and built a power base. Somewhere along the line, the voting machines got discounted when he persuaded his district they needed them. There was probably juice involved," Reuben added.

Evie sent Roark a questioning glance.

"Kickbacks, payoffs, bribes. . . Connections, bébé."

"So judging by the faulty board we found—before Jax's father vanished, *someone* knew the machines weren't working right. Thus, the good senator may have bought his first political position through crooked machines. Swell. But you said Sovereign eventually got caught and sued for fraud. Surely their machines are long gone." Evie slapped spinach on top of the tomato and handed two plates to Roark to take to the table.

"Uh uh, sugar." Reuben sipped his tea and shook his man bun. "Those machines cost too much. By the time the court ruling came down a dozen years later, Sovereign had sold hundreds of thousands of those machines, and Swenson and his cronies were already ensconced in political office—a lot of those first crooked machines were in his district."

"And I bet, from the first sign of trouble, they had people persuading election officials that the machines were easily repaired." Appalled, Evie mulled the implications.

"And his kinfolk quietly started DVM with the same basic machines and sold them on the east coast, where hardly anyone knew about the California scandal."

"Except Jax's father, who died in a car crash right about the time Swenson formed the new company." Evie bit back a curse by biting into her sandwich.

Even her ADD-afflicted mind couldn't find connections between ancient voting machines and poor Mr. Pendleton, but if Jax's father and his partner had been murdered. . . Wouldn't the killer be too old to murder anyone else?

Ten

SITTING AT LA RAISON, AFTERTHOUGHT'S ONLY CLAIM TO FINE DINING, JAX JOINED in a toast with his newfound friends. Quiet Bill Wright, the banker, tipped his glass of tea to Jax's wine glass. Geoff Hayes, his accountant landlord, lifted a beer.

Paul Clancy, mayoral candidate and town council member, held up his martini to give the toast. "To the latest business in Afterthought, the new firm of Jackson and Ives, may you be as useful to Afterthought's well-being as your predecessor."

Jax had just laid down his life savings as a deposit, so he hoped he was successful. Backing out was not an option. "I thank you all for persuading Mr. Norton's family to settle quickly."

He still hadn't quite determined why or how Clancy had become involved, but Jax supposed it was good to know all facets of his newly adopted home.

Clancy laughed. A gold eagle pin on his lapel caught the light and sparkled. Jax had to drag his gaze away. Was the eagle actually holding a fish in its talons?

"Norton's widow is well-off, and his son simply wanted the burden off his back. I don't think they expected anything except paying storage fees on those files forever."

Swell. He could probably have offered half as much. Jax smiled anyway. It was all about connections and goodwill. "I'll need to bring in some furniture, but right now, there's room to store the files. I can relieve the family of that burden. I have a team who can digitalize the paper."

Clancy lifted his martini glass to that. "Understand you used to work for Stockton and Stockton. I got my start there, back in the day."

Jax hid his shock and a twist in his gut. Was this why Clancy had attached himself to the party? How did he play this? As far as he was aware, Clancy was an investment broker, not a lawyer. "I was only there a few years. My father worked longer, though. Perhaps you knew him? Franklin Jackson?"

Clancy drank his martini, hiding his expression. When he put the glass down, he had his poker face on. "Sure, you look a lot like him. Who is the Ives in your office name? A relation?"

Jax set his glass aside before he broke it. He had so many questions. . . None of which he could ask, not until he knew Clancy better. "Old friend of my father's who made buying my office easier." Factual lie but a metaphorical truth. "Did you work with my father much?"

Clancy shrugged. "He wasn't too interested in investing. Nice guy but hardheaded. Jackson could be like a dog with a bone."

Yeah, Jax was getting that picture. Like father, like son, good to know. Lifting his glass again, he debated his next question—when Evie walked in. His jaw nearly dropped into his drink.

She'd yanked her boisterous orange curls into a tight knot on top of her head. That alone made her almost unrecognizable. The blue blazer, gray mini skirt, and heels. . . Jax's instinct for danger warred with animal lust. The only reaction he could manage was to stand when she approached.

The other men weren't as quick to acknowledge her. Her rose lips quirked, and she mockingly gestured for them to remain seated. "Gentlemen, I hope this is a happy occasion. Mr. Clancy, good to see you. Bill, Geoff."

"Would you like to join us?" Jax asked, actually hoping she'd agree so he could get her measure of Clancy.

"No, thanks, I'm meeting with Miss Ward and her campaign manager." She nodded toward a table in a far corner.

Jax didn't know who Ward was, but *campaign manager* sounded ominous. Surely Evie was over the mayoral kick by now?

"Will she set her next ad campaign here?" Bill finally opened his mouth. "I know she spoke about it."

Neither of the other men seemed much interested.

"Oh, you haven't heard?" Her crystal blue eyes lit from within and her mouth curled at the corner.

Jax's gut twisted. He knew that Evie look. His table companions might have known her longer than Jax had, but they didn't know her as well. The respectable suit and slicked-back curls couldn't disguise the evil genie within.

Mild-mannered Bill, the banker, fell for the act. "I never hear anything until it's all over. My wife complains I'm a very bad gossip."

"Oh, Alice will like this. Be sure to tell her." Evie's smile broadened wickedly. "Miss Ward filed her intent to run for mayor an hour ago."

Jax watched his table companions with interest. The banker seemed genuinely pleased. The accountant looked shocked but intrigued. Clancy, the only current mayoral candidate besides Mavis—looked as if his head might explode.

A grin teased at Evie's lips, until she turned to Jax. "The guys have a few things to tell you. You should probably answer your phone."

She swayed off—not bounced or ran or the usual Evie things but a deliberately provocative sway as she headed for the other table.

Jax got her message. She wasn't that hard to read. She despised the current town council—represented by Clancy. She wanted Jax to turn his head and open his eyes. So he did.

The lighting wasn't good, but the tall, elegant woman welcoming Evie looked a little too sophisticated for a small town like this. The diminutive Black man standing up and pulling out a chair wasn't anyone Jax recognized. He, too, had a polished city appearance. Suits like that didn't come off the rack.

Huh. Maybe Afterthought wasn't quite the backwater he imagined.

Behind him, Clancy threw back his martini and spluttered. "They'll make this town a laughingstock. Excuse me. I need to make a few phone calls." Without offering to pay his bill, he got up and walked out.

Clancy didn't think Blacks should run for office? Half the town had brown skin! Jax was starting to understand why Evie wanted Clancy defeated.

"Well, if your girlfriend is siding with the freaky part of our fair town, you've lost any chance at gaining the county's business," Geoff said pragmatically, chugging his beer.

Freaky side? "Not my girlfriend," Jax responded automatically, even if he might want her to be. Antagonizing the establishment wouldn't help his pocket, but he'd enjoyed the sick look on Clancy's smug face. He might be more like his anarchic friends than he'd thought. "Evie's family will never support any of the mayor's cronies. So it's pretty much a given that if there's a freaky side of town, she's on it."

"What about her mother?" Bill asked anxiously. "I thought Mavis was running."

"Only because no one else was. I'm guessing this means she'll step down, unless there's animosity there too?" Jax wasn't liking the idea of losing business before he even started, but he wasn't insane enough to oppose Evie and her family. He'd learned that lesson—

The Malcolms might be on the wrong side of normal, but they knew where the bodies were buried—*literally* upon occasion. Yeah, he'd rather have them on his side than Clancy and the mayor.

Geoff snorted. "No animosity there. Mavis got Larry started on his fashion career. If her family is supporting the fag's campaign, Clancy has good reason to turn tail and run. This election might actually be interesting."

Fag? Jax winced at the archaic slur, then worked through the implications. *Miss* Ward had been born male—at least in the town's eyes. Afterthought had just become much more interesting.

"Well, my policy is to avoid politics." Cutting off any more derisive remarks, Jax gestured at the menu. "I invited you to dinner, gentlemen. I hope we'll be working together in my bright new future."

He didn't pull out his phone until he excused himself to go to the bar for more drinks.

Roark's voice mail was almost gleeful. "The Swenson family is still a Stockton client, and your idiot ex-firm hasn't changed your passwords. Their files are a treasure trove. The family claims Grandma Swenson is coo-coo and wants her locked away before Senator Augustus announces his run for *president*. The good senator signed those contracts between Sovereign and your father thirty years ago, while he was still just a Realtor. Read da contracts sooner dan later, lawyer man."

Jax had no idea what the Cajun idiot was aiming at—but he could guess, and his gut twisted, a certain sign of trouble.

If anything shady had occurred thirty years ago, they were sitting on a powder keg that might blow up a presidential campaign.

Evie's eccentric candidate for mayor paled in comparison.

∿

EVIE TIMED HER DEPARTURE FROM THE RESTAURANT TO COINCIDE WITH JAX'S. IT had been pure luck to find him there. He'd been uncommunicative all day—apparently for good reason, judging by the company he was keeping. Macho Man worked fast to already be on the inside of the movers and shakers. Well, she supposed, all that took was a barrel of money.

"I gather you have momentous news." Evie took his arm.

She had walked here. Apparently, so had he. Mosquitoes buzzed in the humidity of the mild June night, but home was little more than half a mile away. She fell in step with his long strides.

Jax slowed down to accommodate her. "Seems you do, too. What's with the new mayoral candidate? Clancy looked as if he'd swallowed a snake."

Evie chuckled. "Loretta and I drew up lists of potential candidates. We gave up being logical and went with someone who has a big bubble and a rainbow aura. Larraine Ward has outside clout that Clancy can't even begin to wield in his small-minded territorialism. We were sitting with Desmond Redfern, a bit-time campaign manager from Atlanta."

"And *Miss* Ward is known to the locals as Larry?"

She heard his skepticism and shrugged. "Gender has no business in politics."

"Agreed, but this is a small town, and it does. If I want to keep on the good side of the courthouse and its cronies, I'll have to move into my office and pretend I don't know you."

Evie stiffened. "Your call." She'd probably have to kill him if he sided with Clancy. Or evict him. "You have an office?"

"I am now officially a local businessman." Jax dropped an arm over her shoulders. "I hate politics. What was Roark's message about Swenson? *Senator* Swenson?"

She relaxed a fraction, although she still frowned. She didn't like hurting Jax's new business. She probably should have considered that—if he'd bothered telling her he was starting one. "I'll let R&R have the pleasure of explaining. They did the footwork. Roark helped me deliver a turtle house to Ariel today. Did you give her a turtle? She's like a kid with a new toy. She even came out of her cave to show us where she wanted it."

"Turtles need houses?" Despite his sarcasm, he sounded pleased.

"Probably not." His arm around her stirred sensations best left unstirred. She stepped away at the town's one stoplight as they crossed the road. "But if she regularly puts food inside the house, the turtle is less likely to wander off.

We put it near a camera so she can watch. I was amazed that she didn't hide when Roark showed up."

It had been fun watching them. Roark had pretended he was just a delivery driver doing his job, ignoring Ariel. Ariel had surreptitiously watched his every move while pointing out what she wanted. She'd eventually fled inside, but for Ariel, it had been a breakthrough.

"He acted as her taxi driver a few times. She's seen him with me. He's not a total stranger." Jax slowed down as he passed an office building and gestured. "My new office is in there. I'll need furniture."

She wasn't entirely certain how she felt about him setting up business in Afterthought, but her pulse responded by racing. "I suppose clients here won't be any more wicked than in the city."

"And a few of them might even be innocent," he countered wryly. "I've mostly done fraud research, with a little family law on the side, though. I'm not a defense attorney. I suppose boring, safe stuff will leave me time to look after Loretta's affairs."

"And Loretta?" she added, just to see if he understood the kid needed a father figure.

"I'm not good with kids, but I'll be here. It's the best I can offer."

Elated that the uptight lawyer accepted that much responsibility, Evie tugged him to a halt and smooched his bristled jaw.

Jax responded by pulling her into his arms and kissing her—a real kiss and not a pacifying kiss. A kiss that burned right through her middle and had his aura shooting sparks. A kiss that let her feel every hard inch of him and wonder if his office had room for a bed.

"I'll help you find furniture," she said breathlessly when he finally set her down and dragged her onward while they both caught their breaths.

He responded by yanking out the clamp holding her hair in place, tumbling her curls into her face. "That was an impressive act back there, but you don't have to pretend with me."

Evie ran her hands through the mop, massaging her head after the tight bun. "I didn't want to shame Miss Ward by looking like a ragamuffin. I had to borrow the clothes from Prissy. I should probably try harder to look normal for Loretta's sake, shouldn't I?"

"Nope. Only do it if it makes you feel better. You'd even look good in one of those overstuffed quilted parkas." He returned his arm to her shoulders.

"That's because, underneath that control freak exterior, you have an absurdist streak that enjoys abnormal. Others don't appreciate weird so well. If I mean to get respect and run a successful business, I probably ought to practice normal." Evie tried to decide if she liked his proprietary arm. Mostly, she enjoyed the buzz of having a hot hunk this close. His square shoulders were twice her size.

He laughed. "You think you ought to dress normal for a ghost-busting business?"

She shrugged, more interested in his news. "So you bought Norton's practice?"

He squeezed her shoulders. "Yes, I am now the impoverished owner of a once-successful law practice. Do I need to dress normal, too?"

"Depends on who you want for clients. If you want rich people, yup, sorry. You'll probably have to join a Charleston country club too. Otherwise, wear Birkenstocks and let your hair grow out and the rest of us won't care."

"That's small-town attitude. In Savannah, some of the richest people I know looked as if they'd just dragged in from a box car. I grew up with suits, so it makes no difference to me. Give me some hint about Swenson. Roark is likely to be unavailable when we get back."

"You sweet-talker, you. How likely is it that someone from a sheriff's office would call to verify I'm a client of Stockton's and ask for my address to sign a statement?"

Sensing his sudden tension, she didn't bother tuning in to his aura. She could read him without her extra sense these days.

"Not likely. The police should have better things to pursue—unless they have someone breathing down their necks. I gave them an address. They shouldn't need more." He muttered a few obscenities under his breath and picked up speed.

"I'll call Conan, have him look into it," he said as they approached the house. "I need to talk to R&R about this Swenson business. Will Loretta be awake? Should I say good-night to her or anything?"

The chill she'd felt at his reaction to her caller warmed at his offer to acknowledge Loretta as something besides a client. If her head didn't spin off her neck at *his* mixed reactions, she might develop pneumonia from her own. "She'll be reading under the covers. Lights out was half an hour ago."

He chuckled, waved at Mavis babysitting in the front room, and followed Evie upstairs, rapping lightly at Loretta's door before opening it. "Just checking to make certain you're still here."

"I'm here," Loretta called back. "Tell Evie to clear the attic so I can have more privacy."

"What, with all the ghosts and goblins? You tell her. Goodnight, sleep tight." Jax shut the door.

"That is probably the sexiest thing I've heard you say." Evie beamed at him in approval.

"I want to hear more about your Miss Ward, but not while I'm trying to resist kissing you again. This house is becoming claustrophobic."

Evie thought Jax was looking at her with the same hunger she felt, but she understood his resistance. They were adults. They'd figure this out.

She shoved him away. "Go, play with the boys. We haven't even dated yet."

Leaving him looking startled, she entered her own room. She might be lousy at internet research, but she was a good people judge.

Paul Clancy had turned as muddy as the mayor just before he stormed off this evening.

Jax was playing in a shark pool.

Eleven

"*Voila*, furniture." In the early morning light, Evie gestured at the attic full of dust-covered treasures.

After an evening listening to R&R's revelations and poring over old contracts, Jax thought his head needed a refresh button. Setting up his new office had been his intent. Evie's attic was not exactly what he had in mind.

"I need to furnish an office, not a bordello." Jax studied the clutter without hope. "Is that the lampshade you meant to plant on my head a few months ago?" He gestured at a maroon pleated monstrosity with dangling beads.

"Exactly. Wrap that gold shawl around you, and you could be a lamp, spying on your enemies. You need to think creatively." She pushed her way deeper into the shadows of the enormous, hot attic.

"I have no enemies." Jax figured he was better off staying well away from the temptation of Evie in short shorts near old bedsteads. Her crack last night about their never having dated. . . Led him to believe she might be as interested as he was in some kind of relationship. He wanted sex. He feared she wanted a daddy figure for Loretta.

"Will Goodwill take this stuff?" the kid asked, poking around with distaste.

"Bonfire," Jax suggested, kicking at a box of rags to see if anything heavy was in the bottom.

"Garage." Roark shoved aside a few cartons to reach a mahogany inlaid wardrobe. "Huge empty carriage house goin' to waste."

"I'll have a car someday," Evie called back. "I want a red Miata convertible."

"That won't take the space of a thimble." Reuben hefted a carton, then apparently deciding it was heavy, kneeled to examine it. "We could be here forever."

"Unless I see office furniture or junk to be hauled to the curb, I'm outta here." Jax checked out Reuben's box of trashy novels, then looked into the wardrobe over Roark's shoulder. "Does Afterthought have a theater group? Great costumes in here."

"Great-Aunt Val's from the sixties or Great-Grandma's from the twenties? I'm guessing my mother is still wearing her old clothes." On the other side of the attic, Evie heaved a stack of old drapery off a table.

"Both. Did no men ever live in this house?" Fascinated despite himself, Jax dug around on the wardrobe's shelves—all feminine millinery, no boxes of jewels, fake or otherwise.

"The cellar, remember? That was my great-uncle's domain. Admittedly, he didn't last long."

Loretta squeezed in and helped herself to a feathered concoction. "I could have plays up here!"

"Here they are!" Evie pointed at what appeared to be sturdy oak hidden by trunks and ancient paintings. "Lawyer bookcases."

"You had lawyers in the family?" Jax abandoned the wardrobe and wended his way through the junk into the danger zone of Evie.

"Books. Glass fronts protect books. Val meant to put these shelves in the room she called a library but moved on before she got around to it. Books aren't my thing, so I never followed through. There's a library table under here somewhere too."

"Huh." Jax rapped on the solid old wood and examined the intricate glass panes. "Most of my journals are digital, but these would add an air of respectable permanence."

"Here da library table." Having given up on the costume wardrobe, Roark lifted boxes off a substantial oak table. "Look at the size of those planks—old timber."

"Chair!" Loretta called from one of the turrets.

Jax turned to see her wearing a feathered hat and bouncing in what appeared to be a leather Morris chair that could hold three of her. It might take a crane to haul that out.

"Your clients will love that. You'll need something more modern for your desk." Evie joined him in admiring the chair's solid oak frame. "A little leather softener and it will be good as new."

She smelled of ylang-ylang and baby shampoo—sexy and innocent. Jax thought it might be deliberate. Last night's kiss burned through his brain, obliterating sensible thought. She'd turned him on since he'd first met her, but last night. . . Had given him hope he didn't deserve.

"The thrift store will have more modern stuff, maybe even some of Norton's original décor," Evie suggested.

"Not if it reeks of cigars." Jax pictured the modern, glass-and-steel office he'd left in Savannah and tried to see himself in an old-fashioned one with real wood and leather. It suited the old building with its wood trim and bricks.

"You'll look rich and established," Evie said for him. "You can tell people they're family heirlooms. It's a shame all your parents' things were sold off."

There it was, his need to connect with roots he didn't have. He had photos of his childhood home and memories, but they were fading. He couldn't afford sentimentality. "I just want my bank account to look rich and established. Free furniture helps, if we can haul these things down the stairs."

Reuben, the engineering expert, had already cleared a path over to Loretta's turret and the Morris chair. "French doors," he called, pounding at rusted door handles. "Balcony. A few ropes. . ."

Evie was past him before he had the doors completely open. "Oh, look, I haven't been up here in forever! That balcony is outside Val's master suite."

Master suite? The house had a private suite? In the turret, of course, and stuffed with family discards like the rest of the house.

"We need a winch." Reuben headed for the attic stairs. "Best check the balcony ain't termite infested before you drop massive stuff on it."

Before Jax started envisioning a suite with turret and balcony and Evie in it, he headed for the stairs too. "Tell me where to find the thrift store, and I'll stop by later. I'm having George's files delivered today."

"Are you sure there aren't any ghosts up here, Evie?" he heard Loretta ask as he descended the stairs.

"No, I laid them to rest when I was a kid."

Jax hoped she was being facetious. With Evie, one never knew.

He didn't think anyone could lay *his* ghosts to rest. It felt as if the specter of his father leaned over his shoulder, urging him on. Connecting an accident twenty years ago with Pendleton's murder? That was Evie-talk.

What he needed was a desk for his computer, an internet hook-up, and a few hours to better examine those contracts Senator Swenson and his father had signed. And then he needed to go through the papers Pendleton's office had sent. If the California lawyer had died because of those files— Jax didn't want to believe a man was murdered over his father's files, but he didn't like coincidences either.

He checked Evie's security footage on his phone before he left the house. All clear. Maybe they had imagined being followed back in California and that phone call yesterday meant nothing. Maybe Pendleton's death had no relation to his father's papers.

And maybe Afterthought was the center of the universe, and a drag queen would become mayor.

"SENSIBLE SOLUTIONS. WE HAVE A SOLUTION FOR YOU," REUBEN SAID INTO HIS phone mic as he and Roark hauled bookshelves downstairs the old-fashioned way, by muscle.

Evie shook out the old draperies, wondering if they might work in Jax's office. They'd been custom made of sturdy fabric and were well-lined to keep out the cold and heat.

"Yes, Mrs. Winsted, I agree. Owls shouldn't be hooting at your window in broad daylight. We'll be right out. No, I don't think it's your late husband. Yes, ma'am. Yes, yes, let us finish this job, and we'll move you to the top of our priority list." He spoke without even breathing hard as they carried the heavy wood and glass cases down the second flight of stairs.

"Business is booming," Roark said with a heavy dose of sarcasm from the down side of the case.

"The little old ladies like watching big muscular hunks crawling around on their roofs." Dropping the draperies, Evie followed them down. "We'll snag the big cases one of these days. If you can't get the owl to move, tell Mrs. Winsted that I'll be out to be certain it's not her husband. She just wants company."

Evie opened the front door so they could leave the bookcase on the porch. The June heat had hit a hundred already. They'd have to give up on the attic for the day.

"Air conditioning," Loretta said, following them. "Instead of a cook, let's buy air conditioning."

The kid was a wee bit too precocious. "Not sure a place like this can have central. We'll put a window unit in your room. That should be acceptable use of your money."

"Yours, too," Loretta said stubbornly. "And Jax's. Does the cellar get hot in summer?"

"We're good, *chevrette*," Roark called back.

Evie had never had to worry about other people's comfort in her aunt's house. She just kept her shades drawn and turned on the ceiling fan in the evening. But Loretta was used to all the modern conveniences. So was Jax. And the summer promised to be a sweltering one, if today was any example.

"All right, I'll call someone, see what can be done. But the electric bill is likely to go sky-high."

"Solar," Reuben shouted as he aimed for the van.

"More money," she shouted back, before turning to Loretta. "Let's head for the shop. You'll be cooler there while I walk the dogs."

"Can I visit Iddy, too? She likes help with the kennels. And maybe I should bike out to see if Ariel needs help with her turtle."

Jax had started living in the servant's room off the kitchen because he worried about Loretta's safety. An heiress needed security.

A kid needed to be a kid, and she didn't want Loretta living in fear.

Evie wrinkled her nose and sought a responsible reply. "You're good with Mavis and Iddy. If you want to bike anywhere, you need someone with you. What would happen if you got hit by a truck? There'd be no one to call for help."

Loretta frowned. "What if I have a friend go with me?"

"Tell me what friend and let me know when you go and when you'll be back." She hated the words even as they came out of her mouth, but it had to be done. She could remind Loretta about how her parents died, that there were bad people in the world, but Loretta knew that.

Leaving her ward with Mavis at the Psychic Solutions shop, Evie picked up her doggie clients and headed for Witch Hill. Ariel lived on the far side. She debated walking over, but the dogs preferred exploring the pond.

Evie's new phone rang with another unknown number. She hadn't given it out for the business, but Mavis had probably passed it around. She should figure out how to do a contact list. Could they be sorted between business and personal?

While she pondered the mysteries of technology, the call went to voice mail. Ha, another challenge. Determined not to be left too far behind in the tech wars, she punched around until the phone started speaking.

"Miss Malcolm, this is Desmond Redfern. We met last night."

Larraine's new campaign manager, cool. Evie tuned into the message.

"I've had an interesting call from the campaign office of Senator Swenson—from California? He mentioned Mr. Jackson as a friend of his and wanted to touch base to see if we need anything. I am not familiar with Mr. Jackson, but I believe he's a friend of yours?"

Evie replayed the message, uncertain she'd heard right. Jax? Senator Swenson? Ah—*no*?

But Swenson had been a client of S&S and a friend of Jax's *father*—fishing expedition? Had Clancy passed on that information? That made no sense. She really did have a suspicious mind and shouldn't be looking gift horses in the mouth. . .

Jax had put his contact number in her list, along with Loretta's and a few others. She painstakingly saved Mr. Redfern's, then called Jax.

"Yup." He sounded absentminded and irritated.

"Someone from Swenson's campaign office called Miss Ward and offered their aid because they know *Mr. Jackson*. Want to work that out?"

She tried to imagine how he looked as he pondered that, but she didn't even know where he was.

"I have never met a Swenson in my life," he said slowly, as if thinking aloud. "They're still S&S clients but not Stephen's. S&S would never give out my number, but I suppose someone there may have mentioned. . . Nope. I have no connection to Miss Ward's campaign. Why in heck would a California senator have any interest in a small-town South Carolina mayoral campaign anyway?"

"More fishing for information," Evie concluded. "If the call was from California, it may have been the same person who called me. I have a website with Afterthought on it as my address. If they pulled a few strings, I can be found. They may have connected me to you. I don't like it."

"Neither do I. See if the guys can trace that call. At least whoever it is doesn't know where we are precisely."

But whoever wanted to find them was getting ugly close. "Have you found anything in those contracts that might have someone hunting you down?"

"Beyond Swenson's signature? Possibly. There's a clause tying my father's microchips to the patent for the machines instead of to Sovereign Machinery."

"Which means?" Evie began whistling for the dogs, rounding them up.

"Not sure yet, but it might mean my father could yank the patent from the company. I have to read more. I need to get Reuben in to look at actual machines and not just drawings. It's possible DVM is still using the illegal machines *and* the patent. If so, then my father's estate should still be receiving a share of the proceeds. That's a huge suit in the making."

"Ah, the plot thickens. And if those circuit boards are still crooked?" She snapped leashes to collars with one hand, not easy with an eager golden retriever. Maybe she should get earbuds for the phone.

"That's a conundrum to ponder. Should I sue for profits on rigged machines? Let's hope they fixed those circuit boards. I'll get Reuben in to look at the new voting machines somewhere if I can."

"I may think in circles, but I do not understand the criminal mind."

"Because money and power are not your goals." Jax signed off.

Her goal was much more difficult—respect. At least Mr. Redfern had called *her* instead of Jax. Leading the dogs back to town, she punched in her new contact, wondering how she would explain.

She didn't think she could, especially when she got voice mail. "Mr. Redfern, Evie Malcolm here. Mr. Jackson believes the caller from the Swenson campaign may have confused him with his late father. Franklin Jackson and the senator were invested in the same voting machine company."

She decided to throw out a wild card. Maybe not so wild given the apparent connections between Clancy and Swenson. "Given some things we've learned, he advises that you ask to have someone inspect Afterthought's voting machines before the elections."

The elections weren't until the fall. Anything could happen before then.

She left Redfern with Jax's number. She'd rather hunt ghosts. She punched in Reuben's name since Roark usually drove the truck. "Any dead husbands at Mrs. Winsted's?" she asked when he answered.

"Sick owl. We're taking it to Iddy. If we grocery shop, what should we buy?"

"You'll probably want hamburgers and hot dogs and all the gross stuff that goes with them. Pick up some tortillas and Mexican cheese for me, and I'll show you what meat ought to taste like."

"Will do. Juice Jax on inspecting some of those machines, will you?" Reuben urged. "I'm finding some weird sh—stuff—on the darknet."

Evie grinned at the nerdy professor's attempt to be polite. "I think he's on it. The darknet is right here in River City."

She left him whistling the tune. Saving Honey, her mother's golden retriever, for last, Evie dropped her doggie clients off with their human parents and stopped to relieve her mother at the shop.

"I'm withdrawing my application," Mavis announced, straightening the gray knot of her hair. "I couldn't have found a better candidate than Larraine. Her cards are a bit dicey. Have her come in and we'll see what we can do to fix that."

Evie had known her mother hadn't wanted to run. She'd just been making a point in her inimitable way. "I'll try, but she seems to be pretty busy."

"She'll find time. We had someone from the city come by to say the water mains need inspecting and the water may be turned off indefinitely. I'm afraid I cast a forgetting spell on him and hexed his image in the scrying glass."

Mavis was prescient, not a witch. Evie bit back a grin. This was her mother being angry. "I'll call the water department and hex them, too. Sounds like we have Clancy worried."

"While I'm at city hall, I'll hex him, too." In a huff, Mavis left for lunch and gossip.

When Mavis hexed someone, she did it with gossip. Whoever that poor utility guy was, he was about to have a rough week. Clancy could probably chew gossips for breakfast, but they had no good proof that he was responsible for the mains, except that was how small-town politics worked.

Mavis returned from lunch looking satisfied. With impeccable timing, Loretta arrived right after her.

Having made a few calls of her own concerning the utility situation, Evie was confident they wouldn't be immediately waterless. She and Loretta returned to the house for lunch—where R&R were filling the refrigerator with their idea of food.

Rolling her eyes at their pre-packaged, barely-meat patties, she dug in the freezer for shredded pork from a local farm. "There's a grill in the carriage house, or you can wait and see what I do to this."

"Barbecue sauce?" Reuben asked eagerly.

"Not on tortillas."

The men were arguing over their favorite barbecue sauces when the house phone rang. With the receiver propped on her shoulder, Evie opened Aunt Val's homemade salsa. "Sensible Solutions." She used to answer it *Psychic* Solutions, but Mavis was handling those calls now.

"They've just found Fred Clancy dead at city hall," Jax said without preamble. "Your mother visited there shortly before he was found."

Twelve

"You saw Clancy last night." Sheriff Troy studied Jax's nearly empty law office.

Jax sat behind the library table from Evie's attic. The boxes of legal files that had been delivered earlier had all been removed from underfoot. His team had hauled off Norton's more recent paper files to scan, and Jax had shoved the ancient, useless ones into an anteroom. That left little for Troy to inspect.

It hadn't taken the sheriff long to learn about last night's dinner. From what Jax had heard, Clancy had died at noon today and it wasn't yet four.

If the sheriff was questioning people about Clancy, then the death had been suspicious. Since he barely knew the man, Jax didn't think he could be a suspect. Evie and her mother, on the other hand. . .

"I saw him, along with everyone else in La Raison. Have a seat." Jax indicated one of the folding chairs he'd borrowed from his landlord.

The sheriff declined. Jax didn't blame him. Average height, gray and balding, carrying a middle-aged belly, Troy didn't look impressive. But Jax had worked with him before. The sheriff was a reasonable man who simply wanted facts—and knew Evie's capricious family well.

"But you were at a table with him. What did he have to say? Did it reflect his state of mind?"

"How did Clancy die?" Jax asked, in the hopes Troy might open up. He didn't, so Jax pressed for more. "If you want to know his state of mind, then I'm assuming potential suicide?"

Which reminded him too much of Pendleton. Jax had no reason to mention that until he knew more.

Troy grimaced. "I'm gathering facts before the town makes skyscrapers out of anthills. Once news spreads, no one remembers actual facts. They just repeat the last rumor they heard."

Jax could appreciate that. Just reading social media was a lesson in how rumor turned to gospel with repetition. Belief that they'd seen or heard it themselves, or knew someone who did, followed hard on its footsteps. Actual facts were in short supply. "Clancy wasn't there long. He proposed a toast. He seemed interested in my acquiring Norton's practice. I didn't know the man well enough to understand his mood. He left without staying for dinner."

"After Evie spoke to you." Troy waited expectantly.

Jax didn't want to bring Evie into this. Or Ward, for all that mattered. But if Clancy's death wasn't natural. . . "Evie simply stopped to tell me a friend was trying to reach me. I had my phone off. In passing, she mentioned Ward had filed for the mayoral election. Clancy left after that."

The sheriff pinched the bridge of his nose. "I don't know how she does it, but Evie is a trouble magnet. Do you know where she is? I can't find her."

Probably because Evie wasn't ready to be found. She would be gathering information and resources and shielding family. Jax had learned that lesson the first day he met her. He admired the damned woman, even when she was making him nuts. "I'll call her." He punched her contact number.

"Evie finally bought a phone? Just give me the number." The sheriff got out his notebook.

"You really don't think you'll get off that easy, do you?" Jax let the call go through. Knowing Evie's penchant for calling the sheriff directly—with operatic screams—Jax wasn't about to set the poor guy up for Evie's phone.

When Evie answered, he spoke cautiously. "The sheriff is here and wants to talk to you. Should I hand him my phone?"

She laughed wickedly. "Give him my number and tell him to call me."

"Remember, I'm on the right side of the law. Play nice, Evangeline," Jax warned.

"Troy is a grown man. Let him make his own choices." She rang off.

Jax gave the sheriff her number. "It's on your head."

Troy scowled and plugged it into his contact list. "I don't suppose having a phone means she'll call 911 like a normal person. . ."

Jax raised his palms. "I'm just the messenger."

"In the interest of peace. . ." With resignation, Troy called the number.

They could hear the phone ringing from the hall. A second later, Evie arrived in the company of two elegant greyhounds. She triumphantly punched the sheriff's private number into her phone and beamed at them. "I'm learning to like these things."

"One more distraction?" Jax suggested.

The light through the huge office windows was gray from building storm clouds. Evie was a bright ray of orange and yellow in the gloom. What in hell was that she was wearing? A jump suit with shorts? Probably from her aunt's wardrobe. Jax tried to decide if it was all one piece, but he couldn't drag his gaze from her tanned and incredibly shapely legs. Instead of her usual Keds, she was wearing heeled espadrilles.

"Maybe?" She studied the phone as if just discovering it, then beamed at the stoic sheriff. "What can I do you for? I need to take Ward's greyhounds to Iddy for training, and she closes up in half an hour."

"What did you say to Clancy last night that sent him running out the door?"

Evie snorted. "Fine, blame it all on me. I can't even say hi to someone without being accused of whatever happens to them next."

Like her mother, she didn't show irritation but wandered over to admire the view from the windows. Jax knew she could see the sheriff from that position and was probably checking his *aura*.

The sheriff waited her out.

Apparently not finding anything to worry about, Evie shrugged. "I didn't say *anything* to Mr. Clancy. He's never acknowledged my existence and last night was no different. But I daresay he wasn't pleased to learn he had genuine opposition for the mayor's race."

"Your mother was already running. He knew he had opposition."

Evie gestured carelessly. "He'd lined up the water company to turn off my mother's mains. The city used that tactic, among others, to drive my mother and her neighbors from the trailer park. He knew she wasn't any competition. She's withdrawn from the race already. That was why she was at city hall."

"You don't think she was angry about that tactic?"

Evie laughed. "Sheriff, you've known Mavis longer than I have. You tell me, have you ever seen her angry?"

"I know Mavis and she does get angry," Troy said bluntly. "She just hexes people and scares them half to death." He put his notebook away. "Tell her to be careful who she hexes next."

"You don't seriously believe my mother hexed Clancy to death?" she asked in apparent disbelief. "How did he die?"

"You've already heard that from one of the secretaries." Troy returned his hat to his head and nodded at Jax. "Welcome to Afterthought. And don't let her call me every time you annoy her. My dogs don't appreciate it." He let himself out.

Jax couldn't lean back in his folding chair, but he did his best and gazed up at Evie expectantly.

Her bright smile dimmed as the door closed. "Clancy theoretically committed suicide—with a gun to his head, just like Pendleton."

"THERE'S A CAT AT CITY HALL." COUSIN IDDY POURED A GLASS OF TEA AND swirled it. "I could see if it noticed anyone go into Clancy's office."

They'd sent Loretta to bed before holding their family conference. The storm had cleared the air earlier so it was possible to breathe with the Victorian's large windows open. The ceiling fan pulled in a nice breeze. Evie set out a plate of store-bought cookies. It was too hot to bake.

Gracie grabbed a handful. Her sister's telekinetic abilities didn't often apply to these discussions.

"If you find out about anyone, I can check them out," Pris offered, petting Psycat, Evie's Siamese. Tonight, Pris had added gold glitter to her mouse-brown hair. One of these days, Evie was going to figure out what her cousin was trying to convey through hair color.

"We can get Clancy's phone records," Roark suggested. His glass held something stronger than tea.

Evie was almost desperate enough to hold a séance, except she didn't know what spirit to call. Clancy's ghost would be too new to reach out, she suspected. But she ought to try. Or maybe she should do like the mystery book psychics and see if his spirit lingered where he died. She'd only dealt in old ghosts. Even Loretta's parents had been dead half a year before she met them.

Reuben had winched the Morris chair out of the attic but not delivered it to the office yet. Jax sat in it now with his computer tablet. His wide shoulders fit comfortably against the huge chair back. A page started printing from his little printer on the coffee table. "Or we could just learn more about Clancy's connections and who might be breathing down his neck hard enough to make him off himself."

"He was murdered, dear," Mavis said from her rocker in the corner. She fed Honey one of the cookies. "He chose his friends poorly."

Reuben snatched the page of Clancy's connections from the printer, scanned it, and whistled. "Dude, you way better off outta S&S."

When he passed the paper to Roark, Evie sighed and swiped the tablet from Jax to scan the list. "Clancy has always been an investment broker. That's not new. What does that have to do with S&S?"

"Check out his client list," Jax suggested, sipping his beer.

"Half the rich white guys in town." Evie shrugged. "Town council. Your accountant landlord. Your predecessor, George Norton—although one assumes that account will go to Norton's family in Charleston."

"Scroll down, *bébé*," Roark suggested. "Them's just da newer ones."

Her sister snapped the paper from his hand. As a teacher, Gracie understood lists well.

Evie figured out how to use the touch screen and scrolled down. There was Jax's former law firm. "*All* the lawyers at S&S? Or the firm itself?"

"The firm had investments. Several of the names under it are partners in the firm. Some are firm clients. I can be thankful, I suppose, that Stephen preferred to hide his fraud and handle his own accounts. And Loretta's father had his own broker."

"Loretta's father was a Malcolm, dear, even if he pretended he wasn't." Mavis began spreading her tarot deck on a lap table she kept for that purpose. "He knew how to avoid crooks."

"You have no proof Clancy was cheating anyone," Iddy argued. "Being wealthy and connected does not mean you're dishonest."

"The crystal showed him shrouded in blood." Mavis didn't look up from her cards. "He wasn't a good man."

"His aura wasn't open. Greed was his primary color." Evie scrolled down more. "And Gustav Swenson was one of his first clients, if this is in order of date. If Gustav is dead, does that mean the Swensons are no longer clients?"

"Grandma Swenson, the starlet and real estate mogul's daughter, may be in her eighties, but she's alive. Gustav Swenson's account is a trust, probably shared by her kids and grandkids." Jax took back his tablet. "If we're talking murder, we need to know if anyone accessed Clancy's computer before or after his death. We need to know the same for Pendleton. I'll ask Oswin to look into Pendleton, see if he's as good as he says."

"You think Rube and me can't do Pendleton and Clancy too?" Roark asked in indignation.

"I think we need the cases separate until we know they're connected. Does Afterthought have anything like a bar where the city hall folk hang out?" Jax asked.

"Guns and Hoses for happy hour," Evie reported gloomily. "It's too rowdy at this time of night to learn anything. We'd better get out the Ouija board and see who I can summon."

Jax's response to mention of the Ouija board was predictable. "Rowdy it is." He stood and left her with the tablet. "I don't know who's sending them, but we're still receiving digital files from Pendleton's office. Read those. They'll be more useful than ghosts." He gestured at R&R. "Your choice, the bar or start looking into Clancy's files."

"You won't learn anything if I walk in with all them white folk." Reuben headed for the back door. "I'm on Clancy until you get me into some voting machines."

Roark looked torn. "I'm good for rowdy, but da cops will be locking up Clancy's 'puters if I don't dig now. You shouldn't be goin' down alone, lawyer man."

"Fine." Working up a snit, Evie slapped the tablet in Gracie's hands. "I'm going with Jax. It's only Thursday night. How bad can it be?"

Ignoring protests, she dashed upstairs to change into jeans. The bar was air-conditioned, and she wasn't in a mood to be hit on by every Hairy Tom Dick in the place.

She checked on Loretta, flipped the sheet off the kid's head, turned off the flashlight, and set her book on the table. Loretta barely stirred. Evie kissed her forehead and dashed to her room to change.

When she came down, everyone had scattered but Jax, who was scowling. "You're so predictable," she told him, before heading for the front door. "You don't even know where Guns and Hoses is. I could totally scam you into believing I'm psychic."

"Street behind the courthouse. I know how to use the internet. I appreciate that you're not wearing the skimpy shorts but. . . *Karma Police*?" He gestured at Evie's bright yellow T-shirt.

She beamed and wiggled her hip-hugger bell-bottoms. "The *skimpy shorts* were Aunt Val's hot pants. Aren't they cool? So are the bell-bottoms. I need to dig around in that wardrobe some more." She ignored his reference to her T-shirt. That was totally her own.

"Why am I predictable?" He led her to his newly-acquired Harley.

Evie nearly jumped for joy. She'd probably rode on the back of that thing when she'd been a teenager and dating the mayor's son.

"Cool memories," she informed him, before climbing on behind. "You could have walked off without me, but you didn't. You could have told me how good I look in these jeans, but you didn't. You waited for me and scowled. Predictable."

"You would have just followed me. I didn't want you walking these streets alone if there's a killer on the loose. He'd probably murder you on general principles." He kicked the motor into gear before she could respond. "And you look good in everything."

Evie enjoyed the flattery but didn't think the rest qualified as respect. At least he acknowledged her obnoxiousness. She guessed that was a form of recognition.

He parked the bike in the city lot that had once been her mother's home. The noise from the bar could be heard from down the street.

"A wake or a celebration?" Evie asked.

"If those are mostly cops and firefighters in there, as I assume from the name, I'm gonna guess this is a normal night of letting off steam." Jax draped his arm over her shoulders as they entered.

Evie didn't mind. She liked having him close, acknowledging the *zing* between them. And she'd never been in a rowdy bar before. Loud country music hurt her ears. Crowds distracted her to the point of insanity. And getting drunk was a hallucinatory experience when her third eye went uncontrolled. But with Jax at her side, watching over her, she'd learn to deal.

"Your competition, third booth on the right," she shouted into Jax's ear. "You want to tackle them while I tackle the secretaries over at the end of the bar?"

"You think I'm letting you loose in this crowd?" he shouted into her ear. "There are three predators ready to pounce the minute I do anything stupid like let you go."

"That's sweet." Evie stood on her toes to kiss his jaw. Then she ducked from under his arm and shoved him toward the booth. "Go play. I'll let the predators buy me a beer."

She could practically feel him growling as she headed for the women she knew. She swayed her hips just a little to give him something to look at. At this hour, he'd be surrounded by rapacious females soon enough. She'd have to watch him in action.

She'd never had reason to believe men were particularly trustworthy. She suspected she was testing the poor man—while proving she didn't require protection.

"Evie!" one of the secretaries shouted, waving her over. "I never see you in here. Who was that hunk you dragged in and so stupidly let go?"

"Hey, Helena." Evie leaned in for hugs all around. "How's your Cotton getting along?" Helena had a rabbit that Iddy looked after.

"I'm thinking he needs a mate, and you haven't answered my question. We're drooling here. Who's the hunk?" Helena had been a year ahead of Evie in school. Now a divorced mother of two, she apparently didn't get out often enough.

"Damon Ives-Jackson, lawyer, just bought Norton's practice. He's not hiring yet. Want me to let you know when he does?"

She could feel one of the *predators* circling in. She didn't want to be squeezed to death in some mating dance, but free beer would be good. She smiled at the good-looking but too-young cop in the forefront. "Heya, Cal. Haven't seen you in a while. Whatcha up to?"

"Cal, bug off. We're gossiping here," Helena elbowed the young man.

"I just thought I'd introduce Evie around, buy her a beer." Undeterred, he handed over a bottle. "You don't come in here often."

"I don't come in here *ever*," Evie corrected. She raised the bottle. "But thanks."

He tried to take her elbow. She stomped his boot. He glowered. She smiled. "I'm talking to Helena and her friends right now. And I'm with Jax."

She saluted Jax with her bottle. Predictable, as always, he was glaring in her direction. Eying the skinny cop, Macho Man apparently decided she was safe and returned to talking to his new buddies.

"He the new lawyer they're talking about?" Cal leaned in to separate her from Helena.

"Most likely." Evie ducked under his arm and squeezed in between tall, dark-haired Helena and short, blond Dottie, another secretary from city hall. She'd learned obnoxious before she could walk.

"Lawyer, huh? I wasn't looking for a job until he walked in." Helena gave Evie room while she eyed Jax. "Let me know if he has an opening. You're not claiming him?"

"I'm a Malcolm, remember? We don't claim men. But that brings me to another subject." Evie leaned in so only Helena and Dottie could hear. Cal scowled and wandered off. "I would love to find out if I can talk to the recently dead. Do you think there's any way I can get into the room where Clancy died?"

"You think the counshil office ish haunted?" Dottie asked, with a slur that showed she'd been here too long. "It was bad enough when he's alive. Don' need a ghost grabbing my tits."

Evie grimaced at this description of the councilman. "I can lay him to rest, if he's there."

"The cops have the council office taped off, but it's public space." Helena was also more than a little drunk. She studied her beer bottle with glazed interest. "I've always wanted to see a ghost, and I've got keys to the back door."

"Full moon tonight. Never a better time." Evie pretended to take a sip of her beer. She wanted all her senses around her if they were doing this now. "I can't promise anything, mind you."

"Let's do it," Dottie said gleefully. "If he'sh there, I want to hit him where it hurts."

"Speaking ill of the dead," Evie reminded her. "And in the interest of full disclosure, I'm pretty sure you can't hit ghosts. This isn't ghost-busters."

"We can get you into the hall outside the office." Helena was still studying her bottle thoughtfully. "Crossing police tape is probably a no-no."

"Looks like half the city and county cops are in here." Evie checked on Jax again. He was in full discussion with his competition. "Are they holding a wake for Clancy?"

Dottie snorted. "He voted against raising wages. Nah, thish the usual crowd."

Helena caught Evie's elbow and dragged her away from the bar just as two more men headed their way. "I've had enough for the evening. Let's kill a ghost."

Thirteen

JAX GLANCED UP IN TIME TO SEE EVIE'S YELLOW SHIRT AND BRIGHT CURLS—COPPER in the dim light—moving through the bar crowd toward the exit. He didn't know if she was leaving voluntarily with her drunken cohorts, but the male dimwits following her out needed to be headed off at the pass.

He stood and offered his hand to his new competition. "Good meeting you and looking forward to working with you in the future, but my companion is being hustled out. I'd better follow."

He'd learned a few pertinent things about Clancy in their discussion, but not enough to justify letting Evie escape.

One of the men snorted as he followed Jax's gaze. "I went to school with Evie. I don't think you need to worry about those louts."

"They're state cops and don't know her family. You ought to let them learn their lesson," another of the men suggested.

"My policy is to leave with the one I brought." Jax shoved through the crowd to the front door, where two sturdy young men not wearing a uniform followed the women out.

Once he was outside in the humid night, Jax felt like a stalker following Evie without letting her know. He simply wanted to see that she wasn't in trouble. She was half a head shorter than the women she was with—who were wearing heels, of course. And the men following them had a hundred pounds on her.

Before he could decide on tactics, Evie whistled loudly.

Half a dozen mutts raced out of alleys and down the street. She halted to crouch down and hug and pat them. Did nobody in the damned town ever leash their dogs?

This was rural South Carolina—*farmland*. Of course not. He was the city boy here. Evie was on home ground. Jax shoved his hands in his pockets and watched out of sheer curiosity.

Half a minute later, Evie stood and wandered on with her staggering companions.

The dogs remained. Had Jax not known that Evie's vet cousin had trained every dog in the territory, he would simply have thought Evie liked dogs. They weren't slavering hounds but local pets. Still, a terrier could take out an ankle faster than a shepherd and with less invitation. So Jax waited.

The two human hounds tried to push past the pack. The pit bull growled. Leaning against the wall in the shadows, Jax kept one eye on Evie and the other on the off-duty cops. He didn't want the dogs hurt. Judging by Evie's direction, she was headed for city hall. Typical. He'd catch up. The women weren't moving fast.

Human Hound #1 walked into the street. A lab followed, jumping up and trying to lick off his stubble. Human Hound #2 looked as if he'd like to kick the Jack Russell nipping at his ankles. The pitbull growled and paced between the men, while the other mutts just circled, tails wagging.

"Not worth the effort," Hound #2 called, heading back for the bar.

Hound #1 didn't look convinced. Jax memorized his face, just in case. Pushing off the Labrador, the cop stumbled while determinedly attempting to skirt past the pack. The dogs surrounded him.

Deciding this was enough entertainment for the evening, Jax jogged after Evie. He held out his hand for the pitbull to sniff and scratched the poodle's head. He didn't doubt they smelled Evie on him. They let him pass.

"Never follow a witch who doesn't want to be followed," Jax cheerfully advised Hound #1.

He knew she wasn't a witch, but Jax decided the women were right to spook fools.

And understood why witches had been hanged through the centuries. Hound #1 looked murderous. Cops needed to get a sense of humor.

Jax watched from a distance as the dark-haired woman unlocked a back door to city hall. Closing in, he didn't hear it lock behind them, so he took his time checking the perimeter. No lights came on. The few windows appeared to be hermetically sealed. It was a more modern building than most in town. There should be an alarm system, but it wouldn't have been on during public hours when Clancy died.

Finding no sign of trouble, Jax returned to test the back door. It opened freely. No alarm screamed. Neither did the women, but their voices rose in fear and consternation.

Pulse accelerating, Jax jogged toward the front of the building, keeping his eyes and ears open. The halls had low-level exit lighting, but he saw no sign of an intruder. Coming around the corner, he saw Evie's drunken companions gawking at one of the offices. The dark-haired one was attempting to punch a number into her phone. The blonde kept whispering, "Evie, Evie, get back here."

Evie didn't answer.

Jax increased his pace. At his approach in the semi-darkness, the women abruptly grabbed each other and shrieked. Apparently recognizing him a moment later, they shut up. The blonde pointed at the public reception office the councilmen shared. The door was open, and the blinds were up on the interior window that theoretically protected the councilmen and their visitors.

How in hell had Clancy been offed in public view?

The office was darker than the hall. The police tape had been torn from the door and the trash can emptied across the carpet. He'd yell at Evie later. Right now, she seemed frozen beside a desk strewn with paper.

She had her hands in her back pockets, presumably to prevent leaving fingerprints. He'd seen that stance before—when she'd been *talking* to the Navajo ghost in the desert.

In the gloom, he couldn't see much except Evie's bright yellow shirt. Like someone dreaming, she muttered, not loudly enough for him to catch her words. He didn't dare interrupt. When the two women crept closer, Jax blocked them from entering. He didn't know what Evie did, whether it was con or real, but he'd learned to respect her enough to leave her to it.

He was probably as crazy as she was. There was freedom in accepting that, he decided.

A small object flew off the desk, followed by a slightly larger one. When Evie didn't react, Jax produced a handkerchief from his pocket. He got down on his knees in the doorway, turned on his phone flashlight, and searched the carpet. He found a thumb drive within reach. It took a moment longer to catch the glimmer of a gold pin.

A shadow abruptly darkened what dim light there was, and Evie collapsed into a sitting position on the carpet. Jax had to fist his fingers to prevent from breaching the torn police barrier and reaching for her. She seemed more dazed than hurt. Sirens screamed into the parking lot, and his phone's light died. Damn, he should have recharged.

"Any way out of here without being seen?" he asked without much hope.

"I called the sheriff about the break-in," the dark woman reported. "I told him we were here to pick up the birthday presents in my closet."

Jax nodded. "Good thinking. Evie, you need to get your pretty rear out of there now."

She huffed but scooted backward toward him. Jax caught her by the waist and hauled her up, relieved to have her safe in his arms again. "That ought to erase your tracks. Sheriff will think the thieves dragged out a safe."

She elbowed him. "I'm not as heavy as a safe."

Reassured that she was capable of sensible speech, Jax resigned himself to police interrogation. He needed to rethink his connection to Evie if he meant to represent law and order in this town.

Sheriff Troy's night replacement wasn't as sharp as the older man. He idiotically took the women at their word, cordoned off the office again, and placed a guard before sending everyone home.

"Were you really talking to a ghost?" Blondie asked as they grabbed the birthday presents and hurried out the back door.

"A presence," Evie said warily. "I think maybe Clancy was still in shock and didn't know how to move on. I've never been on the site of a recent death. I wonder if the spirit always lingers?"

"What did he say?" The dark-haired woman no longer seemed as drunk as she had earlier.

"Not much. He was confused. Someone broke into the computer. He thinks they stole his phone, too, but that was probably the police."

"OMG, you talked to a ghost!" Blondie stumbled. Jax caught her elbow, but he didn't release Evie.

"Did he say who did it?" the dark one asked.

"That's when he knocked stuff around." Evie glanced at him. "Did you find it?"

"Just a pin," Jax lied. He didn't like lying, but he didn't know these women. "One of those eagle political pins people are wearing."

"My brother has one." Blondie nodded knowingly. "It's Senator Swenson's party. They're promising to cut taxes."

"Don't they all?" Jax asked cynically. "I don't think you ladies should drive home, but I only have my bike. Do you know someone to call?"

"We live in the apartments over there." Blondie gestured vaguely as they proceeded down the street. "We can walk. I want to hear more about the ghost. My life is so boring."

"Not tonight, Dot. I'm wiped. Come in the shop at lunch, and I'll try to remember if I heard anything else, but I don't think so. Ghosts are pretty inarticulate."

Jax stood back as they hugged and said farewells. After watching to see that the two women made it inside the aging apartment house, Jax led Evie back to the Harley. He waited patiently.

She held off speaking until they were home. "I don't suppose Roark hacked the computer at city hall."

"I suspect he was after Clancy's work office and didn't know about city hall. Want to check now or wait until morning?" Under the security light, she looked weary.

"Probably now. Clancy's ghost didn't even know he was dead. He thought he'd just woke up and scared a burglar rifling the desk. I'm guessing that means he didn't commit suicide. When he finally accepted what I was saying, he deliberately threw that thumb drive and pin. I'm thinking that's a pretty impressive feat for a new ghost. He refused to move on to the next plane and vanished. I'm afraid he'll be back."

And so would the killer—if he knew they had the thumb drive. Jax cursed.

EVIE CURLED UP UNDER A SLEEPING BAG ON THE BROAD COUCH IN THE CELLAR DEN R&R had claimed for their own. Despite the sultry night air outside, she couldn't get warm.

She'd talked to a recently deceased spirit. She hadn't thought it possible. All the encounters she'd had before had been with dusty remnants of energy clinging to ancient memories. Clancy had been raging furious—and exhausting.

The men tip-toed around her as Reuben—using a tissue—loaded the thumb drive, and Roark belatedly hunted for connections to the city hall computer. She didn't even need to read their auras to sense their overwhelming curiosity.

"Why didn't the cops take the computer and thumb drive?" Reuben demanded as he hacked to get into the drive's information.

"Public office connected to public information, used by all the council, not just Clancy," Evie told them. "Don't know who the thumb drive belongs to, though. Maybe the intruder?"

Jax came in bearing a mug of tea. She felt better just smelling it. Sitting up, she cradled the hot mug between her palms and let the aromatic steam tease her nose. The man occasionally had uses.

"Clancy's broker computer was just that, complicated client stuff, connected to corporate offices." Roark continued clicking his keyboard. "Betcha dat 'puter got audited regular so there was nothin' personal on it. I figured cops had his home devices. Didn't think he had another."

"If all the council members used the one at city hall, then they probably each had their own passwords to sign in for their private files. He might have kept personal stuff there." Reuben sat back and let his hacker software program run on the thumb drive.

"But Clancy was *killed* in that office. The cops still should have taken everything away." Jax returned to his appointed task of sorting through documents on the pool table relating to his father and Pendleton.

"The cops didn't know Clancy was *killed*." Unlike literal-minded Jax, Evie easily jumped to conclusions based on nothing. "They wouldn't take a computer all the council used because Clancy put a gun to his head. One assumes they'd need a warrant."

Jax grimaced in agreement. "Same with Pendleton. They wouldn't automatically take a computer for a suicide, especially one needed by his office. They probably waited for the coroner's report. The killer has a method to his madness."

"You into that city hall computer yet? Is it wiped?" Reuben watched his hacker program scroll passwords at the thumb drive. "Whoever trashed the office tonight might have brought this drive with them to clean out Clancy's files and dropped it when he got frightened."

"You think Clancy's haint scared him off?" Roark laughed.

Evie threw a pillow at the tattooed lout. "Don't dismiss what you don't understand."

The Cajun pointed at his monitor. "There's da city hall computer innards. Clancy's partition is wiped. Dude knew what he was doin'."

Reuben gave a soft crow of triumph and hit the keyboard. "But the ghost must have made him drop the thumb drive he transferred it to. Looka here."

"If that drive belonged to the person trashing the office, we need to get it back to the police, pronto. They can test it for fingerprints. Do we have enough cloud space to upload the contents?" Jax left his work to peer over Reuben's shoulder.

"Oh yeah, there isn't much here. If this is all Clancy kept on that computer, it's nothing incriminating, just receipts and some ancient Word docs. Think crooks give receipts for payoffs?"

"Expense report receipts?" Jax studied the small screen Reuben was working with. "Lunch tabs. Credit card receipts give a timeline. But we'd need to know what crime he may have committed to see if he had an alibi. Or know the thief's name and crime. They're meaningless as is."

"He also knocked off that pin," Evie reminded them. "He could be indicating the thief wore one."

"That could be any of a few million people," Jax scoffed. His phone pinged and he abandoned the receipt list to check his messages. "Oswin tracked the California F100 plate that you photographed. Belongs to a Donna Ortiz. He also says there is no Officer Reilly in the San Bernardino Sheriff's department. That call to Evie was a fake."

Someone from California was trying to find them. Evie shuddered. *Donna Ortiz?*

Roark opened a window to type in Donna's name. Evie huddled under the covers and sipped her tea. She needed to get over herself and be a proper psychic detective if she meant to demand respect.

What she wanted to do was go to bed and pull the covers over her head.

Jax continued reading Conan's message. "Donna Ortiz is the receptionist in Pendleton's office, so it would make sense that her truck was parked nearby. Conan says he's intercepted messages between Donna—and get this—Marge. Her last name is Thompson."

R&R looked at Jax questioningly. Evie nodded understanding. "Marge—the spa lady in the desert. She wore a purple hat with the Swenson logo. The receptionist had an eagle pin like the one the ghost flung. We're on to something."

"Get me into the town's voting machines, Jax," Reuben said ominously, using Kleenex to remove the thumb drive and drop it into a plastic baggie.

All eyes swung to the muscled nerd sitting cross-legged on the cheap carpet.

"What?" Jax finally demanded when Reuben said no more. "What did you find?"

At the desk computer, Roark called up the file Reuben had just uploaded and whistled. "Connections, we got connections. Anyone want to set up a storyboard?"

Evie wished she had another pillow to fling at him. "Just tell us, will you?"

"Afterthought bought their voting machines from DVM back before your favorite mayor got elected. One of these Word docs is a contract, signed by Clancy, who was on the council at the time. Salesman's name is *Theodore Swenson*." Roark was so excited that he forgot his accent.

Reuben handed the baggie to Evie. "This needs to go back where it was. If Clancy and Swenson are into voter fraud, that's federal."

"No evidence of fraud," Jax responded automatically, typing into his phone.

"I'll have Helena drop the thumb drive in a plant." Evie gingerly accepted the bag. "The cops will think the thief hid it."

"Or an idiot did. If there are fingerprints, they're likely to be someone who had a key, like your friend Helena. And that person isn't necessarily the killer." Jax finished his typing.

"I'll send Iddy to talk to cats." Wearily, Evie dropped the sleeping bag. Dealing with new spirits was debilitating, but the tea had almost revived her. "I'll leave you to contracts and receipts. Loretta is up early in the morning. I don't think I can deal with voter fraud or Pendleton tonight."

"I'll walk you up." Jax removed his charger and pocketed his phone. "If whoever burgled city hall learns you were there, he may come looking for that thumb drive."

Company felt too good to argue as she climbed out of the cellar. "None of this makes sense," she told Jax as they reached the backyard.

"Too many suspects, not enough evidence, too many seemingly random acts. That's why I want Oswin focused on the Pendleton end. This Clancy business is uncomfortably close to home."

"He was probably cheating on his girlfriend." Evie led the way into the kitchen. "There are more cookies in the pantry, if you're staying up all night."

Jax tugged her into his arms and pressed a kiss against her brow. "I don't think we've thanked you enough for putting up with us."

"Mostly, it's no different than having family. Loretta is loving it." Evie wrapped her arms around him and lifted her face.

The short brief kiss she'd intended turned heated and intense. If Psy the Siamese hadn't jumped up on the counter and meowed at them, they might have christened the table, even if she was too tired to think. Probably *because* she wasn't thinking.

"I'm awake now, thanks." Evie pushed away and cast Jax a look of regret as she headed for the front stairs.

He looked unlawfully good in his heavy stubble, with his dark hair rumpled and an expression of confusion and longing on his face.

He didn't know who he was yet. She'd give him time to find out before he learned—as most men did—that living with a Malcolm meant living outside of normal. Right now, Jax was the epitome of conventional and law abiding, which was pretty much the opposite of everything she was.

Upstairs, she checked her email before turning in for the night.

She opened the one from her cousin Orbis, the antique dealer and psychometrist first. He had received the original files from Aaron Ives' security box. "The person who packed this box was grieving, furious, and plotting revenge. I'll keep working through the documents but that file box speaks stronger than anything else. It's as if the owner had just lost his best friend."

Spot on, Cousin Orbis, spot on. Evie forwarded the email to Jax with a note —*How did Ives put the file into his deposit box without anyone realizing he was still alive?*

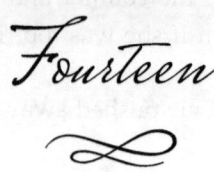

Fourteen

IN HIS IDEALISTIC YOUTH, JAX HAD BELIEVED THE LAW WAS THE ANSWER TO everything. Laws might need changing upon occasion, but the judicial system accomplished that. If people were just taught to stay within the boundaries of the law—

He still believed in the system. He was none too certain about the people wielding it anymore. With no mayor and no county attorney available, he didn't have time to wait for proper protocol—and couldn't trust the city council to cooperate.

That was what was sticking in his craw—*he couldn't trust anyone in city hall.* They were all Clancy's cronies and had been hand-picked by the former mayor now facing fraud charges.

Sitting in his new office Friday morning with Reuben impatiently waiting, Jax rifled through his predecessor's digital files. "County attorneys should be more careful with government documents," he complained. But like everyone else, Norton had parked a lot in his computer. . . "Got it."

Reuben pumped his fist. "Knew you could, man."

Jax pulled up the digital form for requesting an audit and maintenance of the city's voting machines, added Reuben's name and a date prior to the attorney's death, then printed it out. "I am now officially one of the anarchists undermining the system."

"Hangin' with the wrong crowd does that." Reuben folded the letter and tucked it into his shirt pocket.

"The end doesn't justify the means," Jax warned. "But I can't watch anyone else die if this is all about crooked voting machines. I need that motive off the list before anyone else gets killed."

"Or any more elections get thrown to the bad guys." Reuben tipped an imaginary hat and took off with his ammunition.

Evie's email from Cousin Orbis had pushed Jax over the edge. There was a dead man in that mine in California, and he was now positive it was Franklin Jackson. Why he should believe Evie's cousin about the fury, grief, and need for revenge on his father's documents was a frightening question he didn't ask himself. Some things just felt right, and this theory fit—except for Evie's note.

Who else could have put that file into the box? The only answer he could summon was a bank employee. He texted Conan to find out who worked at the bank—the former bank—at the time of the mine collapse. Jax knew it took two keys and two people to access the box, but even he could imagine several scenarios to make that happen—if the bank employee collaborated.

Then he went to work on the old contracts between his father and Sovereign Machinery. He highlighted the pertinent clauses and forwarded them to his contract law professor and his sister. Ariel didn't like face-to-face communication, but her mind was as sharp as his, possibly sharper.

A minute later, Ariel texted back: IF AARON IVES OWNED PATENT, WE OWN SOVEREIGN. AND DVM?

Yeah, his thoughts too.

DID HE KNOW CHIPS WERE USED FOR FRAUDULENT PURPOSES?

He typed back: NO EVIDENCE ANYONE ATTEMPTED TO DISSOLVE CONTRACT

BECAUSE HE DIED she retorted.

Yeah, there was that, even if it was a metaphorical death. Dead men couldn't file suits.

He pulled out the Franklin Jackson will Jax's adoptive father had executed upon his death. Jax read it now with new knowledge of his real father.

Vague clauses of "all land, properties, partnerships. . ." legally covered the law practice that Aaron Ives had sold to Pendleton. The land title, however, was still in the name of Aaron Ives. It hadn't been mentioned directly in any of the wills and his adoptive father hadn't known of its existence.

I THINK WE OWN A RANCH AND MINE, he texted Ariel. WHO PAID PROPERTY TAXES ON THEM FOR THIRTY YEARS?

ON IT

Jax texted Conan, too, to see if his magic crew could determine who paid the taxes, but that was a long shot.

He pulled up profiles on Marge Thompson and Donna Ortiz. Marge lived right next to the land that was still in his father's name. Donna Ortiz had worked for Franklin and should have known Ives. She was in Pendleton's office the day he died. And her truck had followed them out of town.

If Marge and Donna had thought Ives dead and then Jax had shown up looking just like his father and camping on his land. . .

No evidence. No nothing except speculation.

A report from Roark popped up in his email. Jax scanned the document and whistled.

Before he could work through all the angles, a knock rapped at his office door. He needed a receptionist. Well, he needed a desk first. He'd bought one at the thrift store. . .

He got up and let in Evie, followed by the desk delivery people, as if she were his very own genie.

"They said you hadn't picked out an office chair so I brought one for you. You can give it to an employee later if you don't like it, but you need something besides that folding chair." She gestured for the movers to place the desk in front of the big front windows—not the spot he'd chosen.

When Jax started to object, she waved a finger at him. "Good feng shui means your desk should face the door. And you can intimidate people if they have the sun in their face and can't see you clearly."

"Not a prosecutor," he reminded her. He ought to be irritated. He *was* irritated. It was just that he was also fascinated. Evie broadened his horizons in entertaining ways. "And sunlight reflects on the computer."

She gestured for the movers to bring in the next item. "A credenza for the computer. I have draperies for the window, but we need hardware before I can install them. You'll need to sign for the extras."

His credit card groaned, but he took the clipboard and signed away his life, then turned to examine his new acquisitions. She had a good eye. The old oak credenza looked as if it had been made to go with the enormous old desk. Together with the chair, they'd cost less than if he'd bought a single steel and glass desk at the furniture store.

After the movers left, Evie bounced in the Morris chair R&R had brought over this morning and admired his new office. "Very professional. You need photos on the desk."

Jax tested his new office chair—tall back, solid leather, broad seat, spun and wheeled nicely. "Art on the wall, too, but clients are more important. I assume you arrived with the furniture for a reason?"

"Your aura is still too tight," she complained. "You have to relax, smile more often, enjoy the world instead of seeing it as your foe."

Jax pulled the chair up to his desk, folded his hands on top of it, and waited.

She wrinkled her nose. "I take it back. Move the desk to the wall. You're much too good at this. I can't even read your aura properly with all that light."

"I'll pull the drapes when you're here. When I have drapes. What are you avoiding telling me?"

"Iddy took the thumb drive back to city hall, hid it in a plant—and she found the cat. Cats mostly remember people who feed and pet them. So she's getting glimpses of secretaries like Dot and Helena." She crisscrossed her shorts-clad legs in the enormous chair, focusing Jax's attention in the wrong place. "But she says when she carried the cat to the council's office door—they still have it taped off—the cat practically bristled and struggled to escape. She thinks she's reading the impression of someone tall and heavy-set holding it, and a person who might be Clancy sitting at the desk."

"But no clear image that might identify either?" Jax knew not to expect much from Evie's weird family, but every little puzzle piece eventually created a picture.

"Iddy's general impression from the cat was that it had been thrown at Clancy. The poor kitty is pretty traumatized."

Jax rubbed his nose, then turned his laptop around so she could read the email Roark had sent. "We could look up animal abusers who might hate Clancy. But we shouldn't eliminate secretaries."

She leaned forward, studied the screen, covered her mouth, and fell back in the chair. "Oh, my. Way too many coincidences. Marge Thompson and Donna Ortiz are aunt and niece? They don't look anything alike. And Donna is *Senator Swenson's ex*? And she's still working? Wow. Bad divorce settlement."

"Donna was underage when he knocked her up. He was nearly ten years older. Forty years ago, that would have been an ugly scandal for a wealthy family like the Swensons. They probably arranged a quickie marriage to give the kid a name. They split six months after the wedding, right after his son was born. Read the bio on Donna that Conan sent."

"I'd rather fly back there and take a look at them again." She leaned forward and slowly read through the report, shaking her head as she did. "After the divorce, Donna went on to college and still ended up working as a receptionist? Not that there's anything wrong with the job, but it shows an odd lack of ambition on her part. She must have had a lifetime support clause in that divorce. Can I meet this Swenson?"

"Not in person." Jax turned the laptop around and typed, then swung it back around. "U.S. Senator Augustus Swenson and his *eldest* son, state representative Augustus Theodore Swenson, Jr.—goes by Teddy to differentiate from his better-known dad. Gus has other sons by his second wife, but Donna's son is the one who followed in his footsteps. Teddy is running for his second term this fall."

Evie studied the images. "The senator is wearing a toupee. I think they call them toppers now. So, Donna married this guy with the fake tan and the fake hair when she was in high school, and baby boy Teddy must now be in his late thirties. He looks sort of familiar."

Jax studied the image and shrugged. "I've seen the senator in the news, but the California rep rings no bells. He looks like a thug."

As soon as he said it, he got it. He looked up at Evie. "Teddy could have been driving his mother's truck. He has to live in that district to represent it."

"HE *WAS* DRIVING HIS MOTHER'S TRUCK." THE PICTURE RETURNED NOW—THE stocky man at the deposit desk with the angry aura. "I saw this guy in the bank when we were there. And the truck was parked outside. Remember, I thought it was coincidence that the truck went to the drive-through after we did." Evie dug her hands through her curls, trying to see how any of this related.

"If he was in the truck, following us, it's unlikely he was back at the office, shooting Pendleton. I'll check with Oswin, see if he can get his hand on the sheriff's timeline. When exactly did Pendleton die?" Jax began typing.

"We lost Teddy on the highway after lunch, well before we went to that office where you took forever scanning those documents. I saw the truck at the law office while you were doing that, so he must have gone back to the office after we lost him. Pendleton was alive when the bank called him before lunch.

Tight time frame." Evie pinched her nose and tried to recall the two women, the tough old spa owner and the friendly receptionist. She'd not seen anything particularly murderous in their auras.

"None of this has anything to do with Clancy. We should leave it with Oswin." Jax glared at his computer screen.

"Eagle pins, Swenson on your dad's contract, Clancy as the Swenson trust broker. . ." Evie sprang up from the comfy chair, totally unable to focus. "Nope and nope, not getting it. I have to go spell Mavis for lunch. The sheriff wants her to come in for another interrogation, and she's ignoring customers while she throws cards. She needs a break. Dot might come over to quiz me about ghosts. I'll see if I can learn anything about cat-heaving visitors."

Ever the gentleman, Jax stood when she did. "After you've spelled Mavis, and I wish you meant that literally, let me take you to lunch. Loretta, too, if you like. Let the leeches look after themselves."

Evie beamed and kissed his cheek. "R&R aren't leeches. They know how to fend for themselves. You're on. Around one?"

"Does it count as a date if you bring Loretta?"

Evie laughed. "Ulterior motive, good thinking. Nope, not a date. Lunch between co-guardians does not count. I'm not that easy." She glanced around at the furniture accumulating in his new office. "Although it does seem as if you might not be abandoning us again anytime soon."

Although she'd been the one manipulating that. Jax hadn't even bought a *chair*. But he'd bought a law office.

She swung out, leaving Macho Man to the business of law. She knew all he wanted was in her pants. She wanted that too, except she wanted a heck of a lot more. Malcolm women did not do easy sex for a great many good reasons, one of which was that Evie didn't want to raise children without a father as her mother had done. She was having enough difficulty adapting to Loretta. And birth control simply didn't work as well as it should in her family.

A man who could walk away from his job, his home, and his responsibilities for six weeks wasn't a safe bet, she kept telling herself.

Evie took over behind the counter of the Psychic Solutions Agency and Gift Shoppe. Mavis shoved her tarot in its box in disgruntlement and stomped out, practically emitting steam. Everyone knew Mavis was incapable of killing a fly, but Evie supposed the sheriff's legal work had to look good.

Before she could pick up her feather duster, her sister Gracie popped in with daughter Aster in tow.

"Hey, babes, how's it going?" In delight, Evie crouched to hug her niece.

"Is Lorie here?" the tow-headed six-year-old asked.

"Loretta? She's with Iddy. Are you going over to pet the kitties next?"

Aster nodded eagerly. Gracie dropped a stack of papers on the counter. "First, I'm unloading this mess on you. I've been reading through the correspondence files that Roark keeps sending me from the California lawyer. There's an awful lot of legal talk that I don't really grasp. I printed out the bits between Ives and Franklin that seemed maybe relevant?"

Faced with a stack of written material requiring concentration, Evie wrinkled her nose. "I don't suppose you highlighted pertinent details?"

"I don't know enough to know what's pertinent. I put them in order of date, newest first. The ones there on top of the stack talk about mining rights and patents, wills and trusts, and lawsuits involving some company that's threatening them. I can't believe people wrote all those paper letters back then! It must have taken forever to resolve anything." Gracie hauled Aster away from the display of crystals and picked her up. "Jax probably ought to look at it."

"He's taking me and Loretta to lunch later. I'll hand them over. It's odd that they corresponded when I thought they lived in the same town." Evie scanned the first letter. At least it wasn't full of *whereas* and *wherefores*, just the mention of patent rights and a lease agreement with Sovereign.

"No cellphones, email, or voice mail, just answering machines," Gracie reminded her. "If one was living at a ranch and the other in town, mail might have been faster than phone tag. And they were lawyers. Lawyers like paper trails."

Evie sighed as her sister departed, leaving her with a load of guilt on the counter. "What I need is a secretarial ghost to highlight and annotate."

"I'm not a ghost, but maybe I can help?" Dot appeared in the doorway, looking blond and perky and secretarial.

"Not any more than Gracie, I guess. How's your head this morning?" Eager for escape, Evie produced her feather duster and began cleaning the shelves of New Age gift items.

"I drank lots of water and took aspirin before I went to bed. Last night was more excitement than I've ever had in my life. Do you remember anything more about Clancy's ghost?" Dot studied Mavis's crystal ball. "Does this thing work?"

"Only for my mother. And Clancy left no more impression in death than he did in life. I wonder if one needs to actually live, instead of count dollars, to have a soul?"

"But you said he talked to you!" Dot studied the papers Evie had been complaining about, presumably to see if she could highlight and annotate. Probably not a good idea.

Abandoning the shelves, Evie shuffled the papers beneath the counter, while dusting off glitter and assorted accumulations from morning sales. "Keeping in mind that spirits really can't talk the way we do, the best I can describe his spirit is startled, presumably by the intruder. Does anyone have a clue who could have trashed the office or what they might have been looking for?"

Dot shrugged her slim shoulders. "Whoever did it, knew the alarm code and had a key. The building was locked at five and we were there by nine. We could have walked in on them."

"What about yesterday, when Clancy died? Couldn't someone have walked in on him?" Evie figured she might as well learn what she could from some other source than R&R's hacked files. "That was during the day, wasn't it?"

Dot gave a slight shudder. "Midday, lunchtime. Your mother came in before noon and talked to the clerk about the election. At noon, everyone but Clancy and whoever was manning the reception desk left. I'm on reception today, so I left early for lunch. I don't know who had the rotation yesterday but whoever was supposed to be there apparently wasn't. Maybe he sent her away. We all came back from lunch and there was Clancy. It was awful. Did his ghost say why he did it?"

"No, he was just angry about an intruder breaking into the computer. And then when he realized he was dead, he got even angrier and started heaving things. Isn't there any chart showing who should have been guarding the door yesterday?" Evie thought leaving one person in charge of all those city hall files was pretty lax, but she supposed people locked their offices. She hoped.

Dot made a moue of distaste. "If she wasn't sent away by Clancy, I don't like spreading gossip. Let's just say the calendar changed several times and maybe someone didn't remember their turn had come up."

"I suppose that can happen. Have you heard if anyone else has filed for mayor?" Without Clancy or Mavis, Miss Ward had a clear field.

"Everyone is whispering in the halls. They have less than two weeks to file, and you'd think Miss Ward was the devil. I heard Senator Swenson offered her his support, so that sounds as if she must be good." Dot looked a little puzzled at that.

As she should be. Swenson had never come down on the side of women's rights, much less transgender rights or anything remotely out of the narrow-minded norm. "I wonder why a California senator took an interest in a town as small as this? Does he know people here?"

Dot shrugged. "One of his sons has an office in Charleston. That's where his father's family is from. I guess they must have had an interest. Does Ward support Swenson, do you know?"

Evie was pretty certain the conservative senator was the absolute anathema to everything Ward stood for, but she knew nothing beyond auras and bubbles. It was her turn to shrug. "You know what they say, politics makes strange bedfellows."

"Oh, well." Dot seemed a little less perky. "Mr. Clancy always liked me because I kept the cat away. And maybe because I have big boobs. I'd kinda hoped if he made mayor, he might make me his secretary. I could use the raise, even if he was a tit squeezer."

"The cat?" Evie pounced on this tidbit. "He didn't like cats?"

"Allergic. He had an aunt with a houseful and almost went into anaphylactic shock once when he visited her as a kid." Dot sighed.

Anaphylactic shock? From *cat* allergies? Was that possible? Evie needed to call her cousin Iddy.

Dot went on without noticing Evie's distraction. "So much for buttering him up. Ward doesn't know me at all. Maybe if I start wearing some of her designs she'd notice me?"

Evie remembered that Dot hadn't grown up here. She didn't know Ward's background. "I think she'll notice anyone who works hard. I'm not sure Clancy would have."

Dot shouldered her purse and prepared to leave. "Maybe you should have your mother sign up for the election again. I think *she* likes me."

Mavis liked everyone, until she had reason not to. Evie waved Dot off and returned to glaring at the stack of papers Gracie had left her.

She was pretty certain the top sheet she'd been reading was missing.

Fifteen

Jax took them to lunch at the Oldies Café. Afterthought didn't have a lot of restaurant choices, and he figured a kid would be happier here with lively music and cheeseburgers. Loretta ordered a greasy kid's meal and bounced up and down on the bench seat. Evie had practically lived next door to the café all her life and wasn't impressed with his choice. He couldn't blame her. He should take her to dinner in Charleston or Savannah—but that would lead to the overnight debate neither of them was ready to have.

Responsibility sucked sometimes.

"I coordinated Reuben's call to the mayor's office with Helena." Evie didn't even look at the menu. She ordered a grilled cheese, then glanced up at a TV in the back of the room. "Helena said she thought she could talk the mayor's secretary into rubber stamping approval for him to inspect the voting machines."

"Living in a small town has advantages," Jax conceded, ordering the hamburger and fries.

"Connections are easier with wealth and position, just as anywhere else. My family might not be wealthy, but we own a lot of businesses around town, which adds up, I suppose."

"I can't see bubbles on TV," Loretta complained, studying the screen in back. "When I get bigger, can I go to rallies so I can see the politicians in person?"

Jax turned around to see what in hell his precocious ward was watching. "Why would anyone in their right minds want to attend a political rally?" A sea of purple hats in the audience—a Swenson rally?

He looked around. The entire lunch crowd was watching.

"Because I'll never meet the candidates in person," Loretta answered. "And I want to see their bubbles."

"You can't judge a person by their bubble or aura or the color of their skin," Evie admonished. "Actions count more than appearance."

Loretta shrugged and addressed her milkshake before replying. "I know. R&R have twisted bubbles but they're not bad. And Jax has a walnut-sized bubble—but it's growing. People change. What kind of bubbles do politicians have?"

"You're too old for your age. Go ask Gertie to turn the music down to a low roar, please." Shouting about bubbles over the roar of oldies music probably wasn't politic.

"Indigo children are old souls," Evie remonstrated as Loretta dashed off. "You should encourage her curiosity."

"She still needs to be a kid. That's a conservative rally and everyone in here is watching it. What does that say for Ward's chances as mayor?"

"That she won't do well with Gertie's customers, but that doesn't mean much. They're tourists and local establishment with money in their pockets and no need to rock the boat. Ward has little hope of attracting this crowd. But she'll get liberals like my family, the college educated, and a lot of blue collars because of her jobs, and that's a mighty combination—if she even has competition. Have you heard differently?"

"Still just rumors. If you can't see auras on TV, why are you watching?" Jax turned to glance over his shoulder again. Swenson had his family on the platform, all blond, tan, and expertly groomed.

"He's making his candidacy for president formal, and I'm trying to sort out his family. I think the big guy looking uncomfortable in the gray suit is Teddy, the creep who followed us."

Jax studied the screen. "Yeah, he looks more like a guy who prefers a pickup to a suit. But he's *Donna's* son, right? They're letting him up there because he's a state rep?"

Evie shrugged. "Or because he's the senator's oldest son or both. What I'm trying to determine is if the older woman in the blond wig with the face lift is Senator Swenson's mother. There's something vaguely familiar about her, but I can't determine what. I'm assuming the woman with the botox smile is Swenson's current wife. She's nicely placed herself and her kids on the opposite end of the platform from wig lady and Teddy."

"How can you tell they have facelifts or whatever? And isn't that just a shade catty?"

"After a certain age, skin naturally sags. A chin that taut is not natural at their ages. And I'm simply observing, not criticizing. How we choose to present ourselves to the world is telling. If you fake your face, what else are you faking?"

Jax typed on his cellphone and summoned an image of the senator's mother. He showed it to Evie. "Isn't she the one the family is saying is demented and needs to be put away?"

Evie glanced from the phone to the TV. "Your image is just a bad snapshot. Someone caught her without the wig. If that's her, they've dolled her up for the rally, but your picture looks even more familiar than doll baby up there." Evie studied the face but decided she needed a full-figure image and gave up.

Jax glanced from the wrinkled woman with thinning gray hair on the phone to the TV image. "Think they drugged her? She's looking a little glassy-eyed, and someone is standing next to her who could be a nurse or bodyguard."

"Ooo, your mind is even nastier than mine. I like that in a man." Evie produced a packet of papers from a tote bag she used as purse. "Gracie brought these over. She's winnowed through all the Ives-Jackson correspondence to bits she thought might be relevant. I glanced at them, and I think Dot stole the top one, which would have been the newest, the one about potential lawsuits. I'll have Gracie print another if you think these are important."

"Dot, the little blonde from last night?"

"Yup. She says Clancy once went into anaphylactic shock from cat allergies. Iddy says that's improbable, but if there were other allergens present like nuts he might also have a reaction to. . . Maybe the cat thrower rendered him unconscious?"

"I agree with Iddy. Sounds improbable." Jax flipped through the stack and whistled when he reached the bottom. "Yup, my dad was definitely planning on suing Sovereign if they didn't cease using his microchip. Looks like the suit never reached official stage." He checked the dates on the letters. "Because the mine collapsed before one could be filed."

"One more circumstantial nail in the coffin." Evie stroked his hand. "Dot says no one was at the reception desk when Clancy was killed. I'm trying to find out who was supposed to be there."

Before Jax could capture her hand, Loretta launched herself back into the booth. "Gertie says the music is better than listening to swine. I don't think Gertie likes Swenson." Impervious to the discussion, Loretta slurped at her milkshake, then grabbed a fry from the plate the waitress delivered. "Gertie's bubble is shriveled."

"I've created a monster." Evie sighed and patted Loretta's head. "No more bubbles in public places. It's fun for you but other people don't understand. Has Ariel talked to Iddy any more about turtles?"

"Can we go see the turtle? Ariel ordered turtle food, but R&R are working and can't deliver it yet."

"Turtle food should fit on our bikes, so sure. We can do that after lunch." Evie turned to Jax. "Is there anything else we need to take to your sister, do you know?"

"Ariel is learning to accept delivery drivers and ordering what she needs. I have high hopes that once she's settled into this new routine, that she'll figure out how to come into town and buy her own turtle supplies. That she's not ordering them online is a good sign." Jax hoped. He loved his brilliant sister, but it wasn't as if he could read her mind. "Have you figured out how to market your Sensible Solutions Agency?"

He didn't want to talk about murder in front of Loretta. The kid had had enough of that.

"Word of mouth is all I got. If we'd just make enough money to run an ad in the county newspaper—we'd probably still get pest control calls. Maybe it's a sign from the universe." Evie glumly checked the TV over his shoulder again. "Where is that rally being held?"

"Charleston," Loretta answered. "It's on the banner. I wanna see if they have any we can go to." She pulled out her phone and began typing.

"Charleston, huh." Jax checked the TV again. He didn't recognize the stocky guy in the gray suit, but if that was Ted Swenson—he was here on the east coast, only an hour's drive from Clancy and Afterthought. So were all the other little Swensons from the looks of it. He turned around and caught Evie's eye.

She nodded, her thoughts following his. "No Donna or Marge, I'm betting. So maybe the Pendleton case and Clancy are different?"

"We have nothing on anyone," he reminded her. "For all we know, one of

Pendleton's clients or someone he sued took a dislike to him. And if Clancy wasn't a suicide, he didn't sound as if he was a well-liked fellow." And there they were, talking murder in front of Loretta again.

"Mavis says Hank from the hardware store filed for mayor." Loretta spoke through a mouthful of fries. "He's on the council, isn't he?"

"Finish chewing before you spit fries all over the table," Evie chided. "Hank is too old and cantankerous to run for mayor. He's just spiting Miss Ward."

"You can't have an election if no one runs." Unperturbed, Loretta finished her burger.

"If he's on the town council already, someone voted for him," Jax added, just to roil the waters.

"Fine then, we'll see how the town is divided. Come along, kid, we need to visit Ariel." Evie scooted out of the booth. "Thank you for lunch and let me know when Reuben is hitting the voting machine storage unit. I want to be there."

Jax frowned and she grinned. The damned female enjoyed setting his teeth on edge.

Evie and Loretta biked up the lane to Ariel's cottage carrying turtle food and a small basket of peaches. Evie had texted their approach so Ariel could check her cameras and verify her visitors. Jax's sister was waiting on the porch, not smiling, looking a little tense, but eager.

"Her bubble is growing," Loretta said in satisfaction. "Like Jax's. Is he autistic?"

"No, he's a control freak and probably thinks bubbles are messy. But you know what it's like to lose your parents. Imagine how you'd feel if you had to grow up with an old stranger who didn't like noisy kids?" Evie halted when she could see Ariel's aura. Normally, it was so crystal clear that she couldn't detect emotion. Right now, Ariel's aura had a slightly panicked tinge. She didn't like them too close.

"I'd run away." Which she had, so Loretta wasn't boasting.

"You had somewhere to run. Jax and Ariel didn't. They had no relatives." Or they might, back in California, but they hadn't even known their family's name. She could understand Jax's need to know who he was. Knowing family explained a lot of things. If Loretta hadn't found them, she'd be living with people who thought her bubble-talk was crazy.

They set the turtle supplies and peaches on the wrought-iron bench R&R had installed beside the drive. In return, Ariel had left a packet of papers. Evie groaned, hoping she didn't have to read spreadsheets—Ariel's favorite communication.

But Ariel's eagerness indicated she was expected to read them now. Jax's sister usually just waved shyly and disappeared inside until they were gone. That she waited spoke volumes.

"Open it," Loretta said excitedly. "Maybe there's a prize."

"You have a gazillion dollars in the bank, and you want a cracker jack toy?" Evie scoffed, bending the envelope fastener.

She drew out what appeared to be copies of bank statements—to Ironstone Ranch, Bolder, California. Loretta grabbed a handful.

"I can read these. Daddy said I need to learn about money," Loretta explained when Evie lifted a questioning eyebrow. "I had my own bank account. He automatically deposited my allowance in it. But there aren't many deposits on these."

Evie scanned the dates and found the oldest. "These date back *years*. Ariel only printed the December statements." She studied the first one closer and swallowed hard. "We need to get these to Jax, pronto."

"Why just December?" Loretta asked as Evie gathered the statements back in the envelope. "You didn't let me study them. Did the balance go up or down? It didn't look like a whole lot of money. What is Ironstone Ranch?"

Evie knuckled her ward's too-big head and waved the envelope at Ariel, who nodded and darted back inside. "The balance went up enough to keep paying rising property taxes. I think we're looking at a ranch that Jax and Ariel might own, if they can prove Aaron Ives was their father."

"But he's not rich if the ranch only makes enough to pay taxes." Climbing back on her bike, Loretta tried to puzzle out such poverty.

"It's not the money that matters—it's knowing someone is looking out for the land. If we can find that someone, he'll learn more about his father. That's more valuable than money." Evie punched in Jax's contact and left him voice mail saying she'd picked up the papers Ariel wanted him to see. His sister could have emailed them. Was she fearful someone was watching their communication?

"OK, cool. Except now maybe he'll want to move to California?"

There spoke the little kid afraid of being abandoned again. Evie reached over and pulled her pigtail. "I doubt it. Does Jax strike you as a ranch type?"

Loretta brightened and picked up speed. "He couldn't wear suits on a ranch. Let's fix him a peach cobbler so he won't even think about it."

Life should be so simple. When they reached the Victorian and biked up the drive, they found R&R on the wide, covered porch, munching peaches from the basket Evie had left there earlier. They were taking apart a mechanical contraption as they ate.

"New job?" Evie climbed the stairs and warily regarded the oily mess.

"You'd better find us real jobs soon or we'll end up as mechanics," Reuben answered grimly. "Everyone wants their mowers fixed. We can do that, but it's way below our pay grade."

"Snobs. You should be hobnobbing with Jax's California contact, the Conan Oswin person. Sounds like he makes a living at spying." She bit into a peach and contemplated the problem. "Wonder if Swenson's opponents would be interested in whatever dirt you dig up on him?"

"Dirty work." Roark wrinkled his large nose. "Maybe we not cut out for detecting."

"Is finding out what happened to Jax's dad dirty work and beneath your pay grade?"

"No, that's fine, but we can't charge him. If we could get paid for finding Pendleton's killer, now that would be sweet." Reuben yanked an oily part from a motor and grimaced at it.

Evie beamed. "Look for someone who knew Clancy was allergic to cats. The city is bound to create a reward once they realize he didn't commit suicide."

Roark started to complain. Reuben glared at him. "Beats bombing people, dude. Broaden your horizons."

Since they were broadening their horizons simply by venturing from their man cave, Evie left them to it. Inside, she nearly stumbled over a carton of fliers. Loretta pounced on the box. "For Miss Ward! Can I take them around to businesses?"

Evie studied the tasteful headshot of the dress designer and her promise to return justice and equality to city hall, with testaments from employees. Her campaign manager knew what he was doing.

Was it safe to let a kid go alone? She wished she knew more about parenting. It wasn't as if Mavis had paid attention to where Evie was or what she was doing. But then, no one would want to kidnap her. "Do you have a friend who can go around with you? Safer and more fun that way. I'll offer a treat at the ice cream shop for helping."

Loretta immediately began texting contacts. The kid adapted quickly.

Evie's phone rang, and she almost jumped. People seldom called her. She smiled at Jax's name appearing on the screen. Wandering back to the kitchen, she answered it. "Does DNA qualify as evidence that you're an heir?"

Obviously having read Ariel's message, Jax snorted. "How much is umpteen acres of desert worth? I'll ask Conan. He's been keeping an eye on that area for his own reasons. Maybe he'll be interested."

"Pretty smart of Ariel to track it down, though." Evie studied the refrigerator for leftovers needing to be used up. The locusts never left any. Oh well. The allowance from Loretta's trust was more money than she'd ever seen. She knew how to shop. "I wonder where the tax money is coming from?"

"My wild guess is that someone is leasing some portion for oil wells, cattle, whatever. Maybe illegal pot farms pay rent. Ariel is good with financial info. I'll leave her to track that down. I have email in here from Conan with the timeline for Pendleton's death. Like city hall here, his office closed for lunch. Unlike city hall, they leave no receptionist, just hang an Out to Lunch sign and lock up. The secretaries say Pendleton was on the phone when they left. They were celebrating someone's engagement and got back late, after one."

"All the secretaries, even Donna?"

"Donna had to run to the bank first. The bank verified she was there about a quarter after noon. She arrived at lunch around twelve-thirty. The lot of them returned to the office before one-thirty. They didn't check on Pendleton until someone tried to call his office around two."

"Which was when the screaming started," Evie guessed. "We left the bank before noon, stopped at the drive-in nearby before noon, and were eating it on the lake about the time Donna went to the bank. How did she get there if Teddy was following us in her truck?"

"Walked. Not the same bank. Lunch place in walking distance too. Cops don't know about us being followed, so they didn't ask who had her truck."

Evie sat on a kitchen stool and spun it around. "We probably lost the truck sometime before one, maybe as early as twelve-thirty, hard to tell. Teddy had time to go back and do the deed before everyone returned. Maybe Donna sneaked back during the party. Or a stranger walked in off the street. Can we assume the shot would have been heard if the secretaries were in the front office?"

"Gun was only a.22 caliber, they had the audio system playing, and the secretaries were a bit drunk and loud. So I'm gonna leave the timeline open from after he spoke to the bank until two."

"Tricky." Evie spun her stool harder. "Did they trace the gun?"

"No registration and Pendleton didn't have a license." Jax was practically growling at her interrogation.

If he wouldn't communicate on his own, she'd pull it out of him. "I take it no one saw him at lunch."

"Right. His office phone light was lit when they left. They assumed he was on a business call. He only uses his cell for personal. They locked the front when they left, but there's a rear door. They didn't check it since Pendleton could watch that hall from his desk. Office is covered in fingerprints, none of them out of place."

"They're tracing his phone calls?"

"The call from the bank and one from a burner was the only incoming. The call he was on when they left was to a judge. Sheriff's report says the judge answered Pendleton's question about DNA being admissible as evidence that a person is heir to an estate."

Evie whistled. "And the judge said?"

"It depends. Since it's a civil and not a criminal case, and it's unlikely there will be opposition, then mostly, it depends on the quality of the DNA match and the company handling it. The trick, of course, is to find DNA from Aaron Ives. Pendleton did not receive an unqualified yes or no."

Evie frowned. "I think I want to know who the judge called after that. Do we know the judge's name?"

"Oswin had the same thought. He went one step further than the sheriff. The judge is an old pal of Senator Swenson, used to do law work for him."

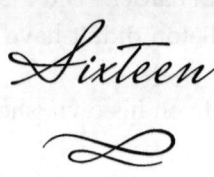

Sixteen

AFTER STAYING IN HIS OFFICE FRIDAY NIGHT, CREATING A MAILING LIST OF Norton's clients to let them know he was now in charge and available, Jax was ready for more interesting action on Saturday morning.

He climbed on his motorcycle as R&R took the steps down from the kitchen, still feeding their faces. Jax had planned on escaping before Evie knew their plans. He could always grab a bite later. He scowled at his cheapskate friends.

"Tell me you didn't tell Evie," he stated flatly.

Reuben, the clueless professor of engineering, licked cinnamon roll off his fingers. "She knew. Mavis says there's bad juju or something and we should stay home."

"Mavis don' know us." Roark, the reckless Cajun, climbed into the van, ready to rumble. "We invite trouble. We'll be in and gone before anyone knows."

"Unless you're planning on breaking in, someone knows. Do you have a key?" Jax idled his bike impatiently as Professor Reuben dangled a key out the van window.

Maybe they could do this before Evie figured out how to reach the storage unit without a vehicle. There should be no reason for trouble. They had the paperwork and permission to inspect the machines. But his gut said the same as Mavis's crystal ball—bad juju ahead. He wanted Evie out of it.

He'd feel a lot better if he could discount voting machines as a motive for his father's murder—and Clancy's suicide. Not that the machines in a tiny town like Afterthought could affect any major election, but it was a thread that had to be tugged just to see what unraveled.

Roaring through the early morning humidity, Jax was debating if they could demand an inspection of any DVM machines in Charleston when the van veered into the city's storage area. A chain-link fence protected a messy accumulation of heavy equipment, pipes, and tin sheds. Surely they didn't keep electronic equipment in a tin shed with no a/c? They'd only find fried wires, if so.

The top-knotted professor hopped out to unlock the gate. In puzzlement, he held up an open padlock. "How many keys they got?"

"Looks like utilities use the lot. Makes sense there's more than one." But Jax's gut clenched as he studied the area.

"Rental van, one o'clock. More dan one person onsite." Roark had always been their front man, with uncanny hearing. "Open da gate, *couillon*. I'm goin' in."

As an officer, Jax had been all about caution and protecting his men. His team, on the other hand, had been all about getting the job done by any means available. Jax could scarcely keep them out of a civilian storage area unlikely to be blown up by enemy IEDs.

He followed the van toward a concrete block building—with its door already open and voices inside.

The Cajun whistled and pointed at the building's roof. Jax tilted his head. Evie waved at him from the flat roof. *Crap on a stick.* Glaring, he ignored her wave and followed Reuben inside. He'd swear she had to fly to arrive before them, but with Evie, dropping from a drone or a kite or. . .

He quit speculating as his eyes adjusted to the interior. Two men in moving company overalls were loading folded-up machines onto a platform trolley.

"I told the mayor's office I'd inspect the machines here." Reuben might be a nerdy engineer, but he strolled through the dim warehouse with the tensed muscularity of the military officer he'd once been. "You don't need to move them."

"We got orders to pick them up." One of the burly movers slammed a machine onto the trolley.

"Those are expensive electronics. You can't handle them like that. I need to inspect them before they leave city property." Wearing a bone-adorned topknot and tribal scars, Reuben rolled up his shirtsleeves, flexing muscles in classic intimidation. Jax wasn't worried about the prof, unless someone pulled a weapon.

"Nothing on the work order about inspection. These are going to the scrap heap. We're behind schedule as is."

This was why Jax was here. Despite his wind-blown look, he could pull off authority in collared shirt and tie. He drew out his cellphone. "Your work orders, please. It's highly irregular to remove machinery without proper authorization, and there is nothing on the city agenda about a recall."

The smaller man in baggy blue grumbled and headed for the door. "Finish loading, Davis. I'll take care of the suit."

Ignoring all of them, Reuben zeroed in on the machines still stacked against a wall. Jax left him to it.

Outside, Evie had affixed herself like a hood ornament to the cab of the rental truck. She crossed her shorts-clad legs, grinned, and talked into her phone. Roark leaned against his utility van, bronzed, muscled arms crossed, observing cynically. Jax kept his Glock locked in a safe in the office, but R&R would both be armed. The trick was to keep his men from going for their weapons.

Baggy Uniform glanced at Evie and opened the passenger door. He produced a clipboard and shoved it at Jax.

The work order came from DVM, not the city. Jax took a photo and pretended to call someone in authority while Baggy Uniform tapped his foot. Delaying so Reuben had time to do his thing, Jax spoke into his dial tone and wandered farther from the van. The work order had no recognizable signature. He'd have the guys investigate once they were out of here.

But it was very much looking like he couldn't eliminate crooked voting machines as motive for murder or suicide on either coast.

Baggy Uniform was on his phone when Jax turned around. Reuben still hadn't appeared. Evie pointed at the road they'd just traversed. Jax recognized the sheriff's car approaching and rolled his eyes. The one time he did something just the slightest bit illegal. . . and Evie pulled the law on him.

BU looked startled but not wary as the sheriff's car rolled to a stop behind the rental truck, blocking its exit. Troy stepped out, and Evie leaped down from the van's hood.

"Better than screaming for me, I suppose," Troy admitted truculently. "Why is anyone here?"

"Because they're stealing the city's machines." Evie beamed brightly.

Jax handed the sheriff the moving company's invoice. "These guys probably don't know that. They're just following orders. But they had keys to get in here."

"And you're here, why?" Troy wasn't a stupid man. He studied the invoice and began punching in the number of the moving company.

"Inspection of the voting machines before an election." Jax hesitated. He was accustomed to working within the law but not revealing all he knew unless required. Telling the sheriff that they expected trouble would be an open invitation to questions.

"Mavis said there was bad juju here," Evie offered. "So we came as support, and a good thing, too."

"Look, we get paid by the job," BU argued. Bug Ugly worked as well as Bulky Uniform. "We need to get outta here and on the road."

Talking to someone on the other end of the line, the sheriff held up a finger for them to wait.

Jax eased over to check on the situation inside the storage shed. Reuben was helping the mover to add the last machine to the trolley. What the. . . ?

"Machines need trashing." Reuben blithely walked out and joined Roark at their van. They slammed the rear doors. . . which had been open to the entrance of the warehouse, on the far side of the much larger rental truck, easily concealing whatever Reuben had been doing—while Evie distracted the driver.

Jax bit his tongue. The sheriff scowled when Roark pulled away, but he knew where to find his team. The movers were a different story.

Jax joined Evie in leaning against the truck while the sheriff was on the phone. "How did you get here so fast?"

"Bikes go where cars can't." She pointed at the hill behind the fence. "Path back there goes straight up to city hall. When someone forgets their keys, they just jog up there and get a spare. Cars have to drive all the way around to take the highway bridge over the flood zone."

"So anyone can get the keys? That's a stupid way to run a business." Disgruntled, Jax glared at the barely visible path through the weeds of an open field.

"That's a small town for you. We know each other. They wouldn't hand keys to a stranger."

"So someone at city hall gave those keys to the movers?"

"Or someone in city hall made copies when they shouldn't have," she admitted. "Internal controls are lax."

"How do you know about internal controls? Did you take accounting classes?" Jax knew he should never underestimate Evie, but she did such a fine job of pretending she was a halfwit that it was occasionally difficult to know what was behind the provocative smile and orange mop.

"I've worked for just about everyone in this town. One of them was Geoff Hayes, the CPA, your landlord. I learn things."

"And you know how to get into my office without asking," Jax concluded, just as the sheriff stuck his phone in his pocket.

Evie beamed. Troy scowled and gestured for the mover to return to business.

Jax lifted a questioning eyebrow.

"*Clancy* signed the work order—the day he died. I'll have to call every blamed person on the council to see if he was authorized. I've told the company to hold the machines until then. They're not happy. How the hell do you two get mixed up in these things? Besides Mavis." Troy grimaced as he said the name.

"Do you really want to know or would you rather just call the council?" Jax asked. If Clancy had signed the work order. . . that was a whole different level of knowledge he probably shouldn't keep to himself.

Troy glared. "I want to know."

"Chances are good, the machines are rigged, and Clancy may have been involved." Jax waited for the ax to fall.

EVIE BIKED BACK TO THE HOUSE IN ABOUT THE SAME TIME AS IT TOOK JAX TO return by the highway. R&R, of course, were already there and unloading the machine they'd stolen. They hadn't bothered to stay and watch the sheriff's head explode over the Clancy/voting machine theory.

Jax's aura flared at sight of the stolen machine, and Evie punched his brawny arm. "Don't. We all know those machines will be trashed, *should* have been trashed. If Reuben can learn from one. . ."

"It's theft," Jax complained, rolling his Harley to the backyard. "*Bad guys* break laws. *We* shouldn't. I only meant for him to take a look at the insides of one."

"Is stealing trash theft? And do you think anyone will notice? And if they've been stealing votes for years, how is the council or whoever any better than we are?" Evie appreciated Jax's honesty, but they operated on entirely different philosophies that would never a relationship make. "The machine is evidence."

"How many people on the council would know if the machines are crooked? We don't even know for certain that they are." Jax opened the recalcitrant cellar doors.

Evie clattered down. Reuben already had the machine in pieces on the cellar floor and appeared to be connecting it to computers.

"It's a DVM machine," Roark reported from his gaming chair. "From the serial number, probably manufactured ten years ago." The Cajun spoke in the clipped tones from his university career. "Council bought them before the mayor's first election, just like the minutes say."

Evie picked up a cue stick and began playing the balls already on the table. "You're hacking council minutes?"

"Public record. Discussion notes aren't here. Just like the contract says, Teddy Swenson was there as rep from DVM. Vote was close. Council doesn't like spending money. If paper was good for their granddaddies, it's good enough for dem." Roark lapsed into lingo in imitation of his fellow citizens.

"Names." Jax leaned against the table, typing into his tablet.

Roark printed out a sheet. Evie grabbed and scanned it, then handed it over. "Council seats should have term limits," she grumbled.

"Can I come down?" Loretta called from the open doors.

"You got donuts?" Reuben shouted back from his circle of mechanical parts.

"I can get cookies. I need money for donuts."

"Kid got pots of gold and can't buy donuts. Not right," Roark grumped.

Jax thumped his buddy's no-longer shaved skull. When Evie had first met Roark a few months ago, he'd sported tattoos on his skull that were now covered with a fuzz of thick black hair. The metal in his eyebrow and ears remained.

"Cookies are good," Evie called up. "I'll make more later."

"You ought to make them eat carrot sticks." Jax went back to typing names into his tablet.

"I ought to make all of you start a garden. Save money and eat healthier." Evie returned to sending colored balls into pockets. "In case no one noticed, the men who voted *against* buying the machines are no longer on the council. And

I was just a kid back then, but I'll make a wild guess that the men who *supported* our crooked Mayor Blockhead and his crooked machines won seats over the next years, giving him a guaranteed approval of anything he wanted done."

Like stealing homes for parking lots, not that she was bitter or anything.

"Not so wild a theory," Jax confirmed, reading from his tablet. "That's the reason you mentioned term limits. Some of these guys—and let us be clear they're all white males in a town that's half Black and female—have been around past their expiration dates. Even if elected, your mayoral candidate will not accomplish beans until the next election."

"I'm pretty sure Larraine knows that. But she'll be a beacon for others. And if those machines were rigged—"

"They are." Reuben set down his tools as Loretta trotted down with the cookie box. "Bless you, grasshopper. Now if only you could make coffee. . ."

Evie whacked his brawny shoulder with a cue. "Buy your own coffee pot or go up and fetch the tea in the fridge. She's not your servant."

Loretta looked ridiculously easy to please. "I can go, but I can't carry pitcher *and* glasses."

"Turnip, don't let them train you to be their slave. Make them teach you what they're doing. Otherwise, I'll show you how to play pool. Either way, they can get their own tea." Evie took the cookie box, helped herself, and set it where the men would have to get up and get their own.

"Damn, you're a bossy witch." Reuben scooted over the carpet to the box, grabbed a handful, then stood up and headed for the stairs.

"You're welcome," Evie shouted after him.

"Can I play on the Pac-Man?" Loretta poked the buttons on the arcade game.

"Dere, see, we teachin' her." Roark took a handful of cookies and returned to his computer.

"Didn't we find out that Clancy was on the council *before* the machines were purchased?" Jax didn't bother picking out a cookie.

Another difference, Evie decided. Jax didn't eat sweets. She probably needed to make sage popsicles for him.

"Again, before my time," Evie reminded him. "I was more interested in sex behind the stadium than the council. Probably still am." She grinned, knowing she was irritating him.

As expected, he drew down his dark eyebrows and glared, then returned to typing on his tablet.

Really, this was a totally dead-end relationship—except for that hunka hunka burning lust thing.

Reuben returned with the tea and plastic glasses. She was probably fortunate that he hadn't just filled his own glass. Obediently, Loretta only filled one for herself and returned to the game.

Evie was going to be a lousy mother. She just knew an Indigo Child needed a wider path for her intellect and abilities than serving drinks to men.

Okay, so now her brain was a Ping-Pong ball. It beat figuring out politics and voting machines.

"Clancy moved his brokerage office from Charleston to Afterthought almost twenty years ago," Jax verified, reading from his notebook computer. "He joined the council prior to the election that put Mayor Block in place. He brought in Swenson from DVM and persuaded the council to purchase voting machines, said he was getting them a discounted deal because Teddy was an old acquaintance."

Jax's biological father had died in a car crash twenty years ago, possibly while attempting to prevent the sales of crooked machines a *second* time. Jax's aura reflected his rage, so they were on the same wavelength for a change, on this topic at least.

Evie did a swift calculation—Teddy Swenson would have been in his twenties when Jax's father died in the crash. Presumably, the senator's firstborn would have been just starting out in DVM/Sovereign. If Donna Ortiz's only son looked as much like a thug then as he did now, he wouldn't have made a very impressive salesman. How had he become a *politician*?

Connections and crooked machines came to mind.

"Do we have a list of towns using these machines?" Evie slammed another ball just to be hitting something. It ricocheted all over the table.

Roark printed out another list and waved it at her.

Jax, on the other hand, followed the more mechanical path. "Can you prove the machines are rigged? And then can we work out who does the rigging?"

Evie took Roark's list of towns and Jax's tablet while the men studied the machine parts and laptop Reuben had set up.

"This PCB is a little more sophisticated than the original Jax found." Reuben pointed to the circuit board. "But they didn't change their methods by much. The board has a mechanical flaw. On its own, it can cause a bad count, but it can't *influence* who wins. The actual rigging depends on the people designing and uploading the ballot knowing how to manipulate the flaw."

He held up the electronic screen. Evie could see wires between it and the board and the laptop but didn't try to figure out the connections. She just listened as she typed with her thumbs.

Reuben turned the screen on to show a ballot with letters A, B, C, D instead of names in the candidate slots. "A voter votes for A and C, hits enter, and the machine counts the vote, right?"

Gnawing on his cookie, Roark reached over and voted for B and D. "Looks normal."

Loretta wandered over. "Is this what a voting machine looks like? It would be cool to have one for school elections."

"Don't touch it, babe. Give me a chance to make it easy." Reuben voted for A and C three more times.

Roark insisted on voting for his B and D candidates in equal number of times. "OK, now what?"

"Now we look at the machine's tally. Basically, the machine is just a calculator totaling how many times a button gets pushed. Really basic stuff." Reuben pushed a button and numbers showed up on the laptop. Even Evie watched—and whistled.

"There were an even four votes for each candidate," Jax muttered.

"But candidates B&D only tally three and A&C tally five. That's a crude example, and basically, all it does is mess up the count, not necessarily in favor of anyone—*unless someone knows the flaw and programs the ballot* so A&C always gets the higher count in *all* the machines. Otherwise, half the wacked-out machines might tally B&D as the winners. Just to win one state, it would take a *lot* of bad machines, in a whole lot of towns, and a whole lot of bad people in each town to rig an election. Pretty nigh on impossible since there are dozens, maybe even hundreds, of different machines and ways of voting. Still, it might work in one small town with all bad machines, like Afterthought." Reuben erased the tally. "It's just a stupid machine. You got to have people colluding to make this happen."

"Collusion *and* crooked machines. That's a lot of long-term planning." Obviously out of sorts, Jax returned to reclaim his tablet. "Thirty years of getting machines in place, people in place. . . No one's that organized. And it still represents an insignificant percentage of the vote, except in local elections."

Evie tapped the screen on his tablet. "Look at Roark's list of towns where they've sold machines." She slid the screen back to her list. "Racial ratios in those towns." She punched *send* to share the list with the others.

Even Loretta left her game to look.

R&R used obscenities they weren't supposed to use while Loretta was present.

Jax simply flung a cue against the wall and walked out.

"All those towns are racially diverse." Loretta studied the ratios of ethnicity on Evie's list. "Why is that bad?"

"Because, turnip, races are often tight in diverse districts. If the machines are fixed, they can reliably swing a close race away from an up-and-coming candidate like Ward to an established candidate already in office, like Clancy. And worse yet, all the investors in DVM are white."

Roark added the crowning touch. "And DVM would only give the insider knowledge to their base. Which means, all these tiny white town councils with insider info can flip an electoral race to *Swenson*."

"As in everything, qualification means nothing. It's always the Man with the money and clout," Reuben said with disgust, retreating to the abandoned Pac-Man machine.

Seventeen

Looking unusually bleak, Evie stood in the open doorway of the empty carriage house.

Still fuming with fury over wealthy bigots, Jax halted beside her. Unused to Evie being anything but cheerful and upbeat, he tried not to dump his anger on her. "What's wrong?"

"Besides the world being a terrible place? I'm never gonna have a Miata." She crossed her arms and glared at the cavernous wasted space.

OK, that was an interesting leap. "You could easily make car payments from the money Loretta's trust pays you." He ought to know. He was the trustee.

She cast him an ugly glare. "Loretta is *family.* I can't take money for taking care of family. I use it for things she needs, although I'm probably stretching the truth with paying the grocery bill. But she needs you and the guys in her life, so I'm calling that expense fair. The rest goes into her savings."

He ought to appreciate her generosity in taking in a kid she hadn't even known existed, but Jax came from a commercial world where one got recompensed for their labors. "You're being paid what the boarding school got. It's meant to cover rent, food, school activities, uniforms, entertainment, salaries, and profit. You're entitled to your fair share. Buy the damned car."

"I don't pay rent. I'm the caretaker and get Great-Aunt Val's house free. I could earn money by renting out her carriage house—or moving all the crap stored in the bedrooms out here and renting them. But I'm still not earning my way. I probably should go back to school."

So that's why she looked glum. Evie's ADHD made school difficult. "Online classes might be easier. You could wash the car, bake cookies, and listen at the same time."

She finally laughed. "Washing the car and baking at the same time might be a challenge even for me. And I don't have a car. Do they have online classes for being a detective? Talking to ghosts isn't getting me far."

Feeling better that he was able to make her laugh, Jax reverted to his usual pragmatism. "Being a detective is mostly tedious, dirty snooping unless you're a cop, and then it's dangerous. You need to be available for Loretta. There probably isn't a lot of profit in ghostbusting. Use the allowance you're receiving to turn the place into a B&B. Take gardening classes and do something with the yard. There has to be a better use for your time than solving crime. That's what the police are paid to do."

"Take up knitting, maybe?" she asked, narrowing her eyes. "Do you really think I could spend my days puttering around the house—especially when we know the powers-that-be are stealing elections? Maybe I should run for council."

Understanding her angry need too well, Jax took her hand and squeezed it. He didn't want to argue. He wanted to throw her over his shoulder and head straight for the nearest bed. At least she didn't yank her hand away. Evie was *not* a stabilizing influence, but holding her hand kept the moment real. Her fingers weren't manicured and silky but warm and strong.

He studied the carriage house interior. "Granny flat. Add insulation, wiring, plumbing, walls. . . You'd have a whole new house, with room left for a garden shed. You don't need a garage for a car anyway. How often does it snow?"

"Money, zoning, and what the heck would I do with two houses?" At least she was looking at the space with a thoughtful frown instead of an unhappy one.

"Consider remodeling as an investment, use Loretta's money, and any rent you collect can go back in her account after deducting an appropriate fee, if that makes you happy. Good tax dodge for her trust. And I looked into zoning a few months ago, remember? Afterthought has none. It would have interfered in Mayor Block's development plans. And I could rent it from you. That way I'd be here to help with Loretta when needed." And he'd have a private bedroom instead of one off the kitchen with people coming and going all the time.

"I'd have to ask Aunt Val." She contemplated the tall rafters. "You never know, she might want to store horses and a carriage again. But the place is tall enough for a storage loft. We could haul all the junk out of the bedrooms and R&R could have real rooms."

Not unless Evie was spending her nights out here. . . But that was a discussion for another day. "Give your aunt a call. We both know people in construction. It doesn't have to be done overnight, but it seems a waste to let it sit here empty while you bemoan a car you don't even need."

"Wait until you're rich enough to buy another Jag, big boy. We'll hear what you have to say then." Dropping his hand, she spun on her heel and marched back to the house.

She wasn't arguing with the idea of him staying here. He'd have to make what he could of that for now—while he pondered who might be the least crooked authority to call about the voting machine fraud that had probably got his father and his partner killed.

How did one go about implicating a presidential candidate in possible voter fraud and murder, especially without evidence?

Delicately, very delicately.

⁓

"WE LANDED AN HONEST-TO-GOSH REAL COMPUTER JOB," REUBEN CROWED, devouring the homemade pizza Evie had put together for lunch. "Your mayor wannabe is one smart lady."

"One smart *candidate*," Evie corrected, sprinkling cheese on another round of veggie-covered tomato sauce. "We should aim for a world where gender and race are irrelevant. What does Ward want you to do?"

"Find the trolls posting on her media accounts and bring 'em down. It could be a real career move," Roark said with more than a trace of cynicism.

Evie pitched a cherry tomato at him. He caught it and popped it into his mouth. "I would love to know how to swat trolls off the internet. They're as useless as mosquitoes and should be zapped. But this job should also be about making connections with important people. Use it wisely."

Reuben snorted up his beer. "Dude don't know wise. They sneer, he blows them up."

"Larraine won't sneer at tats and metal, well, except as a fashion statement maybe. And if you blow her up or off, you're outta here. So behave yourselves for a change." Evie popped the pizza into the oven and sat down beside Loretta to eat her slice while it was hot.

The landline rang. She considered not answering. Only scammers and fake cops ever called these days. And her mother. With a sigh at the expectant expressions on everyone's faces, she slid back out of the booth and grabbed the receiver.

"The sheriff finally figured out that Clancy was murdered, dear," Mavis said with a long-suffering sigh. "I'm supposed to return for questioning. I don't suppose Jax could go with me?"

Evie covered her mouth and thought three dozen foul words before replying. "I don't know what Jax is up to right now. I'll give you his number, and you can set up a time for him to meet you there. Keeping in mind, of course, that he's not a defense attorney."

Evie had dug her fingers into the receiver so hard that she figured she'd left dents by the time she'd talked her mother out of hexing poor Troy and hung up.

"We have a backdoor to the sheriff's computer," Reuben said. "We'll get the deets. You don't worry, okay?"

"Details would be good," Evie answered absently, but her thoughts had already traveled to city hall. Could she try to talk to Clancy's ghost again? Had the sheriff found the thumb drive Iddy had planted? Telling him a large person had flung a cat at Clancy, because the cat said so, would not help their credibility.

"It's Saturday. I should help Mavis at the shop, shouldn't I?" Taking in the adult mood, Loretta worriedly studied them through too-perceptive eyes.

Crap. Evie ought to be down there now. Weekends were her mother's busiest days.

"We'll both go, tadpole. Mavis will need us. Betcha I sell the ugly crystal bug first." There was no point in worrying the kid. Maybe night was a better time to visit angry ghosts. She'd call Helena about a key—

She turned to R&R. "See if the sheriff has a list of who has keys to city hall, will you?" Someone had let themselves in after hours to wipe that computer, and it hadn't been Mavis, the technophobe.

❦

As expected, Jax found nothing in his predecessor's digital files concerning any contract with DVM or Sovereign. The former county attorney had rightfully left any official business at the courthouse. He glared at his laptop. He should probably get a bigger monitor or go blind reading the fine print.

He'd like to have a client or two first.

He'd sent the most current of Norton's paper files off with R&R for scanning. He could go back to the cellar and dig through them. The only paper files stored here were from decades prior to the purchase of the voting machines. Not that any of Norton's papers were likely to contain anything to do with Clancy's death. There ought to be better ways to waste his time.

He glanced at his watch. He had half an hour before he needed to meet Mavis. He was hoping R&R would come through with more info from the sheriff's office before he went. What had changed the charge from suicide to murder?

A knock at the door intruded. This was Saturday, not normal business hours. Wondering if Evie was actually playing polite for a change. . . He laughed at that idiocy and got up to answer the door.

A husky blond man, in an expensive suit that still managed to look rumpled, and a wizened older man, in an unfitted blazer from last century, stood there. The smaller man looked familiar. Jax vowed to learn the locals if he was to build a practice here.

Finally recalling the name of the hardware store owner and newest mayoral candidate, Jax held out his hand to the older man. "Mr. Williams, come in. Hope you're not pursuing votes. I don't think I've registered here yet."

"Can't vote without your South Carolina driver's license, boy. Register to vote while you're there." Hank Williams followed Jax inside, studying the boxes and unfurnished reception area. "George used to have a real pretty secretary in here. And all his golf trophies. Good man."

The younger, husky man cleared his throat, startling the candidate from his reverie and into introductions. "Ah yes, yes, sorry. This is Theodore Swenson, distribution manager for DVM Machines. We were hoping to catch you in today. Swenson needs to return to his home office on Monday."

Theodore Swenson? Jax refrained from expressing recognition—or shock—and gestured toward his office. "I'm unfamiliar with DVM, I apologize." Liar, liar. . . "But I'll help in any way I can. My office isn't ready for business yet, but if you'll have a seat. . ."

What was Swenson doing here? He belonged in California. Or if he was touring with his father's presidential campaign, how did he have time to come to this dinky town?

Swenson had been the salesman who had sold the voting machines to the town. Reuben's refrain of "Ya Got Trouble" popped in mind. If only times were so innocent that pool tables could be considered trouble. . .

The bigger man took the big Morris chair as if it were his throne, leaving elderly Williams to a folding chair. Jax sat at his desk with the afternoon sun pouring over his shoulders. He almost chortled at Evie's cleverness when his visitors had to squint to see him.

"What can I do for you gentlemen?"

"We understand you were present when some of our machines were removed for recycling."

Swenson didn't even attempt to sound genial. A salesman, he was not. But ten years ago he'd sold the town. . . Jax readjusted that thought—Clancy would have done the selling. Teddy Swenson had just been a young representative for his father's company. Clancy had probably known those machines could be rigged, and he and Arthur Block had wanted to control the town council.

He had no proof that Teddy Swenson knew anything about vote rigging back then. Since he was now a politician himself, things may have changed.

Swenson continued. "The sheriff has raised questions about the removal. We were hoping your presence when they were removed meant you had the original contract specifying the terms of the city's agreement."

Hank Williams looked rightfully embarrassed. "The mayor kept a lot of those old files at home, and he's not available right now. Clancy was acting in his place and well. . ."

"Yes, Mr. Clancy's death must be a terrible loss to the city," Jax sympathized, while running through every scenario that would have a California representative and partial owner of a voting machine company in his office. None of the situations he conjured were good. "I had only just met him. Surely his secretary or the mayor's could locate the files?"

A copy of that contract had been on the thumb drive, which meant it had been in the city hall computer under Clancy's name before the intruder wiped it. Surely that couldn't have been the only copy? Or had all the copies been wiped somehow?

"They can't find it," Swenson said impatiently. "Apparently Clancy pulled the file to sign the removal agreement. It's all legal and above board. We just need a copy to show the sheriff."

"And we thought Norton might have one," Williams added. "He wasn't county attorney ten years ago, but he sometimes worked for the city."

He'd have to read the blamed thing tonight. He sure as hell wasn't telling these clowns where to find a copy until he had.

Could Swenson really have nothing in his own files to offer the sheriff as proof that he was allowed to remove the machines? Or was he attempting to remove evidence that the form Clancy signed wasn't legal?

Jax nodded and sounded sympathetic. "I've only begun organizing Mr. Norton's files. Anything in the last ten years is being digitalized. I'll have my IT team go through and search for anything related to DVM or voting machines, if that might help?" If Evie's screwball theories held, he could be sitting across from Pendleton's killer—and possibly Clancy's?

Except none of this made sense. Swenson could just stay in California and build his political career and have nothing to do with Clancy and a tiny town like Afterthought. Over thirty years ago, Teddy would have been too young to have been involved in the mine incident. Jax couldn't see any reason for him to have offed the California lawyer, either.

A pity Evie wasn't here to tell him if Swenson had the aura of a killer, but to Jax, he simply looked like a football player out of his comfort zone.

"You can't just do a computer search right now?" Swenson asked, indicating the laptop.

Ah *no*, not trusting the football player. Jax wasn't about to give away the hiding place for those files. He shook his head regretfully. "Sorry. My team is in Savannah, setting up my cloud account and the new office computers I just purchased." He was getting good at this lying thing. "I didn't expect to have an immediate need for those old files."

Williams managed a glare from under wrinkled eyelids. "If you weren't out there supervising the removal of the machines per the contract, then what in hell were you doing out there?"

Think fast, Jax. "I was asked to oversee the *technician* sent to audit the machines, per Miss Ward's request. Norton's signature was on the audit form, so I assumed it had been approved when the former mayor was in office, but no one had carried it out until Miss Ward asked."

Williams looked satisfied.

Probably knowing DVM's contracts never included audit clauses—Swenson frowned.

Jax checked his watch. "I'm sorry, gentlemen. I have an appointment to meet a client in ten minutes. I'll have my IT department look for your contract, if you'll leave me your cards."

Not-terribly-bright Swenson pitched a card on the desk and lumbered out, leaving Williams to mouth the Southern courtesies as Jax escorted him to the door.

"What will the city do for machines in the next election?" Jax asked as they reached the hall.

"DVM offers a discount for trade-ins. That's one of the reasons we need the contract—to see the original terms. Have your people put a rush on it, will you?" Williams asked crankily.

Ah yes, the old trade-in to keep selling the same product trick, even if the product was a piece of crap. Jax stepped into the hall, locked his door, and listened as the other pair descended the stairs.

Williams sounded apologetic. Swenson said nothing.

Jax texted R&R ordering security cameras in his office. He had a hunch he hadn't seen the end of this.

Eighteen

EVIE HAD JUST SOLD UGLY CRYSTAL BUG TO A TOURIST AND SENT LORETTA TO BUY them both ice cream in celebration when Dot entered. Evie checked on the other browsing customers before welcoming the city hall secretary.

"Hey, welcome back. What can I do you for?"

Dot shrugged. "I was kinda hoping your mother could read the crystal ball for me. I don't think Hank will want me for his secretary. He favors old Bernice. Maybe I should look for a new job."

Had Dot stolen that sheet about Jackson and Ives from the paper stack in hopes of ingratiating herself with someone? Who? Besides Hank Williams, the hardware store owner, who wouldn't understand half of it.

Grumpy old Hank could shake hands and pound a gavel—but someone else was pulling his strings, almost guaranteed. Was there any chance that someone had wanted Clancy out of the way? Was Jax right and they were making this too complicated by bringing in Swenson and Pendleton's death in California? Maybe it was just local politics at its worst.

"I can read your cards, if you like. I'm not as good as Mavis, though." Evie shuffled the deck her mother had left on the counter. Keep Dot entertained, and maybe she could pry more information from her. "Did you ever find out why there wasn't anyone on the reception desk the day Clancy died?"

Dot hesitated over the cards, studying the deck Evie showed her. "Bernice claims Clancy told her to go on to lunch. Her mother is in the hospital, and

154

she'd wanted to drive over to Charleston. She says he promised to watch the desk for her."

"Huh. Sounds like he didn't want Bernice around when he offed himself." Keeping Dot talking, Evie handed the deck over for her to shuffle.

"You haven't heard? The coroner says Clancy suffered from anaphylactic shock and was probably unconscious when the shot was fired. They found traces of peanut dust on the desk, and his doc says he was allergic. I mean, they grow peanuts all around here. If he was allergic, wouldn't you think he'd have an epi-pen?" Dot shuffled the deck and handed it back to Evie.

Uh-oh, so much for the local politics theory. This looked even more like Pendleton's death. Death by allergy wasn't reliable. . .

Evie flipped a simple tarot spread. "Maybe he was only slightly allergic. Did someone give him a bag of peanuts? Or steal the epi-pen?" On top of a cat allergy, even a slight allergy to peanuts might have been just enough to knock him out. The bullet to the brain part, though. . . that was a cover-up, *for someone who knew Clancy well enough to know his allergies.*

Pendleton's death may have been a spur-of-the-moment blow to the head. The killer might have learned from that. Bringing peanuts and flinging cats. . . that was pre-meditated.

Apparently experienced at the cards, Dot winced at the abundance of swords in her layout. "Peanut dust doesn't sound like he was eating them, does it? One of the peanut farmers must have visited while Bernice was away."

Not immediately replying, Evie tapped the ace of swords. "All the other cards show you have a problem and you're conflicted, which you already know, but the ace says you'll discover a solution. Is it possible Clancy sent Bernice away to keep her from seeing his visitor?"

Dot studied the ace. "That's possible. He's done that before. He liked to use city hall as his second office. I wish the cards would tell me what to *do*, not what might happen."

"As I said, I'm not as good as Mavis. Consider this a freebie and come back and have my mother read them for you. If I wanted to talk to Clancy's ghost again, how would I go about it? I'd rather not have people watching me." Evie shuffled the cards back into the deck and mentally crossed her fingers, hoping Dot might come through with a key.

Dot shrugged and pulled her shoulder bag up. "It's a public office. Anyone can go in anytime. But keeping people from watching. . . maybe pull the blinds? Although that's bound to draw attention."

The office was right behind the reception desk and had windows open to the hall. Evie grimaced. "Is there a good time when there aren't too many people around?" Although she really wanted to go there at night or at least when city hall was closed. Spirits were much easier to contact when she wasn't distracted.

"Weekends. There's probably no one there today, which means the doors are locked except to employees with keys. That's not me, sorry. Call Helena, maybe. Thanks for listening." Dot swung out, leaving Evie to her customers.

Evie had all afternoon to fret. She ate ice cream with Loretta, sold knick-knacks to tourists, did a tarot spread for one of the customers who had seen her do it for Dot, and tried not to chew her fingernails. Jax and Mavis were with the sheriff. R&R were helping Ward. She had to get into city hall on her own.

"I can't tell you anything more than I already have." Mavis took the offensive the instant a deputy led her back to Sheriff Troy's office.

Biting back a sigh, Jax took her elbow and steered her into a chair across the desk from Troy. "The sheriff has a job to do. Let him do it. He needs information that you might have and don't realize, okay?"

Troy didn't look grateful for the help but did send the deputy for water bottles. "You were there shortly before Clancy died. We need you to tell us who else was present."

"Why? If he killed himself, what difference does it make?" Mavis wasn't about to make this easy.

Jax bit his tongue and let the sheriff handle her. Troy had known Evie's mother far longer than Jax had. He was here as Mavis's arm candy, apparently. Evie's mother was slightly taller and broader than Evie and wore thick heels and her graying hair stacked high to add height. In full freight train mode, she could out-dowager a duchess, if duchesses wore caftans.

"The coroner said it would have been difficult for Clancy to hold a gun in place while unconscious from anaphylactic shock." Troy played along with the pretense that Mavis hadn't already heard the gossip. "He probably would have died anyway without treatment, so the gun was just a smokescreen. You knew he had a peanut allergy, didn't you? He'd asked you if there was any herbal solution."

Jax winced. Clancy had died just like Pendleton. It might be time to fill the sheriff in—but the connection was so tenuous, he felt like an idiot even thinking it.

"I told him just what his doctors told him. Short of building up resistance, we can only treat the symptoms." Mavis folded her hands over the purse in her lap and sat straight and stiff, the veritable image of an outraged Southern matron, except for the moon and star motif of her midnight-blue caftan.

Jax sat back, crossed his arms, and studied the tiny star studs twinkling in Mavis's ear. He recalled that Mavis's aunt was Evie's Great-Aunt Val, the actress. Drama apparently ran in the family.

"Clancy wasn't carrying an epi-pen, so I assume the allergy wasn't serious?" Troy asked, not bothering to take notes.

Which was why the killer had also thrown a cat—to which he was severely allergic? Jax bit his tongue. There was a bit of knowledge he was *not* about to repeat. He couldn't believe he was even thinking it. Insanity must be contagious.

"I'm sure his doctor can tell you more than I can. Clancy did not return asking for more supplements, so I assume what I gave him didn't help. I imagine everyone who knew him well heard his complaints about peanuts. Personally, I think he wanted to get rid of peanut farmers and turn crops into Wal-Mart." She sounded as indignant as she looked.

Evie was a chip off the old block. What was that old saw about looking at the mothers to see how the daughters would turn out? Interesting.

"Can anyone verify that you weren't carrying peanuts when you went to city hall to confront Clancy?" Troy asked, sitting back in his chair with his hands crossed over his chest.

"All I did was remove my name from the ballot. I might have gone in and hexed him over the water bill if he hadn't been busy, but I wasn't willing to wait around to do so. He was a mean man, and I didn't like him, but I have never so much as *wished* anyone dead. That's extremely bad karma."

Jax raised his eyebrows and waited for Troy to skip the obfuscations and ask the obvious.

"Busy? Doing what?" Bingo, Troy hit the keyword.

Mavis waved her hand vaguely. "Talking. He was a salesman. That's what he did best, talk."

Even Jax sighed in exasperation. "Mavis, you can't protect the entire town. Others would have seen who was in there. Just tell the sheriff what he probably already knows and let us get out of here."

She huffed. "It's not my business to know what others are doing. Clancy was *busy*. I mentally hexed him and left. I am quite certain my hex did not kill him."

"But one of those people in that office might have," Troy insisted. "If you recognized them, give me their names. If you didn't, describe them."

Jax reached over and stopped Mavis's hands from making evil signs. "Even if it was Evie, *tell him*."

She glared. "Fine lawyer you are. Aren't you supposed to tell him he has to arrest me and read me my rights, and I don't have to say anything if I don't want to?"

Jax was quite certain he heard the sheriff chuckle. An officer without a sense of humor might pin Mavis down on the matter of hexing and believe she had sufficient motivation to kill her opponent. Troy knew his suspect too well.

"You aren't accused of anything, and you aren't being arrested," Jax told her. "You are an honest citizen who is doing her duty by acting as a witness to circumstances that led to a crime. The people in that office might know something that will help Troy find a killer. Do you want to leave a killer on the streets? Now tell him."

She drew herself up straighter and glared at both of them. "It was just poor Bernice and Geoff Hayes. They were waving papers and Clancy was shouting a lot. Discussing the town budget sounds a lot like that in council meetings. Troy, you really can't upset Bernice. She's having a hard time with her mother's cancer and all."

"We're questioning all the secretaries. I have a job to do." Troy stood. "Thank you for coming in."

"Is that all?" Looking surprised, Mavis didn't immediately get up. "You don't need my fingerprints or anything?"

"We have your fingerprints, Mavis. You've been run in so many times over the years that we keep them on our Most Wanted bulletin board. We know you weren't in that office." Troy held out his hand to Jax. "I wish you luck if you mean to take Miz Carstairs on as a client."

Mavis hmphed and stalked out.

Jax shook the sheriff's hand. "I'm only here as a friend." Deciding, no matter how distant the connection, he couldn't sit on information, he lingered. "Look, I don't know how there can be any link, but I would be remiss in my duty if I didn't tell you about a similar case in California."

"California?" The sheriff raised his shaggy eyebrows.

Evie would kill him for implicating them more, but it had to be done. "A lawyer Evie and I consulted out there was killed in an almost similar fashion. He was rendered unconscious before someone put a .22 caliber to his temple."

Troy sat down and dredged out his notebook. "Facts."

"I don't have many." Jax pulled out his phone and gave him the number for the sheriff's office.

Troy scribbled it down. "I'm not gonna like this, am I?"

"Since we think it may be related to a thirty-year-old death and voting machines, no, you're not. But I'll warn you that Theodore Swenson and Hank Williams were in my office just half an hour ago looking for a voting machine contract that only Clancy seemed to have. None of this has anything to do with Evie and her family, just mine, so I'd appreciate it if you kept them out."

Troy snorted. "Like that's ever happening in our lifetimes." He reached for his phone.

Dismissed, Jax strode out in Mavis's wake. Maybe he should buy steaks for dinner. It had been a damn frustrating day.

That's when Ariel texted him. MARGARET THOMPSON OWNS M&S LEASING.

Margaret who? Jax texted a question mark.

MARGE. LEASING RANCH.

If his sister got any more taciturn—Jax rubbed his head. The old desert rat Evie said was wealthy—*Marge*. She was leasing. . . the ranch. *Their father's ranch?*

Ergo, Marge might be the one depositing payments into the bank account that paid the property tax.

Did that make her an ally or an enemy? Wasn't she also Donna Ortiz's aunt? Which made Ted Swenson, what? Nephew twice removed?

Steak definitely required.

Nineteen

"Give me an anonymous city any day," Jax declared wearily, lifting his beer bottle.

He was wearing skin-tight T-shirt and jeans, looking ready to hop on his Harley and buzz out of town at an instant's notice.

Evie slapped a salad on the backyard picnic table. It was too hot to eat inside. Until her life flipped with Loretta's arrival, she'd always just grabbed a salad or sandwich and sat on the porch with a pitcher of iced tea. Feeding the hordes. . . required more. "Anonymous—as in, no one is responsible for anyone else?"

"Exactly. I am not my brother's keeper." Jax eyed the salad skeptically. "No kale gave its life for this, did it?"

"It's a chopped salad. You pay good money for this in restaurants or so I've been told. Eat it, and I'll bring you garlic bread next." She didn't know why she was making the male idiots eat right, except that she was grateful Jax had visited the sheriff with Mavis.

"Garlic bread *now*," Roark roared, pushing away from the table and standing. "Ever' ding better wit garlic."

"I'm cutting off the beers at two if you don't behave," she shouted after him as he took the stairs up to the kitchen.

Loretta snickered. "Will you send him to bed early if he sneaks another bottle?"

"I'll leave him to sleep it off in the yard where the rabbits will eat his face." Evie took her seat on the bench beside the kid and admired the way Reuben scarfed down his veggies. At least one of the idiots appreciated a good meal.

Jax's steaks scented the yard. Granted, it was hard to consume greens while salivating.

"Give the dude some space," Reuben recommended. "He didn't blow a gasket after meeting your Miss Ward or when she suggested his nose ring was too last century."

Evie laughed just picturing the scene. "I heard the story from Larraine already. She admires your fortitude and is delighted at how quickly you traced the trolls. And she wanted to know more about you."

Reuben ducked his head and dug into his salad. "Not too many of us queers out here. Like attracts like."

"And that's why Evie doesn't like anonymity. She likes meddling." Jax got up to flip his steaks on the grill.

"*Most* people need friends," she called back at him. "Not everyone is Ironman."

Roark loped back with a basket of hot loaves of bread. "Anonymous is lonely."

"Agreed. But I suppose, after Jax spent the afternoon with my mother, lonely might have its appeal. I probably owe him another beer. Do we add Bernice and Geoff to our suspect list?" Evie snatched bread from the basket. "Although Bernice was probably just asking for time off, if what Dot said was true."

"Bernice was on the list of people with keys. She could have broken in and rifled the computer," Reuben reminded her. "Geoff was on the list, too. Half the town probably had copies. We sent you the sheriff's file with that list."

Evie crinkled her nose. "Try reading all that police jargon with a shop full of customers looking for magic solutions to their problems. I got as far as reading Bernice's claims Clancy wanted her to search files, and she told him she wasn't his secretary. I'll try reading through it tonight. If anyone knows where the bodies are buried, she does. Still, I can't see the motivation. Did Troy interview her?"

"You won't read anything," Jax corrected from the grill. "You'll just interrogate everyone until you have what you need."

"Shut up, Jax." Evie forked a fresh tomato. She was not turning around to drool over his hot bod as well as his steaks.

"Bernice didn't say more than we already know." Reuben tore off a piece of bread. "Sheriff ain't buying voter fraud yet, so he's not asking the right questions. He's like Evie, wanting to interrogate and not read that contract, even if someone went to a lot of trouble to wipe Clancy's files."

"We don't know if voting machines were the reason for his death. That's just assumption." Returning to the table, Jax pulled off a hunk of bread. "Troy isn't a lawyer. He won't understand the contract's implications until they're spelled out. He may have someone on it. He's keeping an open mind. We're not." He sampled the bread. "Not bad."

"Most excellent," Loretta declared loyally.

Evie inhaled Jax's raw male scent along with that of charcoaled beef and hot buttered garlic. Maybe she should move to the city and leave temptation behind. "Thank you, tadpole. An old family recipe handed down from Mr. Pizza Palace. Did Troy interview Geoff? He's a nice guy and my entire illusion of Afterthought will crumble if he's a killer."

"Geoff did time as a juvie before you were born. He was in Iraq. Can't do that wit'out killin', sorry *mon ami*."

Jax took his tempting scents back to the grill. "Hayes is a wheeler-dealer. I wouldn't trust him with my taxes. Once he learned my income sources, he'd use my info for sale or trade. I'll trust a computer first—that's where anonymity works." He brought the platter of steaks to the table.

"Well, everyone needs a hobby." Evie took the smallest piece and cut it in half to share with Loretta. "Geoff calls it helping out. You'd call it meddling. His aura says his conscience is clear."

"When he meddles to help himself, it's *dealing*. If he does it because he genuinely believes he's helping others, then maybe he's one of the good ones." Jax stabbed one of the larger steaks. "Jury's out until I know more. Did Troy learn why Geoff was with Clancy?"

"He was dealin'," Roark said with a snort. "Sheriff's report says Clancy got rich clients Hayes wanted. He says they were dickerin' over different angles to move the clients' business from outta town accountants to Hayes."

"Makes sense." Evie dismissed this as a clue. "Geoff's clients used to be mostly farmers and truck drivers. After H&R Block moved in, he probably saw the writing on the wall and went hunting corporate clients. Clancy had those connections."

"Huh. Who's gonna take Clancy's investment office now?" Reuben asked, finishing up his salad. "Maybe it's as simple as that."

"The clients technically belong to the brokerage Clancy worked for. They'll just send another broker." Jax studied his beer bottle. "Clancy probably knew a lot about his clients—who was losing money, who just came into riches. But that gives Geoff good reason to want him alive. Maybe Clancy was a blackmailer."

"I want to talk to Clancy's ghost again." There, she'd put it out there. This was what she did. "I'll look at that key list tonight and see if someone can let me in after hours."

"Who? The someone who used those same keys to clear out Clancy's files?" Jax asked cynically. "Not sounding like a good plan."

Evie rolled up a piece of bread and flung it at him. "I'll read their auras, okay? If they have an ugly one like yours, I won't tell them what I want."

"Now, now, children." Reuben snatched the bread basket away before Jax could reach for it. "You know there have to be copies of those keys everywhere. Someone needs to suggest that the locks be changed. We're expert locksmiths."

Good idea, except Evie wanted in there tonight, not next month.

Jax intervened before she could protest. "Which reminds me, I think I need security cameras in the office, sooner than later. I bring my laptop home and the most recent files are here, so thieves can't find much yet, but they don't know that. I'd like to know if anything happens while I'm not there."

"Geoff has keys," Evie said wickedly. "They just have to offer him something he wants and anyone can walk in."

"Saves having the door broken in. I'd still like to know who. Swenson wants those machines destroyed." Jax bit into his steak with relish. "I want new locks before I move in confidential files."

It didn't take the ravaging horde long to devour everything it had taken Evie an hour to prepare. The sun would be up for another few hours. Deciding she didn't need nighttime to talk to a ghost in city hall on a weekend, Evie picked up her plate. "I prepared the salad. You clean up. Loretta, you know how to get to Gracie's on your own, don't you?"

Loretta had agreed to keep Aster occupied while Gracie sewed her daughter's birthday dress. The kid grinned and ran for her bicycle, avoiding the clean-up.

"You need a dishwasher," Roark hollered after Evie.

"I need a kitchen counter first," she shouted back as she climbed the back steps. "Otherwise, I got you, bébé."

Leaving her utensils in the sink, she proceeded straight through the house, grabbing her tote bag on the way. She didn't plan to give them time to realize she was gone.

~

Strolling past the overlarge gardenia in the front yard, Evie's look of triumph turned to a glare as Jax met her on the other side of the bush.

"Are you following me?" she demanded.

"Nope. I'm assisting you. That's what you do, isn't it?" Jax fell into step with her. When Evie became predictable, he was in trouble.

"I'm sure you have better things to do. Look at all those files R&R dug out for you. Tons of clues. Just follow the paper trail."

"You could be reading the sheriff's file, but paper doesn't give off auras, and reading isn't what you do, is it? Who do you plan to hit up?" He jiggled the keys in his pocket, satisfied that he was finally figuring her out.

Evie signed in exasperation. "I can always call Helena, but I didn't want to involve anyone else if it could be avoided. That includes you."

"Uh-huh. Stand forewarned, if breaking and entering are on your agenda, you can turn around now. Loretta doesn't need you in jail."

"You don't think I know that? I like to stay on the good side of the law as well as anyone. But I *know* this town. Geoff Hayes isn't a killer. He coaches boys' baseball, for pity's sake. And Bernice may be a bit of a bitch at work, but her cookies carry the church bake sale." She set out on a zigzag path in the direction of town.

"I'm pretty sure the council is not handing over the keys to let you go ghost hunting." Jax wasn't falling for her distraction.

She scrunched up her pert nose. "Look, you're not going to like what you'll see. Just turn around and read contracts and figure out what Swenson wanted. I won't be breaking anything."

"Even the law?"

"Is using a key breaking the law?"

"Probably, if the key doesn't belong to you." Jax thought that might be a gray area, but he pressed his argument. "And there's the small matter of an alarm system. And once you're in there, it's probably trespassing. And then there's a ghost who throws things—"

"Either shut up or go home. I can't read contracts. I can read auras. Let me do what I can do and you do what you do best." Evie turned down a side street of offices closed for the weekend.

If she thought she was hiding from public notice, she should have worn a hat. Jax wasn't about to explain camouflage to an orange-haired genie in bright blue short-shorts and a red tank top saying *I'm not ignoring you. I'm just not paying attention.* Looking at her short-circuited *his* attention.

He studied the neighborhood as if this were a military reconnaissance. She'd certainly chosen a deserted path. "What if assisting you is what I do best?"

"Hogwash." Evie took a shortcut through an alley behind an abandoned gas station.

"I'm not just a desk jockey," he reminded her. "You need to learn to trust me."

"If I didn't trust you, I would have lost you a few blocks back. Trust isn't the problem. A general difference in how we approach life is the problem. Trust *me* on that. You've had decades of practice in closing in on yourself, shutting out others. I don't do that. I literally, physically, cannot shut myself off."

Now there was an insight to ponder. "I thought you could turn off that third eye thing." And now he was believing in chakras and auras and third eyes. Was that lust or insanity?

"Most of the time. Not all the time. I *see* you. That's how I know how uptight you can be. And when you let yourself go. . . Well, then I'm usually better occupied than watching your aura. Once I know what to expect of a person's aura, it sort of becomes a part of them I can't turn off."

That made his skin itch. *Better occupied?* As in, when he was kissing her? Jax hoped so. "That's why two heads are better than one. We can examine a problem from different perspectives."

"Maybe," she said with doubt, before slipping through an opening in a wooden fence too narrow for Jax to fit through.

As if that would stop him. He yanked off another plank and squeezed through into an alley behind city hall.

She shook her head in disapproval but only indicated the trash-littered space. "One of former Mayor Blockhead's complaints was the lack of parking —he couldn't squeeze his Escalade back here. So he tore down an entire trailer park to create a parking lot. Clancy and the rest of the town council encouraged him so they could force the public off the street and make them pay for the privilege of visiting city hall. And then they reserved the choice spots out front for themselves."

"Ward can't bring back the trailer park," he warned. "She's likely to have her own agenda that will set Clancy's sort in an uproar."

"Yeah, but that will be fun, and maybe we can hope we'll push Afterthought one more step into the here and now instead of yesterday." Crossing her arms, Evie scanned the litter-strewn alley. "Either somebody hasn't been doing their clean-up chores, or the trash cans have been emptied."

Jax picked up a few wads of paper and straightened them out. "They could have recycled these by printing on the other side. These are just memos."

"The office shares a printer. Not practical. Afterthought needs a trash company that recycles. I wonder what they were looking for?" Not bothering to check the trash, Evie ran her hand over the top of the door frame, coming up with nothing.

"A dog could have turned the cans over." Jax watched her scout around until she found a large rock and overturned it. From her frown, he assumed she'd been hoping for a hidden key. "Surely no one is daft enough to leave the key to city hall under a rock? And what about the alarm code?"

"Jax, adapt," she said impatiently, glancing around, presumably for more hiding places. "Small town. The criminal activity around here is *inside* this building, not outside. I daresay I could enter every house in Afterthought, given enough time. I'm pretty certain no one stored this key at the front door like half the places I know, but back here, yeah, it's gonna be here just to keep them from locking themselves out when they empty the trash."

She ran her fingers over the decorative cement blocks surrounding the bins, held up a key, and crowed her triumph.

Jax muttered and checked the alley to be certain no one was watching her do this. "Tell Ward to hire R&R to change all these damned locks if she wins."

"Will do." She craned her neck to look inside the block. "Yup, there's the code. The Sharpie ink is fading. I thought that stuff was permanent."

Jax rubbed his eyes in disbelief but said nothing as she applied the key to the door, then reached in and pushed the code she'd found. When nothing clamored, he gave up. It looked like city hall *wanted* to be robbed.

"I could have just watched Helena key in the code the other night, but I was being polite." Evie slipped inside.

Reluctantly, Jax followed. He hated breaking the law, but he hated anything happening to Evie worse. This was how R&R got into trouble with the military —warped priorities.

The central hall had no outside windows to let in the dying daylight, but the low exit lights offered enough to see where they were going. The corridor was eerily silent. The last time they'd been in here, Evie had chatty friends with her so Jax hadn't noticed the silence.

"Shouldn't they turn down the air conditioning when the office is closed?" he asked, feeling the chill after the heat outside.

Almost at the front of the building, Evie halted, put a finger to her lips, and pointed at the window of the public office where Clancy had been found.

Jax instantly stepped in front of her, holding out his arms to keep her from passing until he saw what she did. Except, he didn't. Puzzled, he studied the window. There was nothing there.

Going closer, he felt a draft of cold air.

"He's in there," she whispered behind him. "His aura is a flaming red. Do you believe in hell?"

Twenty

"DAMN," EVIE MUTTERED, STUDYING THE WEIRD GLOW. "IF I BELIEVED IN HEAVEN and hell, I'd say Clancy is teetering on the brink of the latter."

Jax wrapped his arm around her, anchoring her to reality. The uptight lawyer was starting to grow on her, like moss maybe. But she was damned glad he was here. She'd never seen a ghost like this. Scattered remnants of energy, okay. Roaming balls of fire? Not so much.

Jax tried to turn her around. "My personal belief is that heaven and hell are our own creation. Let's get out now. You have no way of knowing what you're dealing with."

Okay, so he wasn't quite buying this assisting business, and she was less thrilled with his company.

"I have no one to teach me but myself." She wriggled free and approached the window. "The apparitions I've encountered are usually ancient energies, fragments of old souls. This thing—is practically alive in comparison. Without a body to orient it, his aura is like heat lightning. I can't even determine what chakra it emanates from."

Jax's silence indicated cluelessness, but at least he wasn't arguing. "Can you ask questions from out here?"

"Probably not. I need to catch his attention. He's just stewing in his own hell right now, still confused, I imagine." If she were truthful, that cold emanation terrified her. Was hell a cold fire?

Jax placed his hands on her shoulders and watched with her, although he probably wasn't seeing anything. "Do you know what you want to ask? What's most important in case he turns dangerous?"

He forced her to focus on her goal. So maybe he had more purpose than moss. Evie relaxed against his strength and closed her eyes to ponder. "Who threw the cat? Because he really doesn't grasp that he's dead, so he won't know who killed him."

"Good point, and ask why. Then just get out, okay?" He squeezed her shoulders. "Or we could just leave and forget about it."

"I have to do this. I'll kick myself for the rest of my life if I don't." Feeling the reassurance in Jax's grip, she was reluctant to pull away. But he'd be around tomorrow. Clancy's ghost might not be. Her goals might be intellectually nebulous, but instinctively, she knew what she had to do.

"I'll kick myself into eternity if anything happens to you," Jax murmured, before releasing her.

That sounded lovely—to a point. "I'm not exactly going to war." Gritting her teeth, Evie entered the office.

She shivered at the icy blast. How did no one notice? The flaming aura blazed brighter in alarm at her entrance. But then the spirit's native caution returned, and a sliver of muddy blue steadied the darkening red.

"Who threw the cat, Mr. Clancy?" Evie approached the desk, thinking the question as much as speaking it. Conversing with energy wasn't an easy task.

"The *bitch*! She promised me." The not-quite-a-voice sparked more angry flares. "She said I'd be governor. Lies!"

Evie waited through incoherent cursing and muttering. Had a *woman* thrown the cat? She searched her memory but Iddy had simply said someone large. Bernice was large. . . If Clancy was merely an emotional firestorm, she might never get anything practical from him.

"*Who* promised you?" She kept her question simple in hopes of a direct answer.

"He'll be president! I should be *governor*." The aura flew about, as if Clancy might be pacing.

Were they even on the same topic? Maybe ghosts merely recycled the traumas or grievances of their past. Names seemed to be problematic, but *president* worked. "Swenson promised to make you governor? With his voting machines?"

"Machines!" The red flared brighter and papers blew around on the desk. "Don't destroy them!"

Evie's strength was draining fast. Did the ghost pull on her energy to speak? She was having difficulty trying to follow and *hear* the aura, while translating these enigmatic statements fast enough to phrase the next question. She was supposed to get in and out. Sensing Jax in the doorway, she needed to keep Clancy's spirit fixated on her. Once ghosts learned to move physical objects, they were dangerous.

And this one didn't seem ready to move on to the next plane, perhaps for good reason.

"Couldn't the company program new machines in your favor?" She hoped she was following his complaint.

"They wouldn't! Not family. I was good enough to kill for them but not to marry them!" The floor-height exit lights blew out.

In the distance, it sounded like the air conditioner exploded and whimpered a dying sigh.

As another explosion blew outside, Evie fled, collapsing in Jax's arms just as the building descended into total darkness. An alarm shrieked.

Lawyer-man swung her up as if she were feathers and raced through the dark to the exit.

Sparks flew from the transformer at the pole just outside city hall. The battery-operated alarm shrieked. Jax could hear more alarms going off all around them. The whole block was probably out.

That Evie had allowed him to sweep her up terrified him. She was all but lifeless, except for shallow breathing. Where the hell did he take her? They'd walked over. It was nearly a mile back to the house or an urgent care center.

His office. The electricity was probably blown, but he could climb stairs in the dark. He had keys in his pocket.

Evie was stirring by the time he reached the building. Apparently small town office lobbies didn't require locks and security guards. What mattered more was taking Evie somewhere safe so he could make sure the fiend hadn't zapped her into eternity.

Demon? Ghost? Or Evie's imagination? He hadn't seen anything except Evie and a few papers flying around in the damned cold draft.

She was struggling by the time he reached the top of the stairs. Jax set her feet down but supported her as he hunted for the lock in the dark. He'd ask for battery-operated emergency lights on Monday. Weren't there fire codes?

"Next time, flashlights," she muttered, leaning into him.

She was alive! And relatively sane. "No next time," he countered, finally opening the door.

Jax half carried her inside. The reception area ought to have a damned sofa. Still supporting her weight, he steered her into his office and the leather Morris chair.

"You could have called Roark with the van. You didn't have to carry me." She sank into the chair and bent over to rest her head on her arms in classic no-faint mode.

"Didn't want his truck anywhere near whatever just happened back there." Jax rummaged in his desk. He didn't do sugar, but he usually had gum and breath mints. He brought her both.

She took the mints. "Water?"

Jax frantically looked around. He'd meant to stock some—*cup*. Bathroom. He filled his coffee mug at the faucet and carried it to her. He really was spoiled when he reached for bottled water instead of a faucet.

Evie leaned against the enormous chair back and sipped the water.

Jax paced. He glanced out at the twilight-lit street. People were emerging from bars and restaurants, looking to see if others were affected by the outage. What the hell had just happened?

He didn't want to push her, but he was going crazy here. He had heard only Evie's murmurs until the air exploded.

"Souls are more emotional energy than intellectual." She finally spoke. "Or this one is. Clancy is in a hell of fury and betrayal. And he said he killed someone, which is probably why I can't send him on."

"Shit." Unable to tolerate separation any longer, Jax returned to the chair and picked her up. She weighed next to nothing, but he already knew that. He sat down with Evie in his lap. "Tell me."

He was honestly believing she'd talked to a ghost. And the ghost had caused an electrical storm that blew a transformer? Or had that been coincidence?

He concentrated on Evie's disjointed run-down of what she'd thought she'd heard. It almost made a crazy kind of sense. "Not good enough to marry?" he asked. "Who would Clancy marry? The bitch who may or may not have thrown a cat?"

Jax tried to relax into the chair with Evie leaning against his chest, but he was strung tight, waiting for more IEDs to explode.

She shifted so he could reach his pocket. "Does your cellphone work? Can you look up Clancy's name? Did R&R do any research on him?"

He didn't want to look at his damned phone, but what he wanted had to wait. Evie focused and sitting still meant trouble.

"R&R have an entire file on Clancy, culled from research and the sheriff's notes." Jax thumbed in his code, called up his cloud account, while reciting from memory. "Clancy grew up in Savannah and Charleston, wealthy family, private schools. He had connections even before he started university."

"I don't suppose any of those files indicate a wife, a significant other, anything? I knew he wasn't married but just considered it as one less motive to kill him."

Jax scrolled through the files, looking for early days, when a man was most likely to marry. "Huh, look at this. He and Gus Swenson went to the same private high school. Clancy followed him to Georgia State. Neither of them is exactly Harvard material. They joined the same country club later. Clancy nailed Swenson's family as one of his first clients when they were both starting out."

"Clancy didn't want to marry *Swenson*." Evie snatched the phone from him. "Doesn't Senator Swenson have a sister?"

"Two, plus a brother. The fish magnate and his Hollywood wife were productive. The offspring mostly live off fish profits. And occasionally help their brother's campaigning." Jax took the phone back and found the Swenson file. "Sisters are married to an oil exec and an Arabian prince, which amounts to the same thing as an oil exec."

"A prince!" Evie crowed. "Clancy didn't stand a chance if royalty was their goal."

Jax took a moment to process all the steps Evie skipped. "You think Clancy may have wanted to marry one of Swenson's sisters?"

"It makes sense. He hung out with them. They were rich. Greed was Clancy's lifeblood. Look." She pointed at Clancy's bio on the phone. "His parents were nobodies—plebian lawyers, nouveau riche with only local connections. Clancy wasn't inheriting billions or a dynasty. But his aura is heavily doused in greed and ambition. You have to figure a man like that thought he could marry billions—and become governor. He said *'I was good enough to kill for them but not to marry them.'* He apparently *killed* someone for those dreams."

"Assuming any of this high-flying fancy is true, Clancy lived on the *east* coast." Jax simply put the fact out there. Clancy was of an age with Ives, Jackson, and Pendleton. If Evie was trying to connect Clancy to murder—Pendleton and Jackson had been killed on the west coast. Only, if any of this had any reality and related to Swenson and voting machines—

Jax's parents had died on the east coast.

Evie hugged him and buried her face in his shoulder. "Can you find out what Clancy was driving the day your parents died? And if maybe he got rid of it shortly after?"

"Circumstantial." But a big hole opened in his gut. If Franklin Jackson had been killed over those voting machine contracts thirty years ago. . . Then ten years later, Jax's father set out to stop the company a second time. . . His father was a careful driver. Jax had always suspected foul play, but he'd related it to his father learning of Stockton's fraud.

Clancy as a killer was probably just Evie looking to tie up a neat package, but it fit.

"We may never know," she agreed sadly. "But Clancy's spirit is enraged and lingering because someone promised him that he would be governor and that someone was a woman. Is there any way of talking to Swenson's sisters?"

"Or his wife or his mother," Jax added gloomily. "I don't move in those circles. I don't think Troy can bring them in for questioning on the basis of a ghost's confession."

"Or a cat's vision. What is *large* to a cat? Are any of Swenson's women large?"

Jax found a photo file and scrolled through. "Good Scandinavian blond. They're not petite. The senator's sisters are in their fifties now, so they've got some heft to them. Gus's wife is younger and must work out. She could have tossed Clancy as well as the cat. Grandma—well, she's in her eighties, isn't she? You've seen her on TV. She might be large, but I think they keep her under lock and key."

Evie took the phone and studied the images. "I need to see their auras. Second guessing a cat and a ghost is impossible. Your battery is almost fried." She handed the phone back. The images were gone.

"I just charged it up." He glared at the blank screen. "Even without auras, you've given us a path to explore that we didn't have before. One puzzle piece at a time."

And he would damned well start fitting the pieces together if it meant determining if his parents had been killed over *voting machines*. He was finally getting a sense of who his dad had been. After reading all the correspondence, he was fairly certain Aaron Ives, the lawyer, engineer, and miner, hadn't been a duplicitous crook or killer but a man trying to do what was right, even if it cost him a fortune.

Did any of this matter while he held Evie in his arms? Her head was on his shoulder, and she wasn't running away for a change. A little life affirmation was required. Jax bent his head and warmed her mouth with his.

She responded with gratifying alacrity.

Evie was pure energy, like the spirits she claimed to see. She poured her soul into her kisses. And then she was kneeling over his lap, and he filled his hands with that insane red tank top and her beautiful breasts. Heaven existed right here on earth.

He tugged the top free and unsnapped her bra. He had one hand on bare skin when she froze.

Heaven descended to hell in an instant. Even his prick knew to shut down once he heard what had registered in his subconscious while his brain was in his pants.

Someone was unlocking the hall door.

Stealing one last kiss and squeeze, Jax set Evie on the floor so she could adjust her clothing and he could stand. He debated weapons, but he had the element of surprise and experience on his side. He'd leave the Glock hidden. He left Evie digging through her tote, presumably for whatever she considered defense. He hoped she knew how to keep pepper spray out of his eyes.

He'd left his private office door open. He leaned against the wall beside it so he could watch the front door in the reception area. There was just enough twilight through the large front windows to see. He held up his hand to Evie, who approached with her keys between her fingers and a can of something dangling from the ring. They might have different perspectives, as she claimed, but when it came to the basics, they were on the same page.

His landlord, Geoff Hayes, stepped in as if he owned the place, which he did. Jax vowed to replace the door lock with one that had a security alert. He'd made certain the rental contract allowed it. But Hayes had the right to inspect his property if there was any chance of damage—like from an electrical outage.

He watched Hayes cross the reception area to the anteroom where Jax had stored Norton's ancient files, the ones he meant to shred. Once the intruder disappeared into the file room, Jax gestured for Evie to stay and crept out to a better viewpoint.

A flashlight illuminated the file room. Jax gave his landlord time to ascertain that the place wasn't on fire or in any imminent danger. When he still didn't emerge, Jax crept to the doorway. Hayes was crouching over an open file box.

Without warning, Jax stepped into the room and wrapped his arm around the accountant's throat. He jerked him upright and yanked the flashlight-wielding arm behind his captive's back.

"Evie, call the cops. We have an intruder." He knew the damned female was right behind him. He'd have done the same, so he couldn't complain. Too much.

"Wait a minute! It's just me, Geoff. I'm only checking the electricity." The accountant struggled to get free.

There wasn't much chance of that. Jax had years and muscles on the older man. "Huh." Pretending he hadn't recognized him, Jax loosened his hold, capturing his prisoner's flashlight as he did so. Heavy flashlights made good weapons. He turned it on his landlord and reluctantly released him.

Geoff hastily backed away.

"It's just an outage," Jax said accusingly. "And you were in my client files."

Geoff threw up his hands innocently. "I stubbed my toe, that's all."

Evie sauntered in. "Geoff, you know I know when you're lying. Don't disappoint me now. I want to believe you're one of the good guys."

The accountant looked at her almost pleadingly. "You know I am, Evie. You know I don't bill my older clients half what I should. I buy ads in all the school yearbooks and newspapers. I was just trying to help a friend."

Evie crouched beside the open box and sneezed. "Good grief, I hope you're shredding this stuff, Jax. The rats have already done half the job."

Jax leaned against the wall, keeping the light on his landlord. "Those files are well past the age of usefulness. I need a truck to haul them to the shredder. What friend, Geoff?"

"A friend, that's all. He thought maybe you hadn't looked through everything thoroughly and wanted me to be certain you didn't have it."

Jax snorted. "Hank or Swenson? The contract isn't in there, unless Clancy somehow got his hands on Norton's storage shed and hid it in forty-year-old files. How likely is that?"

Geoff relaxed and ran his hand through his hair. "Norton occasionally worked for the city back in the day. There was some chance he had it. And I thought it couldn't hurt to help the family of a man who might be president someday. Just think of the connections we could make—"

"Geoff, Ted Swenson will go to jail before that happens," Jax said in exasperation. "Grow a backbone. Swenson is asking you to commit a crime. Legal files are confidential, even if they are only moldering rat droppings. Good men don't dirty their hands for *connections*."

Evie abandoned the file box to take the flashlight from Jax and hand it back to Geoff. "You have no reason to trust Jax. I get that. But trust me when I tell you that should Jax find that contract, he will see it into the proper hands. And I'm thinking you won't want to be anywhere around when that happens."

The contract was already in the sheriff's hands, if he'd only look at it. Jax wasn't convinced Troy would understand what he was reading. But he appreciated Evie's confidence.

With the light off his face, Geoff's expression wasn't visible. He sounded distinctly nervous when he replied. "Hank won't be in trouble, will he? He's just trying to find the contract so the sheriff will release the machines."

So Ted Swenson and DVM could destroy them and hide all evidence of their tampering, right.

Lights flashed on in the street below, and the air conditioning began to wheeze again.

From the open office door came a distinctive "Yoo-hoo." Evie's mother appeared a moment later, as if she'd personally conjured the return of electricity. "Evie, Jax, are you in there? You had a call from a Conan Oswin in California. He claims your cellphone is dead, but it's urgent that you call him back."

Twenty-one

Evie checked that Loretta was safely tucked in bed, with Psycat sprawled across her toes. She relished the momentary normalcy—before Jax hooked up his phone and returned Oswin's call and the world descended into chaos again.

She'd just had the most electrifying experience of her life, almost literally. She needed a little bit of normalcy to give her time to process the fact that *she really could reach out to the recently dead*.

Did that mean she should learn to be a mortician? She was fairly certain that would never work.

Conjuring a scary scenario where she dressed a corpse in pink, while its ghost nagged about how much she hated pink and the stepdaughter who'd forced it on her, Evie returned to the kitchen. She fixed a big pot of coffee for the men and a huge mug of hot chocolate for herself. She needed the sugar. Clancy had drained every ounce of energy out of her. Top that off with Jax's melting kisses and Geoff's treachery, and her head was already whirling.

If damned Geoff Hayes hadn't interrupted. . . She and Jax might have pushed their luck on an ancient Morris chair. Wouldn't Aunt Val get a kick out of that! Evie dropped that inappropriate thought to follow the men down to the cellar.

Rather than keep the call to Oswin private, Jax put his phone on speaker.

"We're all in this together," he explained. "I need all of you to think for me. I've just had my brains fried."

Evie snorted. Was he remembering their encounter in the chair or Clancy? Maybe both. She was feeling a little fried too. Good to know Super Macho Man suffered the jimmer-jammers as well.

But at least he'd hooked up his phone to the charger. Jax never let his phone run down. Had she drained it somehow? That might have added to the electrifying experience. Evie didn't think she'd mention that just yet.

She'd told R&R what little she'd learned from Clancy's ghost. Roark had been fascinated and was now on the computer, digging deeper into the stockbroker's background—and maybe even his car from twenty years ago. The professor had grunted and returned to documenting the flaws in the machine spread in pieces on the floor, in the engineering detail required of a doctorate, as far as Evie could tell.

Reuben's document might be as close to evidence as they had, and that only pertained to voter fraud, not murder.

She sat cross-legged on the ancient sofa and opened her notebook, hoping pen and paper might help her focus.

It was three hours earlier on the west coast, probably still daylight, if not business hours. Jax poked the contact number for the man who might in some way be related to him.

"Good, they were about to run away again." Conan Oswin's California drawl emanated from the speaker.

"They?" Jax asked warily.

"Marge Thompson and Donna Ortiz. Marge is probably your great aunt from the wrong side of the blanket as they say in my wife's historical novels. I'm gonna guess wildly that makes Donna your cousin several times removed."

Evie needed to see *auras*. But lacking that. . . "Can you make this a zoom call or whatever they call it?"

"Who's that?" a woman asked nervously.

"My secretary. She's taking notes." Jax mugged at her.

Evie threw a pillow. Secretary, fat chance.

"If I'm meeting relatives, shouldn't we do this on Zoom?" he continued in his lawyer voice.

"No," the woman's voice protested. "I'm still not certain—" Whispers in the background.

"Donna's a bit nervous." Marge's gruff voice came online. "I recognized your father in you the moment you showed up at my door, Damon. But you were calling yourself Jackson, and I thought my old eyes were fading and my wishes got the better of me."

Jax frowned and didn't immediately reply. Evie knew he was too cynical to accept family just because they said so, no matter how much he wanted to know who he was.

Conan Oswin intervened. "DNA. I got Marge's sample and Nadine ran it and it's all right there. If you want to dig up your father's bones, you can nail it even closer, but the relationship is strong enough for our experts. You and Marge are closely related, and she has all the family documentation, up to the point where your father took off for Vegas under an assumed name."

Official verification! Evie grabbed her phone and hastily called Ariel while Jax questioned his previously unknown family. She knew Ariel didn't like talking, but a text simply wouldn't work. When Jax's sister hit ANSWER without saying anything, Evie barged right on. "Jax is talking to your great aunt and a distant cousin. You need to hear this. I'll just leave the phone here so you can tune in."

She put her phone next to Jax, and he nodded gratefully.

Marge's voice emerged over Oswin's. "Your grandfather was an odd duck, liked to keep to himself, said people got in his face. So he found a few lucrative lodes in those mountains, bought the ranch, and lived out there by himself for a long time."

Sounded like Grandfather Ives was a bit reclusive—like Ariel.

Marge continued. "My mother cooked for him. I don't claim to know about their relationship, but he gave her this spread I'm living on when she had me."

"How does my father enter the picture?" Jax asked warily. "Did my grandfather find another cook?"

Marge chortled. "No, when I was a teenager, and he was old enough to know better, he fell for a pretty face. They got married and had your father right off. They doted on him, but your granddad got snake bit and died when Aaron was just a kid. Your grandmom lived out there in the middle of nowhere until Aaron was in high school, but she was always puny. She died before he graduated. He pretty much raised himself anyway. I was out making my fortune and wasn't around enough. I made a lousy half-sister."

Evie was beginning to think they all needed to clear out and leave Jax to deal with his newfound family, but when she gestured at the door, he shook his head vigorously. He was probably still skeptical and would demand Oswin send him DNA results, signed, sealed, and certified.

"You don't know why Aaron changed his name and left home?" Jax asked, sounding more like a lawyer than a newfound family member.

"Not for certain sure, but we know a little bit. Donna, you want to jump in here anytime soon?"

Donna cleared her throat. Evie called up her memory of the friendly receptionist in Pendleton's office who had once worked for Franklin Jackson and who thought Jax didn't look like his father—back when they thought his father was Franklin Jackson.

"Hello, Damon. I didn't know Aaron Ives well," she said nervously. "He didn't come into the office much. Up until I had Teddy, I lived in LA, so I didn't really know Marge or anyone."

Jax frowned impatiently. "You told us Jackson gave you your first job."

"He did. Marge was one of his clients, and she recommended me. My parents' lawyer had to threaten the Swensons to make Gus marry me and give Teddy a name, so I thought maybe I should be a lawyer."

Senator *Augustus* Swenson was not a very august personage. *Gus* was more fitting for a scumball.

Donna continued over Evie's meanderings. "But I couldn't pass the law school test, and Teddy took up so much of my time, I thought a law office might be easier. Franklin let me work with clients and keep up his case notes."

Jax wisely let the woman ramble, but Evie could see he was waiting for information proving that his father wasn't a scoundrel who murdered his partner, stole his identity, and fled.

More murmuring in the background. Donna seemed to be protesting.

Oswin's voice returned. "The Swensons are something of a sore point here. They settled a nice sum on Donna, and they've taken her son in as one of them. You want to use your lawyer skills on her?"

Evie grimaced, remembering the big, untidy lout that was Donna's son. Only a mother. . .

Jax crossed his arms and looked grim. "I'm a *family* lawyer."

Well, he specialized in fraud cases, but Evie could see why he might not mention that.

"I believe families should stick together if at all possible. Donna, I don't care about the Swensons. I just want to know my father didn't murder his partner. Can anyone help with that?"

Donna gasped. "Oh, no, Mr. Ives would never do that, I'm sure! The few times he came into the office, he was always kind. Franklin spoke highly of him. They were great friends. Franklin, well, he wasn't exactly a manly man, you know what I mean? But Mr. Ives didn't hold that against him. He valued his intelligence, as well he should. Franklin was a brilliant lawyer and nice to everyone."

As opposed to the Swensons, who were swine who had to be sued to provide support for their grandchild, Evie thought.

"So, what happened to Franklin Jackson if he didn't sell the practice and move to Georgia as everyone thought?" Jax had his lawyer face on now.

"I thought that's what he did," Donna protested. "Mr. Pendleton said he bought the firm from him. I thought Franklin was all torn up about the death of his partner."

"Tell him about what happened before the mine collapsed," Marge urged.

"Wait a minute." Jax intervened. "Will this involve anything the sheriff should hear? Keep in mind I *am* a lawyer, and I have an obligation to report criminal activity.

"But I don't know anything criminal or I would have said something sooner." Donna sounded a little more confident now. "Mr. Ives and Mr. Jackson had a business making microchips. Gus lived in LA, working in his grandparents' real estate firm—that's where I met him, in the office where my mom worked. He was learning the family business, but Gus had his eye on politics. After I had Teddy, and we moved back to Bolder, Gus visited. He must have talked to Mr. Ives and Franklin about buying real estate for their new company. One thing led to another, and Gus persuaded his parents and grandparents to invest in their microchip business. It's all legal, I'm sure. Mr. Ives and Mr. Jackson were both lawyers and wouldn't have done anything wrong."

"So after they set up the silica mine and microchip business, they and a group of investors formed Sovereign to make voting machines." Jax hurried the tale along. "We know this part."

"OK." Donna sounded nervous again. "Well, everything was going well as far as I could tell. I was in college and working part-time for Franklin when they were starting up. This had to have been thirty-five years ago or so, remember. I was just a kid with a toddler, but I remember the town was thrilled at having a new business. Gus left LA and moved to Bolder to help with the company and be a daddy to Teddy. He ran for a county office and secured lots of new contracts for the machines. I think the company offered a local discount to get the business off the ground." She hesitated again.

"It's okay, Ms. Ortiz," Jax said in his lawyer voice. "Thank you for verifying what we could only guess at. But at some point, something went wrong, didn't it?"

Evie could hear more whispered arguments in the background. She'd wager Aunt Marge was twisting Donna's arm. Marge had seemed like a savvy old broad. Donna was more creampuff.

Donna's voice returned. "Mr. Ives had a girlfriend," she said with resignation. "She was a troublemaker professor from the university, always protesting something. I think she was part Hispanic or native or something. Pretty and exotic looking but always in people's faces. She worked with some political analyst, and when Gus won the district primary for state representative, she blew a gasket, said all the polls showed him losing. She was convinced her candidate had been robbed."

That was Jax's mom, Evie bet. He inherited his need for justice from her. She couldn't stand it any longer. She got up and hugged Jax. He wrapped his arm around her but stayed focused on the phone.

"Aaron Ives was both lawyer and engineer." Jax encouraged Donna to continue. "And he listened to his girlfriend."

"Yes," Donna whispered. "He came in one day, waving circuit boards and furious. There was a lot of arguing behind closed doors. Franklin looked pretty unhappy. I never really knew what it was all about, but there were a lot of phone calls and shouting. They had me print out their contract with Sovereign Machines and fax it to a few people. A week later, the mine collapsed, and it was all over, and we were all out of jobs." She sobbed a little.

"How much can you remember of the day the mine collapsed?" Jax asked soothingly. "I just need to know my father didn't kill his partner."

He wanted a lot more than that, Evie knew, but he was a damned good interrogator. Giving up on her note taking, she leaned back against the pool table with him, her hip brushing his thigh. He lowered his arm to press her closer, and she snuggled into him.

"I don't know. It's all sort of a muddle after all these years." Donna took a breath, sniffed, and after some more encouragement in the background, continued. "This was long ago, when cellphones weren't around much. We didn't have any cell towers, so it was mostly landlines and answering machines. I remember Franklin got a call on his direct line about a time change for an urgent meeting. He had me calling all over, trying to reach Mr. Ives. I didn't think much of it at the time. Mr. Ives was a busy man and could have been in Sacramento for all I knew. I came back from lunch, and Franklin wasn't in his office. I thought maybe he'd found Mr. Ives and had gone to the meeting."

Donna turned away from the phone and argued with Marge some more. Her aunt apparently took the phone from her because she spoke next. "Aaron had a company truck with the name of the mining company on it. I'd see him drive it into town past my house every once in a while. But when he wasn't out running around the state in someone's limo or plane, he often came back to the ranch in his girlfriend's Jeep. Most of the time, he left the truck parked at Franklin's office for him to use, since Franklin didn't own a car. Looking back now, knowing Aaron didn't die, my guess is that Franklin was the one who drove the company truck out to the mine, not Aaron. The Jeep wasn't there. The truck and its driver didn't leave. Aaron couldn't have had anything to do with the mine collapse or Franklin's disappearance."

Evie wrapped her arm around Jax as he absorbed that information. It had been in the sheriff's report in vague terms, but hearing it said aloud with the names switched. . . There were still holes in the story, but the cairn they found said what evidence could not. Aaron had mourned the death of his partner and disappeared.

"Did you see the company truck drive out to the mine? Did anyone else follow him?" Jax returned to interrogation.

"I *told* the sheriff all that at the time, but he didn't listen. An old brown pick-up with a camper bed followed the company truck out there. The pick-up came back. The mine truck didn't. When I heard the explosion later, I tried calling the ranch and the mine and got no answer. I called Franklin's office, and Donna said Franklin was heading into LA for a meeting with Aaron and Sovereign."

"That's what I told the sheriff," Donna said in the background. "I remember now. That was on his office schedule. That's why I thought he was in a meeting."

Holding the phone with one hand, Jax squeezed Evie with the other. "But the sheriff must have reached Franklin at some point, didn't he? Someone had to be questioned or notified?"

Marge scoffed. "The sheriff called the mine inspection people. Aaron's truck was there. They found explosives in it. The inspection people said they reached Franklin, that he was out of state on business, but he verified that Aaron would be the only person in the mine since they were closing it."

"And they accepted that?" Jax asked, not hiding his incredulity. "They didn't ask Franklin to come in and give testimony of any sort?"

"Not for an accident," Marge said derisively. "Especially if strings get pulled."

Donna came back, her voice tentative. "The brown truck Marge saw? Gus's real estate company owned one just like it. Their hired day laborers used it to fix up properties. Once the sheriff questioned Gus, he closed the case. I don't know what Gus told them, I really don't. I just assumed he'd sent someone out to help Mr. Ives close up the mine entrance and then there was some kind of bad accident after they left. Mr. Franklin called the office a few days later, asking me to run some errands and close everything down. He didn't sound like himself, but I figured, y'know, that he was taking Mr. Ives' death hard, like maybe he'd lost a wife, y'know? I don't know how those things work."

From the floor, Reuben snorted and coughed.

Donna continued with a sniff. "But I thought I was talking to Franklin, and that he was alive and mourning his friend."

"Did she take the box of documents to the bank?" Evie whispered.

"We found a document file in a safety deposit box under Franklin's name," Jax said. "Records show it was put in there after the death of Aaron Ives. Do you know anything about that?"

Only a slight lie—Uncle Orbis had mentioned someone grieving had put the papers in the box. The bank didn't have any records that old. Jax was fishing.

"Oh, that was one of the errands!" Donna brightened. "I forgot about that. I did all Franklin's banking business. I had his box keys and was on the signature card. He told me he'd gathered up Mr. Ives' personal effects and put them in a file on his desk and asked me to put it in his personal deposit box and told me where the key was. The bank didn't argue too hard as long as I had the key and they knew me and the tragedy and all. I mean, we all figured Mr. Jackson would be back."

"But then he sold the law office to Pendleton and closed down the company he shared with Aaron Ives and you never saw him again?" Jax finished for her.

Evie suspected a good interrogator did not lead the witness but he'd had about as much as he could tolerate. She covered the hand around her waist and squeezed. They were wrapped together tighter than a pretzel, and along with the relief Jax must be feeling, the closeness felt danged good.

"I was heartbroken that he never came back to the office, but Teddy's grandmother was in town, and she's kind of a big deal, so I . . ."

"Teddy's grandmother?" Evie poked Jax to wake him up.

Jax poked her back. "Teddy's grandmother is Mrs. Swenson, isn't it? Gus's mother? Did she often visit?"

"What difference does that make? I thought you just wanted to know about your father. I have to go now. I've told you all I know."

Evie mock whistled. Even Roark and Reuben went on red alert. When the dense men seemed blindsided by this crass evasion after Donna's earlier honesty, Evie pulled out the tricks she'd learned at her mother's knee. She leaned closer to the phone. "Oh, are we talking about Senator Swenson's family? Don't you just love them? Such good people. And your son is related to them? You know his family is a big deal in these parts. I hear they throw fabulous birthday parties. Did they ever have a big bash for Teddy?"

Donna sniffed. "Of course not. We're divorced, and once that bitch got her hooks in Gus, her kids got all the attention. But Grandma Swenson is fond of Teddy. He's the only one who has to work for a living, and he's following his daddy into politics. She's promised to leave him an inheritance even if every-thing else is tied up in a trust. Teddy can run for the senate just like his daddy if he has enough money behind him. That should let Gus see he should be paying a little more attention to his firstborn."

Evie gave a thumb's up and grinned at Jax, who was frowning hard now. He gestured for her to continue. Where did he want to go with that? The mine. The Swensons. Mama in town. . . "I thought since you said Mrs. Swenson was in town, that she and Gus might have been throwing one of those fabulous parties for Teddy, but I guess he was still little then, wasn't he?"

"He was seven. Gus had remarried, but he was still in Bolder. Mrs. Swenson insisted that they take Teddy out for a steak. Gus gave him a bike that was too big. But Mrs. Swenson gave him some folding cash. They've always been close. It's been nice talking to you. I gotta go now."

Marge came back on. "Mr. Oswin here says the DNA is enough to prove you're Aaron's son. You gonna do anything with this land? It has potential. I've been leasing it for a couple of oil wells. A lot of quartz and crystal back in there, probably a little gold. Not great for cattle, I imagine, and the cabin burned some time back. Vagrants."

"I thank you for keeping the taxes paid," Jax said, recovering. "You could have let it be foreclosed on and snapped it up for nothing, I imagine."

Marge scoffed. "I thought it was your daddy in that mountain. I'm old. I don't need more land. But I kinda miss having a little bit of family around. Donna has her son and stays in town most times. I'm glad to learn that Aaron made it out and had a family. I'm just real sorry to hear that he didn't get a chance to live up to all that potential."

Evie watched the light go off on her phone. Ariel had hung up. She wiggled the phone at Roark, who tuned in to the security cameras at Ariel's place. He shrugged, apparently not seeing anything. While Jax worked out legal details with Mr. Oswin and Marge, Evie kissed his cheek and crossed the cellar to check Roark's screen.

"Unless you want Ariel flying off to California and taking up ranching, maybe someone ought to go out there tonight and keep her company," Evie whispered to the Cajun.

Roark rubbed his nose and watched as a slender figure emerged from the front door of Ariel's cottage to leave lettuce beside the turtle house. The turtle didn't acknowledge the offering. "Yup, maybe someone ought to see she's all right. I can park under that security light. It's pretty big news knowing your daddy had all that and lost it."

"It's looking more and more like those Sovereign contracts might be why Franklin Jackson died. If Jax keeps digging into those contracts, he's likely to stir the hornets again, if he hasn't already." Evie worriedly watched Ariel slip back inside. She was heir to the ranch and the mining company and the patent to those voting machines, just as Jax was.

"Teddy Swenson was too young to have blown up a mine," Roark reminded her.

"But Gus wasn't. Like father, like son? It's hard to imagine a US senator killing anyone, but they're both here in the East now, not back in California where they belong. If they're dangerous. . ."

Roark pocketed his keys, signaled Reuben, and left the cellar.

Rather than follow, the professor took over Roark's gaming chair and began typing into the computer. The printer began spitting out papers.

By the time Jax got off the phone, Evie was studying the photos and documents emerging from the printer. Jax took the stack. Reuben handed him a roll of duct tape while continuing to type one-handed.

These men didn't *need* to talk. They'd worked together so tightly that they communicated by signals she couldn't follow.

She had to stand on tip-toes to see what Jax taped to the wall. First was a real estate ad from nearly forty years ago of the now-elderly Mrs. Swenson as she must have looked when she was in her forties—a large, stylish woman concealing her age with the best cosmetic surgery Hollywood could buy. Included in the ad was her eldest son, Augustus, now a senator but still a Realtor at the time. Tall, blond, good-looking in a rough, lumberjack way, he'd probably sell on his looks alone. His son Teddy may not have been born at this point.

Off to one side, Jax taped the old photo they'd found of Aaron Ives and Franklin Jackson from that same period, when they were just starting. He added another of the Sovereign Machine company sign and town council cutting a ribbon—his history taped to a cellar wall.

Next to those, Jax posted a wad of paper. Evie glanced at the top page—the contract between the Franklin-Ives Microchip Company and Sovereign, the one Jax had said reserved the right for Franklin-Ives to end the agreement for just cause—like fixing voting machines. That contract might have ended Franklin's life and Aaron's business, while Sovereign kept on chugging for a few more years. Someone—Aaron disguised as Franklin?—had reported the fraud and the feds had run with it. It had taken years to put the nails in Sovereign's coffin, but Aaron Ives had his revenge before he died.

Next level down apparently represented a slightly later period. Jax taped a newspaper article about Gus Swenson winning a local election, then one about the mine explosion and an obituary for Aaron Ives. Next to it, he taped a small squib from a local newspaper announcing Pendleton's purchase of the Franklin law office and another local article about Sovereign buying out the Franklin-Ives Microchip Company—from Ives posing as Jackson?

After that came what appeared to be a front-page article about Sovereign increasing production for a huge sale to LA county of the newfangled electronic machines, crowing about hiring more workers. Nice spin job. Most voters would be wary of the machines, but supporting local economy. . . She hoped to make that work for Ward.

Jax started a third level with a big headline about Augustus Swenson winning the election for state senate—several years after Sovereign had been selling the voting machines all over the state.

And he was only halfway through the stack that Reuben was printing.

This could go on all night. Evie could see where it was heading: the closing of Sovereign twenty years ago after being indicted for vote fraud, the creation of DVM from the ashes, ultimately followed by the death of Jax's parents. Swenson's election to the US Senate would fall right in after that.

The connections were coming together.

The evidence was not. Five people died tragically over a period of thirty years without a single shred of evidence to show why or how or who had done it.

Twenty-Two

AFTER SPENDING HALF THE NIGHT CREATING A WALL OF SUSPECTS AND circumstantial evidence, Jax spent the better part of Sunday making phone calls from his downtown office—with his newly installed locks in place. Burning rage and the need for justice seared his soul. He avoided Loretta for fear she'd say his innards looked like a twisted fiery bubble.

He was avoiding Evie, too. She'd kept him grounded last night when he thought he might explode like the Hindenburg. He'd wanted nothing more than to take comfort in her arms, but he didn't have the luxury of seeking comfort while his father's killer still ran amuck.

Now that he was fully convinced voting machine fraud was the motivation, his list of suspects had become clearer, even if ridiculously improbable, if not impossible.

His cell rang. He checked the caller and turned it off. This was his problem. Evie couldn't solve it. She needed to look after Loretta.

He pulled out a legal pad and began drawing a schematic.

A knock on his door sometime later shattered his concentration. He checked the camera R&R had installed—*Evie*. He'd give her credit for persistence, but he wasn't involving her in what might come down to a firefight.

Could he prove Senator Swenson had been in Savannah the night Jax's parents lost their lives? That would give Gus the opportunity for murdering both partners, a continent and a decade apart.

He circled the senator's name and began drawing connections. He was too lost in thought to hear the lock click—but it must have. Fresh air and the scent of ylang-ylang yanked his head up.

Wearing an almost somber turquoise short set, probably from the fifties, Evie tucked a set of keys in her back pocket as she swung into his private office. Jax almost swallowed his tongue.

"Don't do that to me," he said crossly, tearing his gaze from shapely legs and Angelina Jolie curves. "You've shattered my concentration."

"Good. Then I don't have to take a frying pan to your thick head." She curled up in the Morris chair. "Roark's babysitting Ariel. Reuben is digging an internet hole to China. And you're figuring out how to set yourself up as a target. Tell me I'm wrong."

She wasn't. He just hadn't worked out how to do it yet. "I can't set myself up as target with suspects on two coasts."

She made a rude noise. "Teddy Swenson has been on both coasts at the same time we were."

"Teddy wasn't old enough to kill Franklin Jackson. He had no reason to kill my parents if this is about voting machine fraud. He was barely out of college and hadn't been elected to anything then. His father might be involved in fraud, but Gus had no reason to kill Clancy or Pendleton, even if we could prove he was on both coasts at the right times."

"So you figure the motivation for killing your parents and Jackson was Sovereign's voting machines? Maybe Clancy and Pendleton knew something about that?"

He should really resist pulling Evie into this, but as a sounding board. . . She sure beat the hell out of basement walls. "If the new machines were still using the faulty circuit board, vote fraud might be a motivation for the Swensons, but neither Pendleton nor Clancy were involved in their manufacture."

"But Clancy was running for office and apparently knew about the fix," she reminded him.

Jax grimaced. "Maybe Clancy was blackmailing Gus over the crooked machines? Still unlikely that a US Senator would commit murder. He's too visible. I can see Teddy maybe, but he was only seven at the time of the mine incident."

"Two different killers?" she suggested. "Or were the early ones really accidents? Except Clancy's ghost said he murdered *someone*, possibly at the behest of a female."

If one believed in ghosts. . . "Not many females in this scenario, unless we count Bernice. Or maybe Larraine Ward out of sheer irritation if she learned about the machines."

Evie snorted and waved away those suggestions. "Teddy's mother Donna and her Aunt Marge may not have told you everything—or even told you the truth. They were west coast and could easily have killed Pendleton."

"Kinda hard seeing a connection between them and Clancy and my parents on the east coast—unless, of course, they knew Aaron Ives escaped. Could one of them have been covering up Gus's tracks?" Restlessly, Jax rocked back in his chair, his pen and paper forgotten. Watching Evie frown focused him.

"Clancy was old enough to kill everyone on the list—so maybe his death really was suicide if he thought his ill deeds had caught up with him?"

"He went into anaphylactic shock and killed himself? Uh uh. I can buy Clancy being murdered for local reasons, maybe. But the voting machines and the Swenson connection are an ugly coincidence we can't ignore."

Evie leaned forward, offering glimpses of temptation. "Even Geoff Hayes and Hank Williams had connections to the Swensons. The ripples keep spreading."

"But they had nothing to do with decades-old deaths, and listening to a ghost is a real long shot. I need concrete evidence before I can convince Sheriff Troy to call in the feds to even *start* investigating a presidential candidate. Even then, I doubt Troy can pry the senator's itinerary out of a host of bodyguards and assistants. That requires the feds—and at least a tie-in to the murder weapons."

"OK, are there any similarities in the murder weapons?"

Jax called up the latest report Roark had siphoned from the sheriff's files. "Pendleton was shot with a .22, just like Clancy. The guns were found at the scene and had no registration or license. There is no correlation with the presumably accidental deaths of my parents and Franklin Jackson—other than the voting machines and Swenson."

Evie swirled her finger at his computer. "R&R spent the night analyzing close elections in towns using DVM machines. Check the files. Reuben says they have a list of elected officials who may have benefitted from voter fraud. They compared it to the list of investors in Sovereign and DVM. The Swensons are the most obvious, but there are a dozen others and more they probably don't know about. Tracking all of them. . .

"Isn't happening," Jax agreed, glaring at the list he'd called up. He created a file of the most pertinent material and emailed it to Sheriff Troy.

"Any way we can lure our list of suspects into Clancy's presence?" his nemesis suggested with an almost evil gleam in her eye.

Shit. He'd known it would come down to this. "We're talking *killers*, Evangeline Malcolm Carstairs. Killers. *No*, there's no chance."

"You don't want to see if Clancy will try to strangle his killer? C'mon, Jax, I'm safe." She puckered up her nose. "You might not be."

That did it. She was protecting him? "My father's patents. We'll offer them for sale and use Clancy's haunted office for the meeting."

Evie jumped up and threw herself in his lap. He hugged her, then whispered in her ear, "Except if we're setting me up as a target, we'll both have to stay out of sight until all the bad guys are in one place. Clear Loretta out of the house and stay with your family."

EVIE WATCHED R&R LOAD UP THEIR VAN AND HEAD DOWNTOWN TO JAX'S OFFICE. She hoped one of them would drive on to stay near Ariel.

She'd thought about raising hell over his protective demands, but Jax had agreed she could meet him at city hall Monday night. He just needed his macho thing of protecting the *weak*. Since she had no purpose beyond talking to ghosts, this almost made sense. She didn't have to like it, but she could do it. That he thought *she* could protect Loretta was probably his idea of respecting her talents.

It didn't take much effort or talent to round up her family, warn them of danger, and circle Gracie's house with Malcolm abilities. Iddy's raven watched outside. Psycat strolled the rooms of the tiny cottage, sniffing out trouble and maybe a few mice. Pris chose to watch from the cottage's unfinished attic, which was sweltering in the June heat. Evie brought her buckets of ice and lots of fans. Her freaky cousin had zoned out and barely noticed.

Mavis and the aunts took turns staying awake through the night to monitor whatever wavelengths worked best for them. Evie was fairly certain Pris's mother had a police radio frequency along with her more psychic talents. And Mavis had her telephone gossip circle who could be monitoring the entire town, for all Evie knew. Her mother had the ability to summon an entire parade of townspeople at times of need, but this didn't appear to be one of them.

She hated the idea of Jax setting himself up as a target, but she hated the idea of a killer running loose even more. As owners of the patents of the microchip used by the voting machine company, he and Ariel might already be targets. DVM probably owed them a fortune in royalties. If Jax chose to reveal the PCB flaw and software manipulation that Reuben had documented, he could destroy the careers of some very powerful—and not particularly moral—people.

She tried to look cheerful and not fret while she taught Loretta the board games the child's parents had never allowed her to play. Gracie had a/c, so Evie even baked cookies to channel her spinning thoughts more productively.

Monday, after supper, she tossed her niece, Aster, and Loretta into a wild game of Twister while she ran back to the house to prepare for whatever Jax had planned. Her family was more than capable of looking after the kids.

It was stupid, macho Jax she worried about. As her thoughts had percolated all day, she'd realized this killer wasn't into well-planned murder. They reacted to circumstance. They threw dynamite down a mine, drove a car off a road, whacked old men at their desks. . . Well, Clancy's death had required peanuts but not much else.

She was counting on this lack of thought to hope the killer didn't even know Ariel or Loretta or anyone else existed. He or she would be focused on *Jax*. His military intelligence had probably worked that out too, damn the man. If he kept her out of this gathering. . .

They were having a come to Jesus meeting.

Monday evening, in the lingering summer light, Evie biked straight down Main Street where everyone could see her. No car tried to run her over. She considered that a positive sign.

The sheriff's car was parked in front of city hall, in a space reserved for council members. Jax's Harley was here. So was R&R's van, illegally usurping the mayor's space. There was a fancy black Cadillac with dark windows concealing anyone inside and a bright pink Escalade emblazoned with Ward's campaign logo. She laughed at that. If Larraine was here, this might be fun.

So far, she saw no sign that Jax meant to exclude her.

She locked her bike to Jax's Harley. He wouldn't appreciate that, but she wasn't having him driving off into the sunset again. Maybe California had been necessary, but he had responsibilities now. And she wanted his respect, even if she couldn't get it from anyone else. That ghost was going to dance tonight.

To Evie's surprise, Bernice opened the outer door. The stout older woman had worked in the mayor's office these last ten years or more. She ratted her gray hair to make it look fuller and probably used a filler to puff out the frizzy french roll in back. Evie had never seen her with any expression other than a mild frown of disapproval. Tonight wasn't any different.

"I hope they're paying you overtime, Bernice. How's your mother?" Evie sauntered into the air-conditioned lobby. Behind the reception desk, the window blinds had been pulled on the office where they were meeting. The cold draft warned Clancy's spirit was still around and agitated.

"Mr. Jackson-Ives said he'd reimburse me for my time. It's the most I could do for poor Mr. Clancy." Spine stiff as a flagpole, she led Evie to the office door. "My mother is unlikely to recover. We're bringing her home for hospice care."

"Oh, I'm so sorry, Bernice. You know my family will help out in any way you need. You just have to let us know."

"I'll keep that in mind, thank you. Your mother's always been good to us. You're the last to arrive. I think I put out enough chairs."

She was expected! Satisfaction settled over her like a warm blanket, keeping her warm even after Bernice opened the office door to a blast of frigid air.

More heads than Evie expected swiveled at her entrance. Confident that Jax wanted her here, she waved merrily at Geoff the CPA and Hank from the hardware, who'd probably both walked over from work. Larraine gave her a big grin and pointed at her pink cowboy hat with her logo on it. Evie gave her a thumbs up before studying the only outsider in the room—Ted Swenson. Wasn't he supposed to have left town?

Senator Gus was a no-show, dang. Given that Jax was offering up his patents, it was interesting that none of the owners of DVM had shown up. Maybe Teddy acted for them.

Bernice picked up a digital notepad on a chair out of the action and sat down.

Jax sat in the back corner with the flagpole, behind Sheriff Troy at the desk. Evie wiggled her fingers at both of them and slid into the last chair against the wall beside Bernice, sort of behind everyone else. She settled back and opened her third eye to find Clancy. His aura was twirling like a red tornado and bouncing back and forth with no direction.

The sheriff continued speaking. "I called you here because we have a problem. With no mayor and no county attorney to provide advice, you gentlemen will have to give us direction on what to do about the voting machines that have been removed from the city's possession."

"I don't see the problem, Sheriff." Swenson took command, as one would wish a leader to do. He was still pudgy and rumpled but didn't appear fazed by the impromptu meeting. "Our contract specifies that the machines will be removed after ten years. Software updates require hardware updates after that period of time. We built in a replacement clause to cover those circumstances. The council merely needs to vote to invoke it or look elsewhere for their devices."

Clancy's ghost swirled, giving off sparks Evie interpreted as confusion and anger. He wasn't flinging anything yet.

The sheriff handed out stapled papers. "Hank, you're current chair of the council and, like Ms. Ward here, will be affected by the outcome of this decision when the mayoral election rolls around. I want everyone to be on the same page."

Hank and Geoff looked a little shocked at whatever they'd been handed. Evie checked auras. Guilt and confusion colored Geoff's. Uh oh.

The sheriff continued explaining. "If you'll look at the underlined paragraph, you can see that the contract Mayor Block signed, and the council approved, there is nothing about physically removing the machines. I had the county judge read this, and he assures me that the county owns them outright. Now, if the council *voted* to have DVM remove the machines, then as chair, Clancy was well within his rights to act on the council vote. But there is nothing in the minutes pertaining to trading in the machines."

The red tornado swirled in agitation. Wind ruffled papers around the room.

In Evie's head, the ghost's fury came through loud and clear: *He said he'd fix them for me and no one would know if I just signed the release! He never meant to help, bastards and bitches, all of them!*

OK, here's where it got awkward. Evie had learned from a very young age that she couldn't talk to a ghost in front of a roomful of nonbelievers without seeming crazy. No one listened to crazy people—which was why she got no respect. If she was to use her talent responsibly, she had to think this through and behave rationally—even if she wanted to yank all their chains.

Taking a deep breath, she focused on Geoff and Hank. They were still grayer and murkier than usual. The contract had disturbed them—because they thought all the copies had been destroyed? They'd certainly done their best to find out.

Geoff had been with Clancy right before he died. So had Bernice. She glanced in the secretary's direction. No guilt but a shade of. . . uncertainty? Bernice wasn't as domineering as she liked to pretend.

Okay, here's where she behaved like a responsible citizen. Evie raised her hand, and the sheriff nodded at her. Good ol' Troy.

Instead of speaking to him, she looked at Jax's landlord, the accountant who had wanted Clancy's investment clients. "Geoff, what did Clancy want you to do in return for sending you his clients?"

She hid a smug look as Jax raised his eyebrows at this seemingly unrelated direction.

Geoff tugged at his collar. He must have removed his usual tie after work.

When the accountant didn't reply, Troy spoke sternly. "Geoff, removing voting machines could be a federal matter. If you and Clancy had something going on, you'd best clear the air now."

Geoff threw an anxious glance at Ted Swenson, but Fearless Leader merely looked bored. Apparently stonewalling was a requirement for being a politician.

The CPA nervously tugged at his non-existent tie. "Clancy more or less said what Mr. Swenson just said. I didn't have the contract to read, but I believed him. It's standard operating procedure to remove hardware when it can no longer be supported. Clancy said as a candidate, he couldn't bring the matter up with the council. Hank and I go way back, but Hank and Clancy never got along. He wanted me to approach Hank about signing the removal order."

Evie waved her hand again, and the sheriff nodded for her to speak. "Please, Geoff, don't ruin your reputation for a dead man who didn't deserve your friendship. You're not telling the sheriff everything."

Swenson frowned at her, probably trying to figure out who she was. Or maybe why she looked familiar, if his memory was long enough to remember the bank in California. Her hair did tend to be a tad bit memorable. But he remained impervious.

Geoff glanced at Hank, who gestured irritably. Neither man admitted anything.

The ghost was practically hopping up and down in frustration, then blowing around Bernice and muttering. Evie sighed. If she had any brains, she'd learn paranormal psychoanalysis. "Bernice, weren't you there when Geoff and Clancy were talking? Maybe you can refresh Geoff's memory?"

Geoff reddened. Given permission to speak, Bernice scrolled through her digital notebook.

With the voice of someone reading minutes, she read, "Mr. Clancy wants all copies of the DVM contract. He said we should be receiving an email from DVM authorizing the removal of their machines. Mr. Williams is to present the agreement at the next council meeting. Mr. Hayes is to guarantee the necessary votes for the purchase of new machines at a discounted rate after trade-in and install the software updates once they arrive."

The updates that would have put Clancy's name on the winning side of the faulty machines? Or so Clancy had thought, until someone killed him for believing that. *Ugly*.

"That sounds perfectly straightforward." The sheriff looked puzzled. "Except the contract doesn't allow for any of that. And guaranteeing the purchase in advance without bids from other companies sounds off."

Geoff exhaled. "That's how the council does business. Faster, more efficient, if I go around and ask each member what they need for their vote. Since I'm not on the council, I'm an uninterested third party. I'm good at negotiating. Clancy is good at selling. Between us, we get things done. We needed new machines before the election. There wasn't time to ask for bids."

"You ain't ever promised *me* anything," Hank growled.

"Because you're a reasonable man and want what's best for the town," Geoff said reassuringly.

Evie mentally added, *because Hank always voted with the majority*. It was good for business.

The sheriff frowned. "So Clancy sold you a bill of goods about the machines. Mr. Swenson here had the machines removed based on Clancy's approval. And none of you so much as looked at the contract to see if it was legal?"

Clancy's outraged spirit lowered the room's temperature until even the jacket-clad men shivered. But all Evie heard in her head was muttered obscenities—because his fraud had been caught out?

Bernice's irritated aura attracted Evie's ever-distractible interest. "Bernice, what about you? Did you read the contract?"

The older woman looked taken aback at being addressed on council business. When the sheriff waited for her to speak, she replied hesitantly. "Mr.

Clancy was in a bit of a mood after Ms. Ward declared her candidacy. He made a lot of calls and told me to find the contract with DVM about the voting machines. I don't have all the mayor's files, and he wasn't available, so I found a copy in the computer and sent it to Mr. Clancy. It's public information, so I saw nothing wrong in that."

"Did you read it?" Evie asked again, because it was obvious to her that Bernice was holding back.

The secretary nodded. "I usually do, so I can summarize for the council members. This was early in the morning, not at the meeting with Mr. Hayes. I told Mr. Clancy that according to the contract, it was time for the city to trade in or buy new machines. I believe he was on the phone with the DVM office at the time. He repeated what I told him, then started yelling about Mr. Jackson-Ives looking like another Mr. Jackson, that it meant trouble, and then he gestured for me to leave."

Bernice hesitated another fraction, took a breath, and added, "I don't like making personal, unsubstantiated comments." She glanced at the sheriff, who encouraged her with a nod. "Mr. Clancy didn't look well that morning. He's often angry, but. . . He was worried and not quite himself. Under his anger. . . I don't know. He was afraid?"

She glanced uncertainly at Jax. "His voice raised an octave when he talked about Mr. Jackson-Ives."

Jax didn't move a muscle, simply flipped through a file, apparently awaiting his turn.

Clancy's aura slowly swung in the direction Bernice was looking—at Jax. The ghost began to burn redder. *You! You did this! Just like that other troublemaker. . .*

The lights flickered. Evie frantically processed the accusation no one could hear but her.

Clancy had sold investments to Stockton and Stockton twenty years ago. He'd *known* Jax's father while he was alive. Was Jax's father the *troublemaker*? Of course he was.

Facts, Evie. Focus.

"But you returned later to ask Clancy about time off." Unable to hear a ghost, the sheriff prompted Bernice. "Did you overhear what he was saying to Geoff?"

Bernice raised her chin. "The things Mr. Clancy said weren't right. He was telling Mr. Hayes that the contract allowed the machines to be removed, which was a lie. He said Mr. Jackson-Ives had framed the mayor, which is another lie. Mayor Block stole my mother's lot in the trailer park just like he stole from Evangeline's family. We exchanged words, and Mr. Clancy told me to leave or he'd have me fired. So I did."

Bernice was a large woman. . . She knew about the office cat. . . Evie shook her head. She couldn't believe the older woman carried a .22—and peanuts?—in her pocket, no matter how heated the argument got. And Bernice's aura didn't reflect muddy guilt the way the others did.

Geoff shrugged and intruded when the secretary fell silent. "Clancy was always hot under the collar about something. He accused me of bringing in Jax to put him out of office so I could step in. I don't know where that came from. I'm not a politician. I work better behind the scenes. Bernice left in a huff, said she had to visit her mother. Clancy yelled at her 'to go away and stay away.'"

"What happened after she left?" Troy asked.

Geoff shook his head. "He was ranting. He told me the Swensons owed him, and if buying new machines was what it took to get elected, he'd make it happen. I didn't know what he meant except that Clancy liked flaunting his influential connections. The machines do need replacing, and he was alive when I left him."

Clancy's ghost flared in red rage and a thumb drive flew off the desk, smacking Geoff in the middle of his forehead. Geoff's aura colored with guilt.

Evie sighed in exasperation, seizing this opportunity to speak. "It was you who wiped out Clancy's computer, wasn't it? You needed the DVM contract, why? And don't lie, Geoff. I can read you like a book." She felt the men staring at her, but she focused on poor readable Geoff, who'd been trying to find that contract in Jax's office. It wasn't a great leap of logic.

Geoff reddened.

Hank glared at him. "You listened to that little twerp over there, didn't you?" He nodded at Swenson. "What did he promise if you found that contract?"

"Your election," Geoff whispered back.

Larraine briefly frowned, then apparently remembering that caused frown lines, she returned to benevolently observing.

The silence forced Geoff to continue. "Swenson has *contacts*. He promised he'd owe me. I didn't think it was a big deal. The contract was public record, even if the mayor had it squirreled away. At the time, I thought there wasn't any reason Clancy's suicide should prevent us from benefitting from Swenson's contacts. Without Clancy, Afterthought needs a new source of influence."

But he'd dropped the ball—the thumb drive—and blown his opportunity. That was Geoff all over.

"Well, that explains a few things." The sheriff glared at all of them. "I ought to haul the whole lot of you in."

Teddy scowled but continued looking down his nose and saying nothing. Even his aura reflected a dirty brown and gray over a dark blue-green—an unhealthy personality but a killer? She couldn't say.

Hank glared at Jax. "What's your part in this, Mr. Fancy Attorney? Dot brought me that letter about someone named Jackson suing a voting machine company." He glanced at Evie. "Said she found it on Evie's counter. There's more to this story."

Poor Dot, trying her best to win over a potential mayor. Maybe Hank wasn't quite as dumb as he looked.

Jax leaned forward and tapped the sheriff on his shoulder. Troy nodded and moved his chair back to the wall so Jax could take the desk.

Beside her, Bernice straightened as if ready to take meeting minutes. Jax had that effect.

Evie had hoped the ghost would be focused on his killer by now. Instead, Clancy was muttering and spinning furiously around Jax so that he had to hold his papers down. If ghosts could kill. . . Evie held her breath, not knowing if she should shout a warning.

"Thank you for meeting with us, gentlemen. We'll get down to the reason I asked you to attend. I am the current owner of the microchip used by DVM in their machines. I'm also in possession of a document recently filed with the federal voting commission claiming those machines are rigged in collusion with the parties responsible for assigning ballot positions. I will be filing suit for the return of my father's patent rights, as he would have done had he not been killed."

Reuben had been busy if he'd already filed that thesis he'd been working on. And using the word *killed* instead of *died*. . . Evie winced and waited for the explosion.

Teddy Swenson's aura darkened to an ugly shade of mottled gray. He rose and shoved his chair back. "I will be talking to our attorneys. You cannot make accusations like that without consequences."

Clancy turned a fiery red. *Consequences, you little shit! Talk to your daddy about consequences!*

The lights blew out and all the computer screens went black—even the battery-operated ones.

The security alarms shrieked on full alert. Bernice screamed in terror and tumbled off her chair.

Over the racket, the sheriff shouted, "I'll be turning Afterthought's machines over to the feds. The lot of you may want to start talking to your lawyers."

Twenty-three

JAX LOCATED EVIE FIRST, IN A CORNER OF THE PITCH-BLACK OFFICE, AND BLOCKED her from the others. She stood behind him, arms crossed, muttering—presumably at Clancy's ghost. It would be perfect if she could persuade a name out of the bastard, but Jax didn't hold out hopes. They'd stirred up all the trouble they could this evening, and neither of them had accomplished anything—except shooting out the electricity again and nearly draining most of the batteries in the room. Ghostly energy?

"Well, that was highly unsatisfactory if revelatory." In total darkness, with the alarms still screaming, Larraine Ward sounded miffed.

Jax had to agree.

Sensing Evie needed privacy, he remained in front of her, keeping an eye—or an ear—on the others. Geoff was on the phone with city hall's security. Hank had reached an electrician before cursing as his phone died. After giving up on his cell, the sheriff had radioed paramedics for Bernice, who was already recovering and protesting she didn't need help.

All officials proceeding as they ought, not one of them behaving like a killer. Of course, Swenson had left the room—to warn his senator father? Teddy might be a state representative, but he was still the poor working Swenson. He didn't have a trust fund to invest in DVM. He was apparently just a stooge for others.

"The next election may be by paper ballot. Hope that doesn't hurt your chances any," Jax responded to Ward. He could smell her perfume close by.

"I'll have my lawyer look up voting by mail. But you'd better watch your back. What happens if the feds prove Swenson and others were voted in by fraud?" Ward sounded more amused now. He could tell she was waving her frilly pink cowboy hat like a fan. The air conditioning had gone off with the lights.

The frigid pocket of air abruptly disappeared. Jax glanced over his shoulder. Evie was rigid and radiating a cold light all her own.

"They'll all be voted out before the suit ever reaches court," Jax predicted, keeping an eye on Evie.

Ward followed his gaze. "She's talking to the spirits, isn't she? I wonder what her aura looks like."

"Crushed, at the moment, I suspect. She hoped Clancy's ghost would point out his killer." Jax would never have said that to the sheriff, but for some reason, he figured Ward understood.

"Huh, wonder if they hired a hitman? Like I said, watch your back. I'm gonna talk to that smart Bernice. She seems like she knows a thing or two." Ward swayed off.

Jax noted the second Evie started to slump and caught her just as the lights returned.

"He's gone?" he murmured, holding her up while the others cursed and began making more calls.

"Ghosts are not reliable witnesses," she muttered back. "He shrieked about the sins of the parents being visited on the sons and other inanities. I'm convinced spirit energy is little more than shades of a person's most intense memories and emotions. I think I've sent him on."

Judging by the lack of cold draft, she was right. Almost a pity. Clancy had provided free a/c there for a while.

"Let's get the hell out, then. All we've done is uncover an incompetent burglar, a crooked salesman, and insured those machines won't be used again." Once he was certain he wouldn't have to carry her, Jax led Evie out to his motorcycle—where she'd locked it to her bike.

"Where did Roark go?" she asked, not disentangling their wheels.

The utility van was gone. "They were just monitoring the vicinity to be certain we didn't have any uninvited guests." Jax checked his phone. The battery was low but he could pick up Roark's text. He showed it to her.

"They've got the whole scene on video. I don't think we'll get any earthshaking charges out of this."

"And a killer or two is still on the loose. Is it even safe to go home?" Evie clung wearily to him.

"Excellent question. Let's leave the bikes here and walk over to my office." Too buzzed to settle down, Jax didn't want to wrangle with locks or figure out where to go next.

"If you think we'll have another dance on the Morris chair, forget it. I'm wiped. I'll be asleep in seconds." Evie leaned heavily into him as they strolled across the street and past the courthouse.

"I put in a stock of supplies while I was holed up. Sugar or alcohol?" Holding Evie like this, Jax recognized more than the pull of lust. Sure, he'd hoped for another tango on the ancient chair, but after tonight, he owed Evie the respect of taking her out to dinner, at the very least.

If it hadn't been for her, he'd still be wallowing in confusion. Tonight, she'd pushed some of his suspects over the edge and cleared up a few dangling threads.

Maybe he should take her back to California and see what she could do there.

"Sugar. My brains are already fried. They don't need pickling, too." She slumped in his arms as they reached the lobby, causing panic.

"Do I need to worry about low blood sugar and emergency rooms?" He scooped her up and hurried up to his office.

She snuggled against him. "Explain that I just sent a cranky spirit to hell? Probably not."

"Yeah, God complexes are frowned upon by medical sorts." Not bothering to work out the implications of Evie's impossible statement, Jax managed to unlock the door, kick it shut, carry her through the outer office, and drop her in the plush leather chair. His pulse rate didn't drop as he crossed to his desk.

She snorted inelegantly. "Do you think stubborn idiots argue with God at the pearly gates? Arguing with hell hounds probably isn't any more productive. Clancy should have been a lawyer."

"Nah, he was probably just trying to intimidate you. You got nothing out of him?" He couldn't believe he'd just asked that. She really had him running hot.

Jax rummaged in the computer desk and produced a bottle of bourbon and a box of cookies. He needed the bourbon to counteract his admission that she just might have sent a ghost to hell. Her insights this evening had been more than peculiar. And the electrical energy. . . Big Weird. But he worried more about how it affected her physically. He kept an eye on her while he poured water into his new coffee machine.

Apparently not about to faint, Evie grabbed a handful of cookies and talked through a mouthful. "All I got was pure emotion—fury, regret, a desire for revenge, jealousy. He spiraled out of control. He's probably been out of control for a while now, especially if he killed your parents in hopes of being governor someday."

"Where the hell did that come from?" Jax sipped his bourbon and paced, fitting that suggestion into his theories. It almost made sense.

She finished chewing and shrugged. "I'll remind you of Clancy's words— *'The bitch! She promised me. She said I'd be governor. Lies! He'll be president! I should be governor.'* Then he went on to add *'I was good enough to* kill *for them but not to marry them!'*"

Jax winced. He'd been more concerned about concrete facts and hadn't taken ghostly ranting too seriously. "You're trying to make whole cloth out of loose threads."

Evie nibbled another cookie. "Well, yeah. That's what I do. Clancy lived in Savannah, knew your parents, and knew the Swensons. He was ambitious. So were they. If they learned your father was going after the newly formed DVM. . ." She straightened abruptly. "The partners at Stockton and Stockton found out that your father was Aaron Ives and fired him! They had him *investi-gated,* why? For the Swensons? There you are. Clancy had buddies at the law firm, knew the Swensons—"

Jax's gut ground as he fixed tea for Evie. It almost made sense. "And one of them promised Clancy their support in a run for office if he'd dispose of the danger to their new voting machines."

"But he said *bitch,* as if it was a woman, not the senator. The one Clancy hoped to marry? Do we know anything about Gus's sisters beyond the fact that they married oil barons?" She looked at him warily as he handed her the cup. "You're actually accepting that I'm not making this up?"

Jax added coffee to his bourbon. "I can't know what you do because it's not an area anyone knows anything about. But that office was freezing until you did whatever you did. Geoff would have stonewalled like Swenson if you hadn't nailed him with guilt. You knew Bernice was holding back when no one else did. It all adds up. I'm just not sure how. You'd have made a great lawyer."

She snorted again and swished her tea, dipping a cookie in it. "All we need are computer chips to implant in my brain so I can access law books without opening them."

"Yeah, there's that. And most generally, lawyers don't physically tackle their opponents by jumping off roofs on them, then nearly maim them with elbows and knees, before attempting to gouge out their eyes." Evie had done all that and more the day they'd met. "We just think about it."

She laughed. "You do more than think about it. You blew up people before settling down to an office. You tackled a gunman just a few months ago. I'm not seeing you as a desk jockey." She seemed to be perking up a little with tea and sugar. "Should we check on Ariel, see if she's okay?"

"Roark will head out there. It will take time before Swenson and DVM get their corporate acts together and attack with lawsuits. I don't think Bernice or Larraine are our guilty parties, so it may be a while before Clancy's killer comes after us. You should probably call your family and let them know where you are, though." Jax sipped his coffee and leaned against his desk. They needed to sort out their next steps, he supposed, as long as sex didn't look like it was in his immediate future.

Evie was actually wearing something besides short shorts, although stretch capris and a tank top did little to disguise her curves. With her orange curls falling in her face, she still looked like a grown-up, sexy Orphan Annie. He could kiss her now that the color was starting to return to her cheeks.

She dug a phone out of her back pocket and glanced at it. "It's almost empty. I swear, ghosts drain batteries."

Yeah, he was starting to think that too.

She punched in a text. Before she hit send, she glanced anxiously at the door.

The outer office door had opened. He'd had arms full of Evie and hadn't locked it behind him.

He didn't have time to open his gun safe. Jax yanked out his phone and located his security app. His battery was nearly dead too. He heard Evie's message swish as she sent her text. The footsteps in reception didn't hesitate or even attempt to be quiet.

Without being told, Evie dropped out of the chair, grabbed her bag of cookies, and crawled beneath his desk. Her steaming mug still sat on the bookshelf beside the chair, should anyone bother to notice.

With his camera revealing the intruder wasn't a masked gunman, Jax didn't cross the room to hide her tea. He remained leaning against the desk, sipping his coffee, as his private office door flew open.

Despite having seen her on his app, he almost dropped his mug at the reality of the crazed fury framed in the doorway.

She was large, broader, and heavier than he was and almost the same height. The heels and towering blond wig added to the illusion of stature. Jax thought her peach-colored gown was probably silk, with the padded shoulders of a prior century. Grandma Swenson could take a few fashion lessons from Larraine Ward.

"Your name isn't Jackson," was the first accusation out of her bright red lips.

"It is on my birth certificate," he said civilly. "And you must be Marilyn Swenson, Teddy's grandmother. Teddy, you can come out from hiding behind your grandmother's skirts. I saw you come in."

Grandma Swenson didn't budge from the doorway. "Clancy told me you existed, but I didn't believe him. Aaron Ives was an incredible pain in the ass. Seems like you're a chip off the old block."

Trained in combat, Jax knew how to slow his pulse and think, but his fear for Evie added an edge he couldn't entirely control. "And we're hard to kill, aren't we?"

Seeing the woman in person pulled the pieces together. He wondered if Evie could see auras from beneath the desk. If he were to hazard a guess, he'd say former real estate mogul and wannabe Hollywood starlet Marilyn Swenson was the power behind the Swenson throne.

"Ives are too damned holier-than-thou, is what they are, and don't tell me you aren't one of them. I could have twisted that pansy lawyer Jackson around my little finger, but your asshole father and his squaw just wouldn't leave well enough alone. He had a damned lucky escape. He should have learned his lesson and kept his mouth shut. You'd be a rich man today instead of a dead one." She produced a .22 from her purse.

Jax heard another text swish and set his mug down hard to hide it. "Hey, Ted, you gonna let grandma do the dirty deed again? If that gun is traceable to you, the cops will be all over you. They're already getting close."

Grandma scoffed. "It's not licensed any more than the others were. I bought a case of them back in the day. I taught Teddy how to use one when he was just a pup. He's got more of me in him than any of the rest. Gus near fainted when I threw the dynamite down the hole. The stupid-ass shit thought he'd simply *threaten* your father into dropping his suit."

"That's my dad you're talking about, Grandmother. Maybe if you'd listened to him, we wouldn't be here now." From the other room, Teddy sounded almost reasonable.

"Tell me you're kidding, boy." She glanced over her shoulder. "You think we could threaten this jackass into leaving us alone? You want to buy him off, with what?"

While she was looking elsewhere, Jax flung his full mug of hot coffee at Grandma's head and dived to the floor, twisting her pistol-packing arm in the same motion. Like most old ladies, Grandma was fragile, with poor balance, particularly on heels. Her wrist weakened as she howled, staggered, and grabbed at her scalded head. The gun hit the floor, and Jax knocked it in the direction of the desk.

He was under no illusion that Teddy had arrived unarmed.

Furious, Grandma kicked at Jax with the full force of her two-hundred-plus pounds. Instinctively, he rolled, and with the sole of his shoe, slammed her wobbly ankles. Off-balance already, she crashed on top of him.

Bullets flew over his head until Teddy realized his target was on the floor and buried under his grandmother.

"Shoot him, asshole," the old woman shouted, attempting to right herself. "Shoot the bastard and let's get outta here."

"Oh, look, Jax, her aura is a black hole where the ghosts of the people she's killed are gathering. Does this mean I should shoot her? Or Teddy?" Evie's voice purred from beneath the desk, but the hands steadily gripping grandma's.22 visibly protruded, aimed at the howling woman on the floor.

"Your face is coming off," Evie added apologetically to the older woman. "Coffee melts all that waxy stuff."

Grandma howled more, scraping at her burned face—which couldn't be badly burned, protected as it was by layers of cosmetics. The blond wig, however, was a loss.

The howls almost hid the pounding of heavy feet retreating across the outer office.

Instead of saving his grandma, Teddy slammed the outer door in his flight. *So much for looking after family, coward.*

Shoving off grandma's weight, Jax rolled from under her and placed a knee on Marilyn Swenson's back while hanging on to one of her flailing arms. "Don't suppose you brought the draperies and ties over, did you?"

"You're the one plotting, not me. But Troy will have handcuffs." Evie popped out from under the desk, dangling the pistol on one finger. "I don't like this thing. Let me sit on her."

The madwoman wailed and struggled some more. Unsympathetic to her age, Jax yanked her arm harder. Evie sat on her legs so she'd quit trying to roll over.

"You called Troy?"

"I'm really liking not having to shriek to bring him running. Even operatic high notes are hard to project beyond walls. That should be him now. He wasn't far away." Evie pried off granny's high heel and smacked it against a thrashing hand grabbing at her. "It's probably not right to abuse a madwoman, is it? Her aura is totally twisted."

"Helloooo, everyone all right up there?" a high-pitched voice distinctly not Troy's called. "Is it safe to come up?"

"Larraine, you didn't happen to run into Teddy Swenson down there, did you?" Evie called back.

Jax thought maybe he should pound his head against something hard, but the only available object was Grandma Swenson's head, and he'd had to shove it against the floor to keep her from beating her brains out.

"The nice sheriff has him in cuffs. Your mama's here, and a whole bunch of others. I don't want to lead them into a nest of nastiness." Ward's voice was closer now, apparently not really afraid of nests of anything.

"Remind me again why I'm staying in this madhouse?" Jax murmured to Evie.

"Because after this is all over, you can take me to Charleston for a nice dinner?" she suggested.

Oh, yeah, that was a reason he could buy into—an overnighter in the sanity of a city with creative Evie. Holding grandma in place, Jax leaned back and kissed Evie's cheek, the only part of her he could reach from this position.

He didn't even mind when Larraine Ward in pink feathers and heels invaded his office, trailing a posse of Malcolms, with Reuben holding cord ties bringing up the rear.

Twenty-four

"TVs ARE A MENACE TO SOCIETY." EVIE LEANED BACK AGAINST THE BILLIARD TABLE where a smorgasbord of munchies was congregating. She crunched a carrot stick coated in a decadent asparagus dip. Her cousin Pris's catering was heading upscale. "I never wanted one in my house."

"It's in the cellar, not the house." Reuben adjusted the angle of the big screen against the far wall. "If you want to admire our videos, it's gotta be large enough to appreciate."

"I need to read the law, but I'm pretty sure videotaping people without their permission is illegal." Larraine Ward, dressed casually in spangled jeans and cinched tunic, settled on the big couch. "And if it's not, I want you to put cameras in all my offices."

"That cat's well out of the bag. Security video is everywhere." Jax helped himself to a sandwich and leaned on the table next to Evie. "They're perfectly legal in public, if you own the property, but not where there is any expectation of privacy, like a bathroom. So any space open to the public is perfectly fine, unless specific regulations forbid it. You have every right to allow cameras in offices you own, but Starbucks can forbid you to set them up on their premises."

Ward flicked her long fingernails over her pearl cellphone, taking notes. "I like that. Maybe I'll just start with those nanny cams. I suppose using them for blackmail isn't kosher?"

Jax waved his sandwich. "You put those videos up online, and everyone in them will come after you with guns and lawyers. They might not win, but it won't be pretty."

Loretta bounced on a vinyl ball she used as a seat. "I don't like videos. I want to be right there when the bad guys are interrogated so I can see their bubbles."

"We'll just let you meet them on the street and you can report back to us," Evie said reassuringly. "It doesn't do any good to tell Troy if the bad guy has a shriveled bubble. First, though, you should learn what a shriveled bubble means."

"Jax's bubble isn't shriveled anymore." She eagerly watched Reuben setting up the TV and didn't even glance back at Jax. "It's growing."

Evie bumped his hip. "Is Ariel streaming this?"

"I gave her the link, but she's busy sending me financial statements from DVM and Sovereign and calculating how much they owe us in royalties. We may be my first client." Jax abandoned her to unfold chairs for the arrival of more of Evie's family.

Mavis was already ensconced on the most comfortable seat next to Ward. They were exchanging notes on campaign logos and the astrologically best days to hold rallies. Gracie carried in popcorn, then filled her plate with the scrumptious hors d'oeurves Ward had paid Pris to provide. R&R had already eliminated most of Evie's cookies.

"Aunt Val sent this, did you see?" Gracie produced her phone and showed a headline from the Charleston paper announcing a federal indictment for voter fraud against DVM and its directors, including the Swensons. Beneath it was a subhead broadcasting *local investigative firm* responsible for uncovering illegal dealings, possible murder charges pending.

"We're not local," Evie pointed out. "We're not even a Charleston suburb—yet." They might have been, eventually, if Mayor Blockhead had sold Witch Hill to the developers.

"Your *company name* is in the paper. Update your website and install a better phone system." Gracie wandered off.

"Bet they didn't mention ghostbusting," Evie muttered, but she was relieved that they wouldn't. She didn't want every widow and grieving child calling to ask where granny left the will.

"You don't get respect because you don't respect yourself," Jax said through a mouthful of smoked ham and sourdough. He finished chewing before adding, "If you hadn't talked to Clancy's ghost, we'd never have gone in that direction, and Grandma Swenson would still be on the loose."

"It was a family affair." Evie twitched a little at his comment, but she supposed there was some truth in it. She was twenty-five and hadn't accomplished much, but maybe there was hope. "I can't believe Senator Gus Swenson was with his mother when she threw the dynamite and covered up the murder for years. I suppose he'll claim he didn't know Jackson was in the mine or that she ordered Clancy to get rid of your parents. Hard to say on that one. She should have been the politician, except women got no respect back then. She had to work through her husband and son and grandson, so persuasion was her best asset. Clancy's ambition made him easy to persuade."

"Courthouse gossip says Clancy wanted to marry the daughter who ran off with the sheik." Ignoring the carrot sticks, Jax grabbed another tiny sandwich. "Mama Swenson apparently promised he'd be governor instead, if he'd just remove the threat to DVM's future. Roark sent Troy some info he dug out about Clancy's car from way back then, not that it's of much use now that Clancy's dead. Clancy reported it stolen. The cops found it with the front end crushed."

"Does it help having evidence that Clancy killed your parents?" Evie asked him anxiously. His aura was glowing with justice.

"It gives me big shoes to fill knowing they died fighting fraud," he admitted.

"Shhh," Reuben gestured for silence and flipped the switch.

The scene from city hall played out. They'd edited it for effect, but Evie had been there and saw no reason to live through it again. She stirred the dip and refilled glasses around the cellar. She settled next to Jax again when the clips from his office came up. Watching grandma fall on top of Jax again still wasn't amusing. She reached for his hand and squeezed it. He squeezed back, then fed her one of the cute sandwiches with strange paste in the middle.

She appreciated the part where Sheriff Troy wrestled a terrified Teddy Swenson back into Jax's office to see grandma trussed with computer cords and screaming curses like a dockworker. Reuben had bleeped out the obscenities with a different musical note identifying each word, so it now sounded like a bad xylophone tune. The note assigned to "ass" was a bass one and began to sound like a tolling bell after enough repetition. Evie giggled at that.

"She said I had to shut Pendleton up," Teddy tried to explain in the video, over the xylophone beeps. "I didn't know what she'd done. She just said the old lawyer could ruin us all, and I had to keep him from sending personal files to our enemies. I thought she was talking about sending dirt to my opponent in the next election."

"How did she even know Pendleton was sending the files?" Jax asked on the film.

Evie had time to admire how sexy he looked in rumpled shirt and loose tie. His shirt had come loose in the struggle with grandma, and coffee stained his trousers, but he looked as cool and collected as if he'd spent the day pushing papers.

"My mother called her," Teddy said in disgust. "She was excited that Franklin's son had come to visit, and then they started gossiping about how much he looked like some Ives person. Grandma made me tail him and take a photo to send her and to see what he was up to. She got real worried when she saw the photo of him leaving the bank with that legal file."

A splice from Conan Oswin's video cut in showing Donna Ortiz talking to some unknown observer. "I didn't think it hurt to tell her about old files from dead men," Donna said on the film. "We were speculating that maybe Franklin married Mr. Ives' girlfriend to give her baby a name. I had no idea that Marilyn thought she'd *killed* Mr. Ives! I mean, I don't understand that at all. She had everything! Why would she do that? She'd never even met either of them!"

Which explained how Franklin had died instead of Aaron.

A voice steered her back on track, and Donna wiped away tears. "All I did was tell her that Mr. Pendleton thought it was okay to send all those old files to Mr. Jackson and his client. After all, the files had belonged to Mr. Jackson's father. And then Teddy came in and asked for the keys to the truck, and I just forgot all about it. I had a lot to do that day, and I was running late."

"You have to feel sorry for her." Evie finished the tiny sandwich and reached for another carrot. "The Swensons pretty much ruined her life, one way or another. She worked hard and took pride in her son and tried to raise him right, but money and bad genetics won out."

"Nature over nurture? Maybe, if stupidity counts." Jax wiped his hands on a napkin and actually picked up a cookie.

The video flipped back to the office and Ted Swenson talking over his grandmother's meltdown. "I figured Jackson and the woman really were trouble, maybe even criminals, when they raced the car like demons and deliberately lost me heading out of town. I got worried, so I took the truck back to the office and went inside to talk to Mr. Pendleton. I thought I could use my influence and make him see it was dangerous to the district to send those files."

"Don't talk, you *bleep*!" cried grandma from the floor. "Shut up, shut up, shut up—"

Evie fought a giggle watching the video repeat Reuben's bounce on Marilyn's wide back. He was sitting on her while trying to knot the computer cords around her wrists to keep her from flailing about. Grandma's mind might be deteriorating, but she was still built like an ox.

The sheriff read Teddy his rights, but that only seemed to shake him more. He kept on talking. "I only meant to knock him out long enough to wipe the computer. I thought that would fix everything. I called Grandma to tell her what I was doing, but she kept yelling about boxes and now I'd done it, Pendleton would spill everything. She said if I didn't want to go to jail, I'd make it look like suicide and reminded me of the pistol she told me to carry."

Larraine whistled. "That's one wimpy critter. And people laugh at me!"

"People look at the outsides and never see what's inside," Evie suggested. "A big man like that, Teddy didn't have to work hard to conceal his weakness."

"You're the expert," Jax murmured. "You cultivate small and weak."

"Evie's a silver dagger," Loretta reminded him. "Maybe I should learn to teach others to see bubbles."

"I'm pretty sure that's not possible, dear," Mavis said complacently. "You need to teach them to look beyond the obvious."

Reuben had paused the video while waiting for the talk to subside. Roark impatiently rolled his hand to indicate he continue.

But Evie had been there and heard it all. Taking a plateful of cookies, she settled on the floor and began reading emails, while up on the screen, Ted Swenson confessed to putting a bullet to Pendleton's head at his grandmother's orders. But he refused to confess to the same with Clancy.

Evie had stepped in then, explaining Clancy's ghost hadn't seen Ted as a killer, and that grandma's aura indicated she was the more likely suspect. She did, after all, have a box full of.22s at her own admission, and had known Clancy since adolescence and thus knew his allergies. Grandma had screamed some more. Sheriff Troy had given Evie the side-eye—Reuben's editing brought that look up close—but he'd hauled both of the Swensons in for questioning.

Grandma's attorneys had swooped in after Troy had hauled his suspects to his office, and Teddy made frantic calls. Evie figured everyone in the cellar would go to jail if Troy ever figured out that R&R had access to his computer network and now possessed all the video from his courthouse office.

Grandma had been hauled to a mental institution but not before she bragged about offing Clancy in the same way Teddy had finished Pendleton—as if she'd been planning on blaming her grandson.

They'd heavily edited out the boring bits. Evie watched in sick fascination as grandma ranted about Clancy being a *bleepity-bleep* blackmailer. For Loretta's sake, she was glad they'd tuned out the old lady's curses. Genteel, grandma was not.

"Hollywood in the fifties must have been run by the mafia," she murmured.

"Pretty much," her Aunt Ellen, Pris's mother, agreed. "From what I've seen, it's not much better now. Is that where she's from?"

"Family in LA with enough money to run with the movers and shakers," Jax explained.

"Glad Great-Aunt Val stayed here then." Gracie got up and filled her plate again.

Huh, Aunt Val probably was about the same age as Grandma, but her dramatic tendencies lent themselves to re-enactments and seducing husbands.

"I'll start filming the audience shortly if y'all don't shut up," the professor said grimly, revealing his dark side.

Everyone flung food at him. Evie aimed for his man-bun.

They'd all seen the TV clips of Ted and Gus resigning from their respective political races and the family's appeal for privacy for their poor demented granny, a pillar they'd relied on, yadda yadda. The table full of food got more attention than Reuben's grand finale.

"Good documentary, Reub," Jax called, helping himself to another sandwich while tucking Evie's hand in his. "Maybe you've found a new calling."

"I'm hiring him for my security detail." Larraine hugged the top-knotted nerd. "But making beautiful movies together sounds good, too."

Evie glanced at Roark, who'd been unusually silent this evening. "What's with the Cajun?" she whispered to Jax.

"Bad news from home, I think. He's not into communication."

"Yeah, I kinda noticed that, and he's not the only one." Evie tapped a spoon against the tea pitcher. "Got an announcement, folks, listen up."

When the roar reduced to a low rumble, she figured that was the best she could get. "Mr. Pendleton's family offered a reward for finding his killer. Several attorney and charitable organizations to which he belonged matched it. It looks like the Sensible Solutions Agency will get paid for a change."

Reuben grinned and pounded his fists in the air.

Roark just looked surly. "Dey ain't gonna come after us for hackin'?"

"They don't know you exist and don't care," Jax assured him. "We brought about Teddy Swenson's arrest and confession, end of story."

"Den I'm agonna take some time off." Roark flung the truck keys at Reuben. "Take care of dat van, bro."

"Your bubble is untwisting," Loretta called after him.

Roark gave her a thumb's up and loped up the cellar stairs.

"Well." Evie tore her gaze from that dramatic departure. Roark's aura was bleak but brightening. She tilted her head to regard a frowning Jax. "Too late for dinner, isn't it?"

He broke into the first genuine grin she'd ever seen the stone-faced ex-military lawyer offer. "How about champagne brunch on a yacht in the bay?"

"A yacht? You own a real live yacht?" Evie excitedly set aside her paper plate.

"Adoptive father does. I have the access code. Think we can sneak away?" He squeezed her hand and his lips tilted in a seductive smile.

Lapping waves and brunch at sea. . . and Jax. There was an offer she couldn't refuse. She tingled all over at all that masculine attention focused on her. "*Sneak*. As if I can sneak anywhere."

Evie crossed the room, kissed Loretta's head, ordered her to listen to Mavis and the aunts, then headed for the cellar door.

A few hoots followed when Jax trailed after her.

"You don't mind riding to Charleston on a Harley?" He circled her waist and hauled her up the kitchen steps.

"Ten times rather the Harley than that ostentatious Jag you had. You're starting to grow on me, Macho Man."

"Keep whispering sweet flattery like that and we won't get out of the house," he warned.

Psycat leaped from the counter to Evie's shoulder and nipped her ear. Iddy would have to figure out what the cat wanted. She texted her cousin, then flung her arms around Jax.

"If we don't leave now, the whole famned damily will be up here in about thirty seconds."

"Who needs clothes and toothbrushes?" Jax whisked her off her feet, grabbed his keys, and headed for the front door.

"A golden plan," Evie decided. "I'll call this case a golden plan."

Characters

MALCOLM FAMILY

Evangeline Serena Malcolm Carstairs—sends spirits to light, reads auras
Mavis Malcolm Carstairs—Evie's mother; reads crystal ball
Gracie—Mavis's elder daughter; telekinetic; daughter—**Aster**, age 6;
Idonea (Iddy)—Evie's cousin, veterinarian who talks to animals
Priscilla—Evie's cousin; telepathic
Loretta Aurora Post—ten-year-old heiress; sees souls
Cousin Orbis Jr—antique dealer psychometrist
Aunt Felicia—Mavis's sister; Iddy's mother
Aunt Ellen— Mavis's sister; Pris's mother
Great Aunt Evangeline Valerie Malcolm Brindle—Aunt Val, Civil War re-enactor

BOOK TWO:

Damon Ives Jackson (Jax)— fraud and family lawyer; parents, deceased
Ariel Jackson—Jax's sister
Roark LeBlanc—Jax's hacker friend, former military intelligence

Dr. Reuben Thompson—Roark's partner; degrees from MIT and Duke

Aaron Ives—deceased lawyer and engineer, owner Ives Silica Mine, partner of Franklin Jackson

Franklin Jackson—deceased lawyer; partner with Aaron Ives

Caleb Pendleton—lawyer who bought Franklin Jackson's law firm

Margaret (Marge) Thompson—lives near Ives silica mine

Donna Ortiz—receptionist in Pendleton's office; Teddy Swenson's mom

Grandpa Gustav Swenson—deceased father of Senator Swenson; owned east coast fisheries

Grandma Marilyn Swenson—Senator Swenson's mother, Teddy's grandmother

Senator Augustus Swenson—from California; heir to Grandpa Gustav's fortune

Teddy Swenson—Gus's oldest son; California state representative

Conan Oswin—Jax's distant cousin

TOWNSPEOPLE

Mayor Arthur Block—resigned office over land fraud

Gertie—elderly owner of Oldies Café

Sheriff Troy—sheriff of Afterthought

Hank Williams—hardware store owner; town council member; mayoral candidate

Geoff Hayes—CPA, Jax's landlord

Paul Clancy—town council member; mayoral candidate

Larraine Ward—local fashion designer; mayoral candidate

Helena—works at city hall

Dottie—works at city hall

Bernice—mayor's secretary at city hall

George Norton—deceased county attorney

Desmond Redfern—Larraine's campaign manager

The Indigo Solution
Patricia Rice

Copyright © 2021 Patricia Rice
Cover design © 2021 Killion Group
First digital edition Book View Café 2021
ISBN: 978-1-63632-018-2 ebook
ISBN: 978-1-63632-019-9 print

Published by Rice Enterprises, Dana Point, CA, an affiliate of Book View Café Publishing Cooperative

Book View Café
304 S. Jones Blvd. Suite #2906
Las Vegas NV 89107

BOOK VIEW CAFE

About the Author

With several million books in print and *New York Times* and *USA Today's* bestseller lists under her belt, former CPA Patricia Rice is one of romance's hottest authors. Her emotionally-charged contemporary and historical romances have won numerous awards, including the *RT Book Reviews* Reviewers Choice and Career Achievement Awards. Her books have been honored as Romance Writers of America RITA® finalists in the historical, regency and contemporary categories.

A firm believer in happily-ever-after, Patricia Rice is married to her high school sweetheart and has two children. A native of Kentucky and New York, a past resident of North Carolina and Missouri, she currently resides in Southern California, and now does accounting only for herself.

Also by Patricia Rice

ALL A WOMAN WANTS

About Book View Café

Book View Café Publishing Cooperative (BVC) is an author-owned cooperative of professional writers, publishing in a variety of genres including fantasy, romance, mystery, and science fiction — with 90% of the proceeds going to the authors. Since its debut in 2008, BVC has gained a reputation for producing high-quality ebooks. BVC's ebooks are DRM-free and are distributed around the world. The cooperative is now bringing that same quality to its print editions.

BVC authors include New York Times and USA Today bestsellers as well as winners and nominees of many prestigious awards.

www.ingramcontent.com/pod-product-compliance
Lightning Source LLC
Chambersburg PA
CBHW070529100726
47907CB00004B/1045